BABY MONSTERS

Baby Monsters
Copyright © 2024 by S.A. Lunamir

First Edition

Place of Publication USA
Paperback ISBN: 979-8-9885169-2-7
eBook ISBN: 979-8-9885169-3-4
Library of Congress Control Number: 2024916020

BABY MONSTERS

S.A. LUNAMIR

A lonely and hungry monster floated in the cool ocean water, watching a human child on the pier. It wants the child to come closer.

CHAPTER 1

SCARLET

It was a warm summer night on the California coast. Scarlet had exchanged her dull work shoes for flowery flip-flops when she got out of her car. Now she mildly regretted the change, grit rubbed in between her toes. It shouldn't bother her, but she suffered from a very sensitive foot.

The oceanfront could be reached by walking through all the boardwalk rides, but it was a bit of a trek. She could have parked closer, but she needed to watch for something, or well, someone, someone who should be under the pier where they originally hatched, but no. No—they tended to travel up the San Lorenzo River, but not too far. The little Kraken used the waterway to get to the log ride where it hung out in the splash zone. Or occasionally— and this made Scarlet worry—she would find her in the kiddie section, at a ride called the Sea Dragon. Where small children could sit in dragon shaped boats and go around in a circle of shallow water.

The best way to get the tiny kraken out of the rides clear water was to buy an ice cream cone. The tiny spirit had a sweet tooth but regularly consumed meat.

A children's green beach bucket dangled from Scarlet's arm. Half a bottle of water sloshed in the bottom—enough to keep her charge moist if she needed to be coaxed out of one of the rides. Scarlet worried about her drying out more than she needed to.

Scarlet walked past the water rides of the park, keeping an eye out for the pintsized red and purple monster she sought. But thankfully she was not there. Scarlet entered the shadow of the massive antique red and white roller coaster; it was a Friday night at the end of August. The local schools' term began a few weeks past, so the park was fairly tame.

She made it to the sand and walked to the water's edge. The sand remained warm from the long day of sunlight. The Pacific Ocean always felt cool in Santa Cruz, and the water soothed her feet, especially the sensitive one. She stood at the blue edge. Scarlet's eyes were technically ensorcelled. She could see waves of magic floating along the surface of the ocean. California didn't have many spirits, so the shimmering magic was the one strange thing apparent above the waves. Scarlet's eyes had always been magic, allowing her to see spirits and creatures others could not. But with a spell cast on them to see in the dark that went a bit wrong, she could now see magic in its purest form, and spells, and a few other things she was still getting the hang of. Also, she could see in the dark, that part went right. The spell had been cast on her by a troll in Rome, the troll was now her ally. With a tired shrug, she kept walking. The pier stood farther along the golden beach. And moving around after a long day in the lab felt good. She dumped the drinking water in her bucket and swung it back and forth as she walked along.

Scarlet passed under the outdoor seating area of the bar and grill that sat outside the wharf when she saw a seagull flying strangely—seeming to disappear and reappear several yards away in the blink of an eye. Scarlet glanced at the waves. Her charge bobbed in the clear ocean water concentrating intently on the erratic seagull.

The seagull knew the situation was suspicious but being opportunistic took advantage of the strange circumstance and grabbed a corndog off a child's plate when it was suddenly very near. The seagull tried to flap its wings and wheel into the air, yet it mysteriously kept moving closer to the ocean. Most of the people at the restaurant paid attention to the now crying corndogless child.

Scarlet picked up the pace to barely below a run. She needed to put a stop to this very risky behavior. The kid the corndog belonged to pointed feebly at the bird. A few people laughed at the seagull. Scarlet saw several cell phones out and pointed at the gull. What if one recorded a video? They could notice the strange movements, and then who knew what would happen.

"Ariel, Ariel stop it," Scarlet mock whispered. She'd pulled out her phone, so she didn't seem crazy. Instead, she seemed to be having an intense conversation.

Plop—the nearly complete corndog fell from the seagull's beak into the water creating a big splash. She heard people cheer behind her at the daring seagull's misfortune. The bird called out a few complaints but did not dive into the water after the food.

Ariel came to the surface holding a cleaned stick. Not even a crumb was left on it. No one but Scarlet could see her, and thankfully no one noticed the corndog stick either.

"Follow me right now," Scarlet said, walking farther under the wharf away from prying eyes.

Ariel dove into the water, surfacing in front of where Scarlet settled on the soft sand. The baby kraken was about the size of a wiry street cat, six pounds of energy and precociousness. She looked like her mother, who Scarlet met in Venice, but not as terrifying. Ariel had hands with three fingers and one thumb, unlike her mother, who as Scarlet recalled possessed two large tentacles where human arms would be. Scarlet couldn't tell if Ariel's thumb would be fully opposable. Ariel was still developing. And probably would be for a long time. Her bottom half appeared very octopus-like. Originally Scarlet wanted to name her Ursula, but Juan insisted on a different name. Instead, they named her Ariel. It was probably best he talked Scarlet out of Ursula. Scarlet felt Juan was her better half, he had great ideas. Perhaps names were prophetic. Ariel obsessed over humans; Scarlet hoped it to be a healthy obsession.

Ariel's facial structure seemed fairly human-like and expressive. A tiny, cute button nose, but a mouth filled with sharp shark teeth. And big gray eyes with an oval pupil.

Overall, Scarlet found her rather adorable. Mostly she stayed pink and purple, but she could change her coloring at will and would shift shades with her mood. When Ariel became angry she turned very blue with purple hands, like a cartoon of a child holding their breath.

Her magics were still coming in. She could manipulate water, which seemed logical, but she also manipulated space. Ariel could get places that it didn't seem possible for her to swim or crawl to. And she could knock things out of a seagull's beak and maneuver those gulls into getting food for her—mostly corndogs, her favorite food, even above ice cream.

Scarlet sighed. "I hope you didn't ruin your dinner." Then she pulled out a bag of McDonalds from her tote.

"Fries," squealed Ariel.

Scarlet didn't have to worry about Ariel ruining her appetite for dinner. The new kraken was a bottomless pit. Ariel wiggled her way up onto the sand next to Scarlet, Scarlet rewarded her with a large order of fries. Scarlet dug out one cheeseburger for herself and set the paper bag aside.

Ariel blinked up at Scarlet. Then she moved her head back and forth. She could use some words, easy words with one or two syllables. She could even put a string of words together, not a complete sentence but a thought. Her language acquisition was not like a human's. Scarlet regularly repeated numbers and body parts for her, however, she seemed to take up names and adverbs better. She couldn't say Scarlet's name yet, but she could say another name just fine.

"Juan?" Ariel asked.

Scarlet sighed. Of course, she liked him better.

"He's coming. He doesn't mind his nuggets being cold." Juan really didn't mind cold fast food. He was Scarlet's fiancé and a mostly normal human. He couldn't see spirits, but spirits loved him, and with Scarlet's troll-enhanced vision, she could see he emitted something, something that looked a lot like raw magic.

Ariel seemed appeased, and then she set about eating her fries. She liked the long ones best, devouring them first and with much relish.

Scarlet wondered if she should try to get Ariel to eat more nutritious fare, or at least hunt fish.

Ariel finished all but a handful of fries and began to play with them. She pushed them around in the sand making car noises. Scarlet rummaged in her bag. She'd brought a few old Hot Wheels, so she got the colorful toys out along with a small ball and a bath-time book. All the toys ended up in the water eventually, so she'd learned to bring water-safe books. Although when that first board book dissolved in Ariel's hands, she didn't seem sad—just interested in the process.

Ariel had a whole game going on when she gave a happy squeal. Scarlet didn't bother to turn around. Juan came up silently and sat close to Scarlet's side. He leaned back, crossing his legs in the sand. His shoes were off, and his pants rolled up past the ankle.

Ariel crawled into his lap and wrapped her arms around him. He put his hand on her head. Almost getting a thumb in her eye.

"Good job, but maybe move your thumb up a smidge," Scarlet said.

He glanced down. Ariel wasn't visible to him, but Juan was better at sensing spirits than Scarlet. He could usually feel them now with his physical body, describing the sensation as a slight pressure when Ariel touched him, but he could not feel if she was warm or cold, smooth or rough. Also, when Ariel became loud, he could hear a sound, but it remained muffled and quiet like a whisper behind you.

"Oh good, you brought a book," he said, smiling. His teeth were blindingly white against his tan skin. He reached over and got the book, his black loose curls falling across his broad forehead.

It was a Disney book about the different princesses. Ariel loved it because Ariel from *The Little Mermaid* was on one of the pages. Juan read through it. Then Ariel took over flipping through the rubbery pages.

While Ariel stayed occupied with the pretty pictures Juan locked eyes with Scarlet, his brow tight. "Did you get the second ballroom as a backup location for the ceremony in writing?"

"What? Oh no. I tried, but Kelly said it's their policy to have one event at a time." Scarlet began spinning her sapphire engagement ring on her pale finger.

"Okay, 'cause rain is possible now. Late tropical storm I guess."

"Years of drought and we will finally get summer rain on our wedding day." Scarlet and Juan had been engaged for over a year. He proposed in Florence—that trip to Italy changed many things about Scarlet's life. At the end of the trip, she even decided it was finally time to tell Juan the truth about herself and her strange powers. But all he'd done was prove himself the better half of the couple. He stayed with her, treated her like nothing changed, and even understood why she'd kept her secret from him.

"It is supposed to be lucky, the rain," Juan said. The book in his lap stopped flipping.

Somehow Scarlet did not feel the rain would be lucky. Scarlet hadn't been able to shake the feeling that her wedding wouldn't happen. And if the sky opened up and rained out their ceremony, she might be right.

Ariel moved from Juan's lap down into the sand. Because Ariel was corporal, eventually he would be able to see her, just like everyone could see Donya, the troll. Scarlet suspected it to be related to size. Ariel was still small enough not to register. Scarlet read about creatures and spirits every chance she got. She enjoyed resources now, books that Grazia, an ancient and now dead alchemist, left her. Sadly, none of those books were in English. Latin did not come easily to Scarlet, but she took an online course last semester. Grazia, in the few days she had known Scarlet, managed to change her will, leaving a sizable property in Rome stuffed with magical artifacts and books in Scarlet's name.

Yet even when she could understand the writing, it didn't always make sense. The methods alchemists used needed to be taught. They weren't even close to the scientific methods Scarlet knew. And Grazia's shade was hard to access in the realm she currently inhabited with the Kraken.

"Kelly quit. I hope the new girl kept that same policy," Juan said after a few minutes.

Scarlet shook herself out of her musings. There were maybe not more important things to worry about, but still big life events in her near future. "You shouldn't worry too much. I mean she said the reason they did that was because the staff couldn't handle two events. The hotel isn't gonna overbook itself. That would be stupid." Scarlet bit her lip, she always had been overconfident. And that over-confidence led to what almost got her and Juan killed in Italy. Donya wanted to eat Juan before she shifted her outlook on life and helped Scarlet.

Scarlet didn't die though, and now she boasted a magical bond with a troll, a large magical inheritance, and Ariel. Although it hadn't all worked out for the best, her foot still hurt and there was an ongoing investigation into her because of Grazia's death. But she and Juan deserved to have their normal human wedding day, which was two weeks away.

Ariel pushed sand into a pile next to Juan. He made swirly patterns in the sand. Then a square window or door. Ariel moved her hands saying, "pop pop." And water from the ocean sprinkled on the lumpy swirly pile. Juan helped form the now wet sand into a better castle. Scarlet watched surprised, that was the first time Ariel moved an object very clearly in front of Scarlet. Scarlet wondered if it was easier to move water for her.

"Please do pop pop again," Scarlet asked.

Ariel smiled, popping herself above the castle, then flopping into the sandy structure. Juan flinched with surprise as the sand scattered everywhere. Scarlet clapped her hands to encourage Ariel, but at the same time, she wondered how strong her little ward would become.

CHAPTER 2

DONYA

Donya conversed with a blueish boulder. She patiently waited for it to respond—boulders spoke on their own time. Meanwhile, a giraffe stared at her. She thought most of the animals in the zoo would be sleeping, but this animal seemed especially wary. Boulders would not take up a conversation from a distance, so Donya stood in the habitat of the giraffe, her nose inundated by the strong smells of the zoo.

"You describe this beautiful half-nymph as blind, but I recall a woman with eyes. The eyes sat wrong, but they were there," the great chipped boulder said.

"Perhaps it is a different woman then." Donya stood from the cold ground, stretching her stony short legs. She could picture Nera, tall and graceful, her eyes taken by her father years before. Her father used magic to occasionally supply new eyes for her, but the eyes degraded quickly. She would not have eyes now, now that her father was dead.

"No, I was not always located in this zoo, I once knew much of the outer world. I could sense her magic, and I know the silver circlet she wore."

Nera did wear a silver circlet, a powerful one that Donya watched gleam in the starlight upon her brow the first time they met. Donya needed to find her. She had not stopped searching for Nera in over a year, even examining her dreams for the woman, for she must make an apology for betraying her. Nera had meant to rescue Donya and Scarlet under a bridge in Florence, but Donya had ruined her plan.

"How many sunrises since you saw her?" Donya could barely contain herself. Her breaths came in puffs, a troll's body is slightly warmer than its surroundings. August in Auckland was cold, especially a few hours before dawn.

"The sun has risen eight times since that day. Go to the docks; the man accompanying the beauty spoke of a ship."

Donya went to the harbor, checked every vessel, and walked the bottom of the sea floor. The stones told her more about Nera. Nera stayed in this place for several weeks. A dark smooth rock described her as blind but beautifully attired—attached to a wealthy human. Although when he wasn't around, she frolicked in the water with the sharks and whales.

The yacht she occupied is called the Fin and Tonic. A name Donya could not understand. The Fin and Tonic refueled the day before and took on supplies, then set out not more than twenty-four hours before Donya arrived at the dock.

This was the closest Donya had been to Nera since Italy.

No stones knew its heading. Or if it would simply return in a few days.

When the sun rose, Donya found shelter under the sea water in the shadow of a dock. She continued to question pebbles instead of sleep. Nera sang often in the waters. She played with sharks and dolphins alike. Many of the stones loved her.

Donya had used several tracking spells since she began her search for Nera. But they came up with nothing. She even tried a version of the spell Heldrig used to pull herself to Nera. But the distance was too far or Donya too weak, and Donya knew Nera covered her tracks. Even in this water, Donya's superior sense of smell should pick up traces of her scent, but there was nothing, not even a hit. Nera was quite powerful. She could scrub an area of her presence, obliterating her tracks. Still running from her father, perhaps, or running from everything. Did she not know that Heldrig was dead?

Donya did not wait for sunset. A few gentle rays of golden light hit her as she emerged from the water. They did not harm her, but felt uncomfortable on her skin. Still, she needed to keep searching. A harpy sat on a wooden beam above where she emerged. It preened its black feathers and let out a squawk.

"Good evening," Donya said. She would be polite to this ancient being, but did not want to ask her about Nera. Harpies loved to feed on beauty, not in the same way as the Kraken in Venice. No, they liked to feed on it in the bone-crunching agony-inducing way. This one smelled of wind and fish guts.

"Good evening, I have information for you. But it will cost."

Donya could be mean too. Most of her strength had returned. She could throw the crone down, pull out her feathers, and make her talk. The harpy would probably respect that. But she didn't need any more enemies. "What is the cost, old hag?"

"The bead," she called. Her voice rang out between a human and a crow's. Her vowels got dragged long and became shrill.

Donya found the bead she spoke of in the bottom of her bag. It came from a bracelet she used to wear. Heldrig had snapped the bracelet as part of the ceremony of their oath to work together. Heldrig kept one bead, and he broke the oath. Donya found the bead at the stone house he kept outside of Rome; she searched that dwelling thoroughly in the days after his death, looking for Nera and then scouring it for clues as to where she would run.

The simple cloudy jade bead bore a small crack. It was not that beautiful, but it held the broken promise and all the potential that promise entailed.

"This bead is too important; your price is too high." Donya dug in the bag; during her search of this island she had found a few old relics. She intended to sell them for extra cash. It was much harder to obtain money now that she did not kill humans. And outright mugging or robbing felt beneath her. "What about this?" It was the blade of a paddle, the shaft broken off long ago, never meant for aquatic use but for a human ceremony. A sleepy yellow stone sat embedded in swirls of meticulously carved dark wood.

"That begot happiness, it will not do." The harpy eyed the sky like she would leave. "Oh, but I love sad beauty. That is why I loved that pale blue woman on the boat, with her scars and songs. She told me many things."

Donya shoved the bead at the harpy. Donya felt the scrape of her talons on her fingers and then listened intently to her story.

Nera headed to Tokyo. She was excited about the lights of the city. The boulder at the zoo had not been mistaken. She used eyes again when the harpy spoke with her. The rich man on the ship supplied the eyes. The harpy could not say if he was a dark magic wielder or if he employed them.

Donya got on the first flight she could book. Eleven hours nonstop. The air felt thick with moisture and heat when she arrived. Dawn blushed through the large windows to her left. She needn't worry about weak sunlight, she'd abstained from human since Italy, even the ones that smelled very appetizing. Although none smelled as good as Scarlet's intended. Donya thought if she could keep from eating him, she could keep from eating any human, no matter her hunger. Still, she would find somewhere devoid of windows to sleep, it was better to be safe than stone.

⨯

It was happening again. A recurring dream. Trolls do not get recurring dreams. Donya grew weary of being the first troll to experience so many things.

She stood in a dusty desert landscape with a white-blue sky blazing overhead, thinking of the time difference between Japan and California. Donya did appreciate this dream, as it allowed her and Scarlet to communicate directly.

The dream was a remnant, built and cast to trap Scarlet, evoked by Nera and her half-brother Mars. Donya had yoked herself to the spell to aid Scarlet and not allow the trap to spring upon her. Donya still felt shame that she only killed Mars, and Scarlet needed to finish Heldrig. But the dream persisted. Occasionally she thought she smelled fresh water on the dry breeze, a scent she knew was Nera's.

She heard footsteps behind her.

"It has been a while. You could call."

Turning around, Donya saw the redhead. She wasn't sure how to respond. She shrugged.

"Did you travel to a different continent again?" Scarlet asked.

"Yes, I landed in Tokyo."

"I'm surprised you came up to the northern hemisphere, summer will be around for almost a month."

The human she was tied to enjoyed excellent second sight, and a fire element and shield that could keep her safe against even the strongest of enemies. But she couldn't sense the supernatural with anything other than her eyes. Scarlet had started to sense Donya, at last, and very minutely, because of their special bond forged in a sword. The bond was no longer necessary to either of them, but it persisted. It probably would persist until the day one of them died.

"I received information that Nera is headed to Tokyo."

Scarlet leaned over poking at the large magic circle forming in the dusty dream earth. "I hope you find her soon."

"I will find her. The time it takes does not matter."

The seal on the ground sat fully formed with deep fissures into the ground for a moment before it flared gold. In the dream, this part happened much faster than it did the first time when Donya had stabbed the great sea serpent form Mars used, and activated the seal sent by the Kraken and Grazia. The fact that the seal still coalesced meant they were connected to this place still as well.

Scarlet studied Donya, then the sky began to shatter. "I always hate this part."

"As do I. You missed it the first time. How goes your quest?"

"Still nothing. I got the best private investigator I could afford. He tried to be honest at first, asking around for the body at all the hospitals and morgues as a private investigator. Now he is pretending to be family. I hope he gets a lead. Do you think if we find Mars' body these dreams will stop?"

"It is the best way to end this. I should not have left his body. Another mistake," Donya said. The sky cracked, and pieces began to fall. Donya had only killed Mars in the dream, not out in the material world, leaving his body an empty shell, a shell that along with Nera pulled them to this dreamscape over and over again. Scarlet murmured under her breath. "What was that?" Donya asked.

"Oh, I'm counting, my eyes are still changing. I've been able to count things very quickly, for a few months now. It's kinda great. I can do my job quickly and perfectly. I have to be careful to slow down and make fake mistakes to look more normal. There's eight hundred and ninety-two pieces of sky. I counted them the last time we were here too. The number stayed the same."

Donya blinked at the human. That spell she cast had gone completely wild, probably tapping into Scarlet's unused potential.

"I'm gonna leave. I hate when everything falls apart," Scarlet said with a wave.

"Farewell."

Unlike Scarlet, Donya liked to watch the dream crumble. In those moments she recalled her sword doing justice. Not only that, it allowed her to recall the immediate aftermath, the first night when she thought she would see Nera, when Donya thought she could help her recover from the large casting of this spell.

Everything went black. It wouldn't be long until she woke up. The darkness didn't bother her, on the contrary, she felt almost energized by speaking to her ally. And still, in the darkness, she breathed deeply and thought she could smell the fresh scent of a stream.

The dream was a problem, a very small problem, yet a small problem at the top of a snowy mountain can become a large problem by the time it rolls downhill. And Donya found herself to always be downhill of a problem.

Her eyes opened in the waking world. Ah yes, she sat in a janitorial closet. The smell of wet cloth and harsh chemical cleaners filled her nose.

She stepped from the closet and no humans nearby noticed. Her clothes were a mess. But she needed currency. She opened her small backpack, pulling out a wad of old euros, money from New

Zealand, and even a few rubles. Donya could smell a currency exchange booth nearby. When she found it no one else waited at the counter. She wouldn't get a good rate, but she didn't need money for much, only clothes and modern travel convenience.

The woman behind the counter nodded at her, Donya needed to show an ID according to the sign with instructions written in several languages, all of which Donya read. Fortunately, she still retained her passport. Donya flashed the forged document. The woman raised her eyebrows slightly but started counting out money.

Donya was thankful for the lack of conversation, although she spoke antique but perfectly good Japanese. The travel and the dream made her feel chalky and dusty. When the woman finished, Donya held a nice pile of yen in her hand. She shoved it and her passport into her worn sea salt-stained backpack.

The first store that smelled acceptable was Uniqlo. She found a stretchy black dress and dark green tights. She tried them on. Her heavy black boots had seen better days, but the leather held up despite all the moisture she subjected them to. She found a messenger bag and decided it would do. She moved her stuff over and changed into the new clothes in the dressing room. She ripped off the tags and counted out forty thousand yen. The number seemed high but who could understand humans and their imaginary wealth?

The dressing room attendant held up her arms in an X motion as she went to leave. But she waved the cash at her and then proceeded to the front counter. She put down the tags and the cash. The young man at the register paled. He did not speak up though.

He rang up the price, but she walked away, flashing a toothy smile at the dressing room attendant who spoke hurriedly to her coworker.

In the mirror, as she left the store, she looked passable, clean, and small. Her hair stuck straight up in dark spikes. Normally she liked to have a jacket, but the heat of summer pulsed in this land.

The airport doors slid closed behind her. The odor was strange, it contained the scents of modern life—industrial fumes, human sweat, false fabric, tar, but an ancient smell persisted. Green, she could smell the plants all around her. They were healthy, growing strong and upright. She could feel the sun had set. But the streets were brightly lit, and a glow hung in the west. It didn't seem like night. It didn't feel like night.

CHAPTER 3

SCARLET

It wasn't that all jobs were the same. No, Scarlet's new job seemed better; they respected her free time and valued her input. But there will always be people problems. Two of the deckhands argued over what kind of line to use on the nets. She thought they both held valid points, but a two-month debate on the subject seemed excessive. Scarlet didn't have any skin in the fight, as she rarely went out to collect samples. But they wanted her to pick a side.

There was another meeting scheduled about the line on Wednesday, and Scarlet dreaded going. She pulled her head back from the microscope and blinked to refocus her eyes. It was Monday. Her wedding was less than two weeks away. She dreaded it too. All the decisions and checking in with vendors—it all felt terrible to her, not romantic in the least.

Juan loved it though. He didn't even seem to mind the building drama. One of his aunties took it upon herself to invite around twenty of his third cousins from LA. Thankfully the cousins had enough sense to realize they didn't get a real invitation. And Bertha, Juan's sister, finally came in handy as a bridesmaid. Bertha was a diva and enjoyed explaining to that auntie that if any of those extra relations showed up because of her—she would need to foot the hundred-dollar-a-head bill.

Scarlet checked her calendar, she needed to go to the dress shop today for one more fitting on her gown. She didn't want to go into the dress shop though. No, she wanted to go home and eat dinner with Juan. The weekend flew by. And that stupid dream made her agitated and short-tempered. She called the PI during lunch, but he didn't have any new leads, the same as the last time they spoke at the beginning of August. He seemed irritated that she checked in, like she pestered him while he'd been busy. But he accepted her money, service was due as far as she was concerned.

To her, the dream became a terrible reminder of how close she had come to disaster. She had been unprepared, relying on her good luck her whole life. That was a fool's game. For the last year and a half, she studied hard. Grazia, the old alchemist who became a shade and now stayed with the Kraken left instructions for her to master reading the tarot, learn Latin, and not be burned by fire. Donya, who barely understood humans but remained Scarlet's closest ally, told her to follow the old woman's instructions, but also work hard with her shield and eyes. At least getting a grip on what she could innately do was a good start Scarlet thought. Donya told her she contained a lot of raw power. If Scarlet mastered that power, she hoped the fear and anxiety she experienced lately would fade away. She hadn't been afraid before, and she wanted to at least get back to a manageable level of anxiety. And yet, she studied but rarely found time to actively practice.

Her phone buzzed—time to clean up and clock out. That was the most annoying thing about his job. They still used a real punch. She hadn't used one since her first job at a restaurant as a teenager. Overtime wasn't approved right now so even though she'd been in the middle of a sample she saved the data and closed out of the access database. She put a lid on the tray she worked through, grabbed her things, and walked to the punch. Footsteps behind her told her all the other lab workers would follow. A few punch stations were scattered around the building, one stood near her workstation by an old grimy window. The window looked out onto a beach. Small waves lapped at the warm sand in the afternoon sun. She scanned the blue card with her name on it. It registered her time, and she made her way out through a windowless hallway. Her coworkers attempted to cheer up the space with pictures of otters and pelicans on the walls by the doors that led off to other labs and offices. The lab sprawled through the old building, all state-funded, but usually fairly empty as half the workers need to be out collecting samples.

A door swung open in front of Scarlet; she sidestepped as Khloe walked through.

"Hi Scarlet, where you headed? A funeral?"

Scarlet's mouth gaped but she closed it quickly. She didn't think she appeared that out of sorts. "Um, a dress fitting."

"That'd put me in a bad mood too."

Khloe stood far taller than Scarlet, she was permanently single and loved to sail. Scarlet could never guess her age—between forty-five and sixty.

They exited the building together and Khloe waved, not stopping for a chat. She was far too sharp. Scarlet always felt worried when Khloe mentioned how quickly Scarlet completed samples. And her high accuracy rates. Thankfully Khloe seemed the extremely logical type. Scarlet didn't think she would guess magic eyes were Scarlet's secret weapon. But perhaps this would be a question she could ask the tarot, after the wedding, when she had more time.

Out in the parking lot, Scarlet's old Toyota needed a bath. The fob sat in her hand, but she didn't use it to open the door. Feeling guilty for putting off her practice of more difficult magic, she formed a tiny bar of shield and pushed the unlock button inside the door. This skill came to her far easier than anything with fire, which she found annoying. Fire she could see and understand. Her shields worked with her mental image and imagination, her imagination that she had ignored for many years. She tossed her stuff in her car and made a mental note to get it washed next Monday. Maybe she should even get it detailed, sand dusted the floorboards, and built up in the crevices and cup holders.

The lab perched right on the water; an impractical place for it to be, but nice, nonetheless. On the breeze floating in from the waves, Scarlet could hear singing. She didn't think anything of it.

Her mind was on several other things, but still, she noticed it. No words were decipherable, but the song seemed filled with sadness and desire.

About an hour later Scarlet was starting to sweat.

"Lean over and jiggle your chest as hard as you can," instructed the seamstress, her curly black hair bouncing as she imitated the movement.

"Like this?" Scarlet asked, leaning over in her ivory lace dress.

"More lunge." The seamstress backed up to a wall of dresses, in lace and satin, ranging from white to ivory to soft baby pink.

Scarlet lunged. Nothing popped out—that was what she hoped for, probably the seamstress too.

"Good, now stand up tall and windmill your arms."

Scarlet stood, following directions. One of her straps gave with a pop.

"Oh dear, yes, we will need to put industrial snaps on that side."

"You can sew the straps on," Scarlet said.

"That would work but if you want to remove them they will be on there. I don't want you taking scissors to my work with a few glasses of champagne in you."

"Does that happen?" Scarlet asked, stepping away from the triple mirror and bright lights.

"More often than you would think."

Scarlet moved behind a curtain and peeled off the dress and shapewear. The shop was in Carmel-by-the-Sea. She thought longingly of all the restaurants she could have picked up food from and surprised Juan with, but no, no, he would have salad waiting for them. The McDonalds they enjoy at the beach on Friday would be the last fatty food either of them got to have for almost two weeks. Both of their mothers nagged them about salt and water weight. Scarlet wasn't sure if water weight held any scientific validity. But as she pulled up her pants they did seem to fit better. Scarlet came out from behind the curtain ready to leave.

"Give me at least two days, then come back anytime to try it again," the seamstress said as Scarlet walked to the front door.

"Sure, sounds good, and thank you for all the hard work." Scarlet gave a quick wave.

Outside she checked her watch. It was only five. Juan would be home in thirty minutes. She could do a short walk. The late afternoon sun felt warm and the breeze fluffed her hair pleasantly. Moving around could help clear her head. She tapped her watch to record her workout, then began power walking downhill.

She always forgot how hilly Carmel was, and how dangerous the drivers could be. Tourists foraging for an open parking spot paid little attention to pedestrians or stop signs. And more tourists wandered into traffic to cross the road to another wine-tasting venue or art gallery. An old man with a comb-over almost jumped a curb next to her in a candy apple red car. It looked fast, too fast, even with its fender stuck to the curb.

Scarlet thought of the cheese shop, all that pepper jack, asiago, mozzarella, and gouda sitting, waiting for someone to buy it and then eat it.

No, she headed toward the ocean. Walking helped her think and focus. Her attention felt divided lately. The thing with Mars's body, all the studying of magic, and the wedding.

Finding Mar's body had been delegated to a professional, a professional that could hopefully be relied on. His website boasted over a hundred good reviews, and he was a retired detective who even worked with the FBI on several high-profile cases. The studying probably should take a backseat to the wedding. Even though the wedding could be viewed as less important overall, it was more urgent. How could a one-day event take so much time and energy to put together?

Her phone buzzed again. Elyse, one of her bridesmaids, and oldest friend texted her a thumbs up. Scarlet and all the bridesmaids shared their workout data. Most of them tried to keep her motivated. Although Lettie said if the dress fits why keep trying? Scarlet agreed with her but didn't want to bloat up and have it not fit on the big day. Scarlet was more of a reader than a runner. Even now she thought of the photos she'd taken of the text in one of her ancient books. There was a section of text that she found impossible to translate. She wanted badly to sit on the beach and work out a word or two. The section was on transference, a subject she could wrap her mind around far better than the more outlandish transmutation. Many of Grazia's books were on transmutation as alchemists were truly obsessed with turning cheap metals into gold. She took a funny step on a root-raised section of sidewalk and stubbed her toes on her sensitive foot. The shock of pain helped Scarlet focus, she needed to lean in and concentrate on the wedding.

Trying to read Grazia's books distracted her from that, even if the information helped her reach her long-term goal.

A song drifted up from the water—the same melody as earlier. She wondered if it was opera. Back in Moss Landing, she'd thought someone played a record out in one of the sailing boats or yachts. It seemed too much of a coincidence to hear that same aria again twenty miles away.

What could it be?

Scarlet's breaths came faster. Cardio three times a week could only do so much for her. But it wasn't just the hills and quick pace. No, something had to be wrong. That singing. She put her hands over her ears. But the sound did not diminish.

She made it to the sand, heedless of her tennis shoes.

Maybe a dozen other people relaxed on the beach, several couples meandered hand in hand. She studied them. Either they didn't notice the singing, or they were not bothered by it. She wouldn't give the melody a second thought if she hadn't heard it this clearly twenty miles away.

She came to the water's edge, the waves had picked up, and sea-foam frothed up on the sand. But there was nothing—nothing unusual. Boats out on the bay. Happy people on the sand. Magic floating like a shimmering haze in the air. But nothing else. She scanned the broad blue bay and shore again. The singing continued. Goosebumps raised on her arms.

She pulled out her phone and called Juan.

"Hello," he answered after two rings.

"Hey babe, on your way home yet?" Scarlet started her ascent up the beach away from the water.

"Just leaving work. How did the dress fitting go?"

"Fine, I called to say go right home, okay? And I'll be a bit late."

"What's up?"

"Maybe nothing, but I need to go check on Ariel," she said, around gasps from her exertion.

"Alright, drive safe. Wait are you running?"

"Walking quickly. I gotta go, can't talk and walk this fast."

"Okay but give me a callback and explain soon. Love you."

"I will. Love you too."

Scarlet ended the call and put her phone in her back pocket for easy retrieval. Creepy songs floating along the coastline were not what she needed right now. Normal things were what she needed. Sweat dripped over her ribs and her jeans clung to her thighs as she strode to the car up the incline. Maybe she was overreacting. If she was, at least the stress would probably make her lose more weight, she thought with a wry smile.

CHAPTER 4

DONYA

The city of Tokyo did not seem to know true darkness. Electronic billboards flickered, cafe signs lit up, 7-Eleven storefronts emitted a bright glare, and many things glowed neon and multicolored. But history and stone peppered the city as well. And a wealth of spirits to talk to, surprisingly helpful spirits. Donya spent all night searching while chit-chatting with a nine-tail fox who smelled not vulpine at all, but like cherry blossoms and plum wine. A tengu followed them; he did not seem unfriendly. He flapped about on his large wings, his red face studying the fox, then Donya. His eyes often wandered to the sky. He repeated the end of a sentence Donya said a few times, and when he spoke his Japanese seemed even more antiquated than hers.

Dawn approached when the tengu took off into the sky without a farewell. Donya watched him circle a few times. Tengu were rare, only living on a few small islands, but they had distant relatives all bearing that long nose, and all guardians of mountains. This one smelled of cedar, the fragrance faded quickly after its departure. She couldn't see much of the sky between the wall of shipping containers she stood by. The fox watched silently but smiled a fox grin as the tengu glided upward.

"I must depart too," Donya said.

"I don't think that fellow liked you," the fox said.

"Not my problem," Donya didn't care if another mountain dweller liked her or not.

"Watch out for groups of them, they can be irritating," The fox fluffed its fur. "Which way will you head on the quest for the beautiful nymph?" the fox asked in what sounded like a human woman's voice now.

"I will stay here. I arrived here before her. I do not know if the ship will come directly to this port."

"The port is quite vast. You could easily miss her." The fox's nine fluffy tails shrunk to half of the length.

"I can see that. We have walked all night and these ships are too large, with their great metal boxes. I do not think the Fin and Tonic will be this large. I should have asked the harpy for more details."

"You have the ship's true name." The fox's fur now seemed shorter than it had before.

"I do. I could call out to it. I have heard that ships have souls."

"All the luck to you. Enjoy your stay in this land, but mind the dangers."

"Yes, danger only ceases once you are dead, or for a troll, stone," Donya said.

The fox nodded vigorously leaning her head down in a low bow as a farewell, then with a smooth motion she stood on her hind legs and transformed into a beautiful woman. She still sported her shorter tails and whiskers, but most humans would not notice. A tight red dress stretched across her new voluptuous form and her dark red hair was cut into a pixie style. High heels clicked on the pavement as she walked away.

A bridge stood in the distance, but it rose too high. It didn't look like it would cast deep shadows to hide Donya, so she continued to walk. Lights sparkled off the water. What would she need to call to a ship? Her grandmother's henkie blood could not help her with the salty ocean water, but one of her grandmother's spells could be used. Donya remembered being taught it. It was for objects, not people, but she could change it a little, add the use of her sword, a very versatile magical tool. She did not normally rely on circles and complex spells, her magic being as easy as breathing. For this spell—she could call shadow, but tonight would not work, time was too short. A pine bow and river water, she would use shadow in place of a few of the herbs her grandmother used. There would be no finding those herbs here anyway.

She had turned away from the ships and came upon Aomi Minami Terminal Park. The city life began to pick up, you could hear it in the din coming from the tall buildings. A train squealed on metallic tracks in the distance. Donya found a muddy pond with a low walkway over it. She crossed this wooden walkway and found the perfect spot. The water lay shallow, and the shadows were deep and cool. Trolls preferred to be cool.

❧❧

The Sumida River emptied right into where Donya rested throughout the day. She walked upstream to find a good spot to collect water. Then, using her nose for hours, she finally found the remains of a bonfire at one of the shrines. The grounds had been swept spotless, but this ash must have still been too hot to clean up properly. It lay piled on a spot of moist dirt by a massive tree. A paper charm encircled the ancient tree, she could feel the talisman. The shrine didn't want her on its grounds.

It hurt her to feel the rejection of this place. She had abstained from human for over a year despite her hunger. Her thoughts drifted to the tengu from the night before. Taciturn, like herself, most of his utterances felt foreboding. It was the fox who'd spoken with her. No matter, it was quiet and dark here. She took the ash and left a small pinecone on the stone steps leading up to the temple. Perhaps that would appease the powers she had unintentionally offended.

Her ingredient list completed; she only needed a site. It appeared that the temples were not to be used for her magic, so she would need to find another park. The park she spent yesterday in would not do. It lacked the connection she needed. She kept walking. Every-thing was brightly lit and felt wrong. As she moved, she thought of all the circles she knew. Midnight came and went.

33

People on the streets avoided each other. The drunk humans did not especially shun her. A young human with spiked hair fidgeted with a metal object in his hand; he smelled especially good to her. Donya steered her feet away from him. Her mouth watered. All this wandering would get her into trouble eventually.

Donya was strong now, she knew that. She could afford to use her strength on what seemed a frivolous spell. It came to her perfectly. It was only a few words, and she splashed water on her hands from the jug of river water. It allowed her to use her hands as dowsing rods, working well for locations, in this case the location of where she should do her spell. Her grandmother used it to find the location of water or good feed for the cattle she loved. Normally Donya did not need it as the earth let her know where to do a spell, but on this island, she needed a bit of extra help. Donya's right hand tingled. She walked in that direction.

Donya had traveled to the hills and rivers her grandmother lived in while searching for Nera when she could find no more leads on where Nera was off to. But Donya's grandmother was not in her river. No cattle remained in the area. The humble human hamlet that used to keep the cattle lay abandoned. Donya knew her grandmother still walked about, not yet dead, just very ancient. Perhaps the elderly henkie found a new stream and another cow herd.

Eventually following the tingling in her hands, she came to another seaside park. In it stood a statue she recognized. Confused, she walked closer. A symbol she had seen in America of a woman holding a torch above her head sculpted out of bronze. She thought of it as very much American.

This was the right spot. She didn't have to rely solely on her own abilities. She had an ally.

She circled the area. A large neon sign that said "love" glared. She moved away from that. Although it appealed to her in a strange way, it did not aid her in this.

No, she found a patch of verdant grass not far from the symbol of a distant land. She drove two fingers into the sod and trenched her circle. It was a simple one she knew. Balanced, it was good for answering a question almost a true locator spell but only required a true name to find an answer. She poured the ash in the center, and sprinkled the river water in the cardinal directions, starting with the north and ending in the west. The pine branch was small, she could eat it all in one bite. But instead, she ate slowly, pulverizing the bark and sticky needles. The circle wavered with the magic of the earth. Then she unstrapped her small sword from her back. She carried it close to her stony skin. It was not sharp. It slept. She drove it into the ground and asked it to wake up.

Minutes ticked by, more minutes than usual for the sword now. Donya had practiced awaking it many nights, but the change in area affected the opal sword as it affected her. The sword awoke with its fire and shadow. The circle had been charged but now it pulsed with red and black.

Donya opened her mouth, spoke a word of power, then said, "take me to the Fin and Tonic." The sword let out a burst of fire, causing Donya to blink but she did not let go of the hilt.

She didn't expect to actually be taken. This circle called out. Donya hoped for a feeling of the location, much like the tingle in her hands from earlier. Or an image of where it was and who was on it sketched in the dirt and sod in front of her. Instead, she hit the deck hard, shattering through the wood like a boulder. She caught herself mostly on the hull of the boat, one foot punching through. She left her foot dangling out into the fresh seawater for a moment. The sword glowed in her hand. It felt lively and wide awake. She was impressed with its power. It had grown up. However, it apparently now took commands too literally. It must have gotten that from the human.

Donya could feel her connection to that other half out there through the sword—strong and warm. Too strong. The sword enabled them to transfer power between them, an excellent conduit and vessel.

She couldn't focus on that now. Footsteps pounded above her, and a shrill alarm blared. Right now, she needed to decide if she should pull her leg out of the hole and allow more seawater to flood in, or continue to be a stop-gap. Troll minds moved slowly; Donya's was no exception.

A blinding light hit her face from the hole above her. Until that moment she hadn't noticed the pitch blackness around her. There were no engine noises under the sounds of panic. And the boat rocked slightly.

She couldn't understand what the man above her yelled. Inhaling deeply, she smelled Nera. Donya pulled her foot out. Water instantly rushed in. She moved to a hatch and threw open the door.

"Nera." Her mouth moved before she had even decided what to say.

Donya emerged in a dining area. A beautiful table and chairs sat waiting, fine silk covered the chairs and the tablecloth matched. The lights were off and through the windows, she could see a dock. It was not Tokyo.

A man charged into the room shouting. She understood what language it was now—Tagalog, not one she knew. The human languages she had studied were mostly northern ones. Some of these languages fell into disuse and went extinct, but Donya would never forget a language once learned.

She pointed to the hatch, and he rushed that way.

She went up from where he came. A man stood on the deck, and Donya caught Nera's scent on him. He must have held Nera's attention for a while. Tall, handsome for a human, with a strong jaw and large but elegant hands. His eyebrows were knit together, an expression Donya understood now. He looked worried, but not that worried. Donya wanted to rip his heart out and feel while it shuttered to a stop. Then of course grind the warm muscle between her teeth.

"Nera," Donya repeated.

"My Nera, my Nera is gone. Do you know her?" He asked.

His English sounded very flat. Like he did not curl his tongue. Australian, Donya guessed.

"I know her. Where did you lose her?" Donya asked, not moving toward him. She noticed it felt warmer here than in Tokyo.

"Here, we stopped, it is a lovely town. There's ice cream. A waterfall lands in a river not far from town. I wanted to take her to hear it. But I got caught up in a meeting," he said.

His brow furrowed. His eyes glistened with tears, appearing truly distraught. Donya didn't care. She wanted to hit him at least. No, eat him. Maybe not as flamboyantly as before but at least crunch his bones between her molars. She was very hungry. He smelled off though, a smell that came from the mad occasionally.

"You should move on. Once she leaves it is unlikely she will come back."

"She came back before, if we stay here, she will come back," he said confidently.

Donya nodded. An angry man came from below and spoke quickly behind her.

Donya scented the night air. She couldn't waste any more time with these humans. This was the closest she'd come to Nera in over a year. Her scent lingered discreetly in the boat but out on the night air Donya could find a trail. If she moved fast, she could find her. Who cared about a sinking ship.

CHAPTER 5

SCARLET

Scarlet tried not to break speed limits. But it was hard to stay in control. Juan had called her, as she traveled north on the freeway in Watsonville. She needed to turn around. He sounded sure Ariel was with him. Scarlet used the next off-ramp and merged south; traffic in this direction went far slower. Scarlet kept her weaving between cars to a minimum.

Juan couldn't see Ariel of course. But water kept splashing at him from the fish tank. And there were corndog sticks on the floor.

She wasn't afraid for Juan. Ariel wouldn't hurt him. But how the devil did she get to the apartment? Was she afraid, or had she figured out how to travel longer distances and gotten excited? Ariel learned new things all the time, which could be it, Scarlet thought or hoped. Scarlet's frayed nerves felt calmed by this. But then she thought of the melody from earlier. It had to be the singing that drove Ariel to get to the apartment.

Traffic inched to a crawl outside of Moss Landing. From this spot the open ocean was visible, and the air smelled of the marshes. She rolled down her window and tried to listen. Hearing wasn't her specialty. Nothing sounded off, just waves in the distance, no strange singing. Traffic continued to creep along at five miles an hour.

A few months ago, Scarlet found a passage in a book about shielding magics. Her shield should be able to appear and protect things even far away from her. But for it to work she would need to be able to sense those she wanted to protect. Donya always lectured her to work on her other senses. She couldn't close her eyes while driving, even driving very slowly, but she let herself relax and tried to mentally picture her sunny little apartment. Her old couch, the worn carpet, the really sad cabinetry, and Juan cleaning up corndog sticks.

It was a nice mental picture, but she couldn't do what she wanted to do. She could make her shield appear anywhere in her vision. Shields were tools, and hers wanted to be useful. It did what she wanted very easily.

The afternoon light streamed by her so golden it almost felt buttery, she gazed out at the land with the shimmering magic flowing over the ground and floating in the air. One of the books Scarlet found in Grazia's vast library called the stuff "Ged." Scarlet wished she had found another name for it first, something that sounded elfish or more magical. But the word Ged stuck in her mind. She asked Donya if she'd come across that word. Donya couldn't recall it. This winter Donya was supposed to go back to

Italy, Scarlet would meet her there, and they would go through Grazia's collection together. Donya must answer Scarlet's questions. It was a boon from the time Scarlet freely offered her seeds. Donya knew a lot, but occasionally she didn't know the answer to Scarlet's questions. When this occurred, it was because Donya never had thought on certain subjects or hadn't bothered to learn about them. But they could learn together, with the help of the old books, and a visit to the Kraken and Grazia in that other realm.

Scarlet drummed her fingers on the armrest below the window. No spirits were visible which was usual for California. Ged avoided the eucalyptus trees. She never liked those trees, they made her sneeze and smelled like cat piss.

Traffic picked up again, still not moving quickly but almost going the speed limit. She passed the old power plant towers and then the fruit stands. Then the two-lane highway turned back into a multilane freeway, and she hit the gas, breaking the law just a bit by keeping her speed eight miles above the limit. No cop would pull her over for that. Well, not in California anyway.

Scarlet came to her exit before long. She had moved her right hand to take a sip from a water bottle. The opal sword materialized in that hand, Scarlet opened her hand, and dropped it. The darn thing did that whenever Donya used it, forming a double of itself in the hand of the partner that was not holding the real sword. The double was just as useful as the original, however the moment you released a grip on it, it would dissipate. With her already jumpy nerves Scarlet felt like screaming or crying over it. She sped through town and came to a halt in her parking spot in front of the apartment complex. She bounded out of the car and took the stairs two at a time. Not something she was used to. Her breath came in gasps when she made it to the second-floor landing. Her next-door neighbor stood in his doorway pulling a laundry basket from his apartment.

"Hey, neighbor," he said.

"Hi, Trun," she panted.

"Doing a workout for the upcoming nuptials?"

She drove her key into the lock. She had been expecting Juan to watch for her and open the door. If he wasn't, what did that mean? "Uhhuh, need to fit into the dress." She did not want to get stuck talking. "Gotta get inside, I'm late for a call with the florist."

"Can't wait to see the big day," Trun said, then he hefted his laundry and awkwardly descended the stairs.

Scarlet opened the door, and was greeted by a merry tune. Sebastian sang *Under the Sea* from the big TV in the living room. Juan sat on the couch bouncing along to the beat. Ariel perched on his lap, kicking her tentacle-like legs and humming happily.

Scarlet stood gaping for a moment. The corndog sticks indeed littered the floor. As she stepped in, she saw that there was more mess than Juan noticed. Plants knocked over on the balcony. Corndog wrappers sprinkled the stovetop and kitchen table. And water dripped down the walls, not a lot, the amount a small tentacle would flick at a person or a cat.

The cat was wet.

Mostly his tail, but he licked it morosely as he sat at the top of his cat tree.

When the happy tune ended Juan and Ariel finally focused on her.

"Oh, good you're home, I'll go unpack dinner," Juan said.

Scarlet marveled at his ability to miss the expression on her face. The tightness of her jaw. Although even she couldn't place the emotion running through her. Relief, anger, annoyance, they seemed to all swirl about warring for the winning emotion. She walked over and picked up Ariel off Juan's lap.

"How did you get here?" Scarlet asked her. She didn't expect an answer. Ariel was a baby after all. But maybe she could get the point across.

Ariel's attention drifted back to the movie. They had played it every day when she stayed here for a month last winter. Scarlet had been worried she wouldn't get enough to eat in January when tourist levels were low, and the ocean temperature dropped. But Ariel languished in the fish tank—bored and lonely all day.

Scarlet paused the movie. Ariel blinked, her big eyes focused on the remote in Scarlet's hand. The tips of her tentacles turned from pink to violet, but she shifted refocusing on Scarlet.

Scarlet repeated her question. "Ariel, how did you get here?"

Ariel's cheeks puffed up, "swim swim swim," she said. Then held up her hands and opened and closed her fingers. "Pop, pop, and pop," she continued. The last word of each triplet was slightly higher, almost like a question.

Scarlet nodded, understanding that she swam the shoreline and then used her spacial magic to pop herself along. Pop pop was very useful. As the crow flies the apartment sat near the ocean. And there were ponds on the way, the biggest one by the library.

"Ariel why?" Scarlet asked.

Ariel turned chartreuse, then faded her color to match the couch that Scarlet now huddled on. It made her blend in. Except that Ariel sat on Scarlet's blue jeans—the visual suggested a couch puddle in her lap.

She wasn't going to get an answer to that one.

"It's okay, you are here now, and it looks like you ate." Scarlet could feel her shoulders dropping. "Was it hard to get here?"

This question had Ariel changing back to her pinkish hue. She nodded enthusiastically. "Yes Yes."

If it was hard to get here her reason must have been important. Scarlet decided to ask again later, after Ariel rested.

"Here it is," Juan said, coming around the corner with three plates balanced.

He set Scarlet's plate in front of her on the low coffee table. It was a salad, a nice one with chicken, walnuts, and cranberries. He had the same. On the third plate was a warm corndog and a chocolate cupcake. That plate, he gave to Ariel.

Ariel sniffed at Juan's salad then stuck her tongue out.

Scarlet felt about the same, but she knew human adults needed to eat salad. She poked her romaine lettuce. Then speared a cranberry with her fork and placed it on Ariel's plate. "Try it," Scarlet said. It was the tastiest part of the salad.

Ariel eyed Juan who happily ate his salad on the other side of her. Then she looked pointedly at Scarlet's untouched plate.

Scarlet forked a leaf and another cranberry and placed it in her mouth. She attempted a smile as she crunched on the mixture. The cranberry was dried and sweetened, the dressing contained olive oil and lemon. It wasn't that bad.

This appeased Ariel. She placed the cranberry in her mouth and bit it. Her chubby cheeks sucked in.

"Even dried they're sour but still good," Scarlet said. She used the cranberry as a way to stare intently at Ariel. Her pink didn't appear as saturated as normal. And the violet in her tentacles was completely gone, instead, they looked dark, almost black. Scarlet wondered if she felt weak after using so much magic. Even now Ariel continued to use her magic. Scarlet knew from minding her niece that kids don't always know how to slow down when they are tired.

"She didn't like it?" Juan asked.

"She made a face, but I'm sure she loved it," Scarlet answered.

"Movie," Ariel squealed, picking up her corndog and using magic to wiggle the remote. The black on her tentacles crept up a millimeter or two.

They would put her to bed early Scarlet decided.

Juan grabbed the jiggling remote and pressed play.

Scarlet put another forkful of salad in her mouth and eyed the cupcake. Maybe Ariel would share a bite. They did need to work on sharing.

The dream surrounded Scarlet again. It began as it had the first time, in the ocean. She preferred when the dream started in the desert. The ocean seemed more awful after the fact because it was something she loved but that had been used against her. Going to the pool no longer worked for her. She would have canceled her gym membership altogether if the Tuesday night yoga teacher wasn't so nice. She missed laps but didn't have time to figure out her fear with all the other things she needed to work on.

She swam slowly. Wondering when Donya would arrive. She had never yet been alone while repeating the dream. Scarlet always hoped the water would drain away quickly. It felt like something lurked past the kelp. She couldn't decide what to do, so she swam up. She swam up and up. It took a long time to get to the surface in the dream, kelp didn't grow this deeply in the real world. But dreams don't make sense, so why would dream magic? Finally, she broke out into the air and sunlight. She bobbed in the swells.

Tomorrow would be a shitty day at work. This dream made her wake up feeling unrested and cranky.

Something grabbed her foot and she screamed.

Donya broke the surface next to her and her scream cut off.

"I have said before, nothing is here to harm you in this place," Donya reprimanded.

"Then why does it feel scary?" Scarlet snapped.

"Blood magic will have that effect on its creations."

"Weren't they trying to frighten me here?" Scarlet asked.

"I don't believe so. This should have been the dream—water, sunlight. You needed to be bound but I doubt they wanted to frighten you."

"What about the monster eel you fought, and the shark, and the sea snake disguise Mars used? Those wouldn't be in a normal dream."

"I doubt Heldrig would know what is in a human dream, Nera either."

"Huh," Scarlet shrugged in the water. She could kick and kick in this dream and never grow tired. If only this burned calories. "Ariel traveled all the way from Santa Cruz to my apartment."

"Very mobile, and quite the show of strength for one so small and new."

"I think it's because she's afraid," Scarlet said.

"Why?" Donya asked. Her face showed no emotion.

"Today I he—"

The song started.

"That, that, what is that!" Scarlet half-shrieked.

Donya cocked her head—she was not very expressive, but her eyes seemed wider than usual.

"I know that tune, calm yourself."

Scarlet did not feel any calmer. But she stayed quiet.

"That song is not inside the dream. It is from long ago. It summons in the language of storms."

Scarlet shivered violently in the water although she was not cold. "None of that made me any calmer."

A crack began in the sky.

"Good, I am glad you will be waking. That song, it is a summons."

"A summons to what?"

"I do not know. We will need the sword. The song is here because you can hear it in your sleeping ears." Donya activated the sword she held, as she always held the sword in the dream.

The shadow of the sword appeared in Scarlet's hand.

"It wakes up quickly now. It is eager," Donya said.

The water drained away from their feet, leaving the dried cracked ground. The symbol appeared. Scarlet counted the pieces of the crumbling sky again. "Eight hundred ninety-two, again."

Scarlet's heart beat like a drum. She had never wanted the dream to end this badly. She watched as the sky cracked open and chunks of blue fell.

"Be ready when you open your eyes," Donya warned.

CHAPTER 6

DONYA

Donya woke long before sunset when the dream shattered. It was far too bright for her to move. The sword felt warm in her hand, and it shimmered even in the thick shadow. It stayed awake. She couldn't tell what had happened, Scarlet lived, that much she knew. Donya wondered if the same spell she used last night to make it to the Fin and Tonic would work to cross the sea quickly to Scarlet. The spell was meant for objects, but with the sword, the spell had been altered to not just show one the image of the object or know its location. Perhaps the spell could now be used on a human. And the sword would want to see Scarlet. That way would be faster than a plane. She would need more ash and pine boughs. Few conifers grew in the area, she couldn't smell a single pine on the breeze. The air held more warmth and moisture than Tokyo. Though her place on the earth lay farther south, still, she seemed to be in Japan.

Donya felt a pang of covetousness for that summoning. The one who sang it could be quite far away from Scarlet and yet she could hear it. Donya knew no summoning spells, only tracking. She tried to push the feeling and thoughts of summoning from her mind.

The sun heated the stones she could see from her shadowed hiding place. A large pillar in the middle of a vast green space made an appealing shadow Donya liked to watch move over the plants. Last night the stones told her the humans built this monument to unite the eight corners of the world. She was confused as the world had no corners. But the stones were adamant, proud of the story of their lineage and place of power. She did not argue. And if the earth held extra power in this place that could help her to move across the ocean, moving that far would be difficult even with the strength she possessed, and perhaps tapping into Scarlet's reservoirs as well.

The minutes ticked by. She thought of how she would find a phone and call Scarlet once the sun set. Her apology to Nera would have to wait. Nera's trail the night before had gone cold, Donya was sure Nera doubled back a few times and then her scent disappeared into a river. In her gut, Donya knew by tonight Nera would have covered her tracks again. She had failed to utilize her best opportunity to find Nera.

Donya pulled at her hair which helped it form the spikes she normally wore. The moss in the shade smelled nice. She stroked a thumb over it—soft as velvet. She found herself humming the tune from the dream. It was a song of summoning as she had told Scarlet, chanted and crooned at one of the great holy nights long ago. When the war god died at the end of the year, the time of the goddesses began. It hailed from the language of storms. It brought the cold and the rain. It closed off the world for many, making it a time of family, of mending, of potion brewing, and of ale drinking.

It was not sung any other time or for another reason.

Who would know that song? And who would sing it outside of its proper time? They must be summoning more than rain.

Scarlet seemed truly terrified by the harmless tune. Many of the very troubling incidents that Donya had in fact brought on Scarlet did not bother her as much as they should have in Donya's opinion. Lately Scarlet seemed more careful in her actions, which was wise, humans are very breakable with their squishy warm insides. Donya felt a hunger pang and deliberately changed the direction her mind headed.

But that timid new nature had a drawback. Scarlet was slow to practice and master her abilities, both the old and the new. Donya had not pressed her about this. A mistake on her part. If Scarlet was adept in her sight, she could see the threat in several different ways. Donya would help her with this as soon as she arrived, although it would not be easy as Donya had no strength in vision magically or otherwise.

Perhaps Scarlet did not let Donya understand the depth of her troubles. They had not known each other that long, and though they were allies, could a troll and a human have friendship between them? Scarlet did speak of her wedding more often to Donya and in a way that made it sound like a problem. She invited Donya to the special day. They spoke about it not long after Donya woke from her winter rest. Donya hadn't thought much of it at the time, but perhaps she should go. How often would a bond like theirs occur? A troll and a human.

Donya found herself smiling at the thought of a wedding. The smile on her cold lips caused her mind to wander back to Nera who made her smile too. Nera who could be down the street from her. Perhaps she would be playing in a river or a lake on this island and Donya would find her if she just kept up the hunt. The world was large. If she left now would she ever find Nera? She made it difficult, years of escaping her father meant nothing short of a family tie and blood magic could find her. Although Donya did have most of her true name; that was something. Maybe if a deity tried, they could locate Nera. Trolls worshiped no gods or goddesses.

Nera was still running. Probably running from her, she thought. Donya had used many spells over the year and a half that she searched for Nera. There was no way Nera didn't know someone sought her. And there was no way she didn't know of her father's death. The ripple of his death spread wide. As Donya was a known acquaintance, many spirits and creatures asked her about it. She kept vague, not letting on that she helped in his end. Though she had not helped as she would have liked. Donya would have liked to be the one to smash his body to dust. Scarlet got all the luck.

Donya needed to find Nera. It was important that Donya apologized properly and made amends. Although she still didn't know how she would make amends. She rolled onto her stomach and thought about how now she would have much more time to make that plan. Gifts perhaps, or the acquisition of something Nera needed. Donya poked her fingers down. The old layers of moss were thick, but her fingers closed around a pebble.

She brought it up to the surface.

"That is better. I haven't seen the sun in a century," the pebble said.

"Happy I could help, most rocks don't notice if they are in the sun or not." Donya breathed a sigh of relief at having a friendly rock to talk to. Her thoughts were causing an uncomfortable tightness in her stomach.

"Not me, I always liked the sun, I rolled along the bottom of a river for many years. My river housed a dragon. He loved to play in the sunlight and lay on us rocks."

"What happened to your dragon? And your river?"

"The river was rerouted for the construction of apartments. I don't know where the dragon went. You are well met troll. I am Hisa."

"Well met Hisa, I am Donya."

"It is not often I have seen trolls, too warm here, but shouldn't you be a night creature?"

"Yes. I awoke from a dream. And now my thoughts will not let me rest." Donya resituated herself on the soft green moss.

"What thoughts would those be?"

"If I should go to a human wedding." She set Hisa on the moss beside her.

"I must be the luckiest river rock that ever existed. What a story. A human wedding. If you were invited you must go."

Donya thought about this for a moment. Hisa was correct. To not go would be rude. Trolls lived tens of thousands of years, there was time to pursue Nera. Donya would move herself tonight, like she did for the ship. And it would be good practice for the sword. Repeating spells made them stronger and faster.

"I will go."

"Did the bride or the groom invite you?" Hisa asked.

"The bride."

"You must take her a silk kimono."

Donya had seen a few kimonos in the tourist areas of Tokyo. None smelled of real silk. She did not think Scarlet had much interest in fashion. Still, it would be appropriate.

"Is that a human tradition here?"

"How would I know? I am no human," Hisa said with a laugh.

Donya cracked a smile. "You seemed so insistent."

"Silk is only the fabric that seems most like sunlight and water. And the cut of a kimono is very pretty."

"That it is."

❧

It wasn't full dark, but Donya left her hiding place, Hisa in her pocket and her sword strapped to her back. The sword felt heavier than usual, and Donya wondered at what Scarlet had done with it. First, she needed to check on Scarlet and let her know she would come to her. Phones were very convenient. More convenient than spells. Then with her human forewarned and hopefully still bodily sound Donya would call out her true name and use it to pull herself to California. No reason to wait on a plane ticket when she could use the new spell. The sword would help. And this time she would land gracefully and not damage any structures.

She bought a calling card at the first convenience store she came across. The town was busy, people chatted softly, rode bicycles, entered cars, closed doors, and lights flicked on. All of it filled the air with the din of life. It took Donya until true dark to find a payphone. They were few and far between anymore. During her walk, she noted the many palm trees and more tropical flora of the area.

She followed the instructions on the card and dialed Scarlet's number. It went to voicemail.

She repeated the steps.

It went to voicemail again.

Donya impatiently waited for the beep. "I will come to you."

Donya found herself cursing under her breath as she left the phone. Her cheery mood had been unwarranted. She needed ash and pine. Once again, she headed to California.

CHAPTER 7

SCARLET

Scarlet woke with the sword in her hand. She swung it in a wide arch. Fire shot out of the tip. A lick of the flame caught her cell phone sitting on the bedside table, it clattered to the floor and sizzled.

After the bright flash of fire, Scarlet stood stunned and dazed. Her night vision showed her there was no threat in the room. Juan still slept on the other side of the bed, Scarlet's shield extended over him. Her cell phone smoked on the floor. Ariel was awake in the fish tank in the other room. And although Scarlet couldn't see her, she could hear her making little calls, and what Scarlet's sleepy brain thought was a whimper.

Scarlet kept the sword pointed down and rushed to the living room while reeling in her shield. The shield bothered Ariel, but Scarlet would put it back up if she saw anything strange.

Ariel's head and face were a bright white, shifting to gray in her body and black at the ends of her tentacles. All of her tentacles bundled up tight and she clung in a corner of the fish tank. All the fish huddled around her.

"Shah shhh, Ariel I'm sorry. Did the fire scare you? It startled me too."

The sword was not normally this awake and rambunctious. Although she rarely practiced with it, Scarlet could feel it wanting to be used again. It felt light in her hand, almost like it wanted to be raised, to be pointed at something.

Ariel nodded her head. Her tentacles relaxed and she stuck them over the side of the tank. Her eyes were on the sword.

"This is mine. It won't hurt you. Your mama helped make it."

"Mama."

"Yep, that's right."

The song started again. It had been quiet. But from the open window, the melancholy tune drifted in.

All the hair on Scarlet's neck raised. She looked at Ariel. Her tentacles once again bunched together.

"Ariel, is that song why you are here?"

Ariel only watched Scarlet with wide eyes.

"I think that might be a yes." Scarlet stepped closer to the tank and scooped up Ariel with her free hand. The small spirit used her arms and tentacles to grip tightly onto Scarlet. Ariel was cold and wet, but still, the closeness was comforting. Even though they were both afraid they were not alone.

"I'm glad you're here," Scarlet said.

Ariel nuzzled her face into Scarlet's shoulder.

"Let's peek outside."

Scarlet turned around. Juan shambled up behind her, sleepily holding out her phone.

"I heard voices and smelled smoke. What happened?"

"I'll explain later, it's good you're up. Put down that phone and follow me."

"Babe, what's in your hand?" Juan asked.

"Oh, this? You can see it?"

"The shining sword, yes, yes I can see that."

"Good, I think. Okay stay behind me and follow us outside."

Juan bobbed his head, placing the smoldering phone on the tile of their little bathroom floor.

Scarlet made her way outside. She hoped their neighbor wouldn't hear anything. It was a quiet complex.

The moon shone on the wooden decking, no wind stirred the nearby trees, and yet mist was moving in low to the ground. And the song sounded as loud as if it came from a car below them in the parking lot.

"Ocean," Ariel said pointing west with a chubby finger.

Scarlet could feel the sword tugging on her arm. She walked out farther, away from the tree branches to her right. Juan stayed in the doorway, his eyes on the sword.

"Here goes nothing," Scarlet whispered as she raised the sword.

For a moment nothing happened. She peered up at the weapon, feeling like a failed She-Ra. Did she need to concentrate or something?

The song ended with a mournful trill. Scarlet repositioned her feet, preparing to swing the sword down since it wouldn't be doing anything else. "Do something," She whispered at the sword, feeling anger flare for a moment, all the sword had managed was to kill her cell phone.

The sword heard her, and a fountain of shadow erupted from the tip.

Ariel let out a wail and leapt from her arms, scrambling up Juan's leg.

Scarlet stood immobilized, unsure of what was happening. This shadow was like Donya's magic. It looked wet and fast. Would it fall back to earth like a toxic rain? Scarlet watched it float in the night sky shaped between a nimbus cloud and an amoeba. It moved suddenly with a lurching undulation toward the west, where the ocean lay.

Scarlet slowly lowered the sword. She kept a tight grip on the hilt letting it finish what it had started, it twinkled in the low light. Minutes ticked by and the melody ended abruptly.

"It stopped, maybe you killed it." Juan whispered.

"Go back inside, get some rest," Scarlet said quietly to Juan. Who looked sleepy.

He wandered inside still holding Ariel close to his chest.

Scarlet tried to reach out with her senses, but nothing tingled, all she could do was watch the sword. Its colors shifted to shimmering purples, that rippled over its surface. It felt like fifteen to twenty minutes passed by Scarlet's arm grew tired from holding the heavy stone sword. Then the light works stopped, and she was sure it was finished with whatever it had done. Scarlet let go of the sword and as it was the double it disappeared.

❧❧

Scarlet felt sorry for herself. She had not bought any kind of insurance for her old phone. And summer was a terrible time to purchase a phone. A new model would come out in time for the holidays, and it would probably have a new camera. And she was tired from working all day. She wanted to go home and eat chocolate. But the new phone in her hand had a better camera than her old phone, and it was waterproof making it safer to take on the honeymoon. Scarlet kept her phones meticulously backed up, so she knew she hadn't lost any documents or photos.

Three voicemails popped up as she walked to her car. The phone loaded files and apps from the cloud slowly without Wi-Fi access. She didn't recognize any of the numbers. She checked the most recent one first.

It was the bakery. They wanted to make sure she was set on the black forest cake for two layers. An entire day when vendors couldn't get in touch with her this close to the wedding hopefully didn't cause any disasters.

She called them back immediately. "Hi yes, this is Scarlet Burke. Is Rochelle in?"

"No, she left for the day."

"Okay, can you leave a message that yes I am sure about the black forest cake?"

"Yep, I'll write it on a sticky note and leave it at her workstation."

"Thank you. Have a great evening." Scarlet hung up. She sat in her car, the shopping center parking lot was almost deserted. It was hot inside, but it felt good on her tense shoulders. She took a deep breath appreciating a moment of solitude and silence. The wedding was ten days away. They needed to submit the final count of guests in the next three days.

The next missed call was one sentence. "I will come to you."

It took Scarlet a heartbeat to recognize Donya's voice. The line crackled. She played it again.

"Fuck" Scarlet yelled at the top of her lungs.

"I knew it. I fucking knew it," she continued to mumble to herself. That song. It was bad. Evil, darkness, a trap for her and Juan. It had to be. Why else would Donya come?

Sweat trickled down her back. The keys dangled from the ignition. She turned the car over and cracked the windows. Unfortunately, she couldn't run home and hide. Her next stop was to get more corndogs and salad at the store.

The sun glinted brightly off of windshields, and birds sang in the trees lining the streets, but Scarlet's knuckles were white on the steering wheel. Her inner monologue wouldn't slow. This was the time before her wedding. Couldn't she be allowed to enjoy it? How lucky are the brides who only need to worry about cake flavors and rain? She needed to worry about missing bodies, songs drifting along the coastline, and incoming trolls.

She remembered the third call but was merging onto the highway. The speed helped calm her frantic thoughts. She merged over to the fast lane. The ocean was bright blue to the left of her. It would be great if the weather could be this perfect on her big day. The climate on the central coast was pretty stable, but that rain in the forecast worried her.

A highway patrol car always hid on this stretch of the One. A patch of dirt and tall trees made a convenient hiding place. Scarlet let off the gas when she saw him. They never pull anyone over for barely breaking the speed limit. She passed him and nothing happened.

Her mind bounded around to a million different things at once. But one of the connections her brain was trying to make besides remembering to play that last message was that she needed to reread the section in the *Liber Unguium* on transference. When she got home she would. Donya had explained the principle to her once, that the sword could and did transfer their magic types and eventually could even move objects between the two. It stemmed from her fire because fire moved everything in the universe.

She wasn't changing her mind about focusing on the wedding. But if she could send a message to Donya it would facilitate another phone call, maybe one where Donya could tell Scarlet why she wanted to come, if Scarlet should be scared out of her mind.

One thing first. She played the last message as she grabbed a cart for her shopping.

"Hello Scarlet, it's Guy. I have news. On your cousin, or whoever that man was you wanted me to find. I found him. Well, I found where he was, until he left. That's right, came out of the coma months ago. Give me a call when you have a chance."

Scarlet stood at the entrance of the store mouth gaping and the slow realization that she wasn't overreacting—everything was much worse than she had even thought.

CHAPTER 8

DONYA

"Her name is Scarlet, that is the best one," Hisa said.

"She is a very pink human, I am not sure the red blossoms will compliment her color." Donya stood in a dark shop. She had sniffed out the fine fibers and asked the stone walls to bend for her. The shop was very small and neat, she did not want to do any damage. Many of the buildings here were old, but the scent of fire permeated the structures. Like they had burned many years ago.

It took a while to narrow down the kimonos in the shop, all were made of the finest silk and none were ugly. Donya found shopping for the human very difficult, she recalled the last time she needed to. When they had been in danger. When Donya needed Heldrig to have a more difficult time tracking Scarlet.

The question before her was the dark blue silk kimono with white starbursts skirting the bottom or a white silk kimono with red camellia blossoms. Both garments were very fine and made with skill, the starbursts seemed as though they belonged in the night sky and the blooms could have just been plucked.

"And then you must decide on the Obi," Hisa said.

"This is quite difficult. Finding all of the materials for the spell was easier."

"And you do want to be off, fine the blue kimono but I must insist on that pink Obi over there, the Obijime and sash packaged with it will all work wonderfully."

"Perfect." Donya saw the beauty of the choice, the starbursts perhaps would remind Scarlet of the Ged she could see. An ability unique even amongst spirits and ancient beings.

Donya flipped over the price tag. She fished out more yen than needed and left it on the counter. Behind the counter, she could see a neat stack of shopping bags with the store's logo embossed on the front. She took one and began to fold the silk up.

"You really should wrap them in tissue paper," Hisa instructed.

"I will find a place to have them professionally wrapped when I get to California. Right now, I only need a container." Donya would not dishonor herself or Scarlet by giving a shabby gift.

"What will you wear to the wedding?" Hisa asked.

Donya had not spent much time with this stone, but she felt like Hisa was very good at reading others. "I will find a garment that is suitable in California."

Hisa stayed silent.

Closing her eyes Donya thought of what she would wear, perhaps a suit made of fine wool. But as she breathed in the sweet smell of the silk all around her, it still held that green hint of mulberry sap. She changed her mind. Donya could picture what the caterpillars had feasted on as they grew plump in a far-off place. Those larvae died to make all the beauty here. Donya took a few steps still smelling the air. Her fingers brushed the soft silk, and when she opened her eyes she found the singular black kimono in the shop meant for a woman. She studied the design, a mountain decorated the bottom. It was not like her mountain, which was snow topped with tall evergreen trees rimming its base. No, this mountain lay covered in trees mostly green but with a few bright red maples mixed in. Those leaves were rendered in fine detail with gold threading showing the veins. She liked it. And she still had a few minutes to kill, she wanted to complete the spell with the sword at moonset.

"Good, now grab that white Obi, it does not have the accouterments like your friends. Give me a second," Hisa said.

If Hisa was a being with hands Donya would have imagined her tapping her chin while circling the display of Obijime, the beautiful cords that went over the Obi.

"Yes, the golden cord to pick up the gold in the design and that patterned white sash."

Donya grabbed both, but hesitated at the sash. It felt protective, and it reminded her of the tengu on the first night in Tokyo. Donya moved her hand to a solid smooth deep purple one. It would set off the black.

"You have excellent taste," Hisa said.

Donya got the impression that Hisa enjoyed this entirely too much. Donya retrieved more cash from her bag, she would need to obtain more money soon. She left it with her first stack and placed her outfit inside the bag gently on Scarlet's wedding present. "Where would you like to be left? I am going to the seashore, I can leave you in the waves or outside this shop. I see a water garden you might enjoy."

"I must see you off. The beach will be fine, it has been ages since I have been in salt water."

It was a quick walk to the seashore through the tiny town. It amazed Donya the difference in human habitation. That there could be a city like Tokyo and then a tiny town like this in the same culture. Nothing hung about in the night, it stayed quite like her mountain. When they reached the sea, the waves lapped at the rocky shore, Donya climbed up the craggy surface and started to make her circle. The rock of the shoreline would not allow her to thrust the sword into the earth as she had in Tokyo but there was a large tide pool. She would dip it into the water, it was a slight adjustment. If she tried to bury the opal sword into the rock it would get scratched. Lately, she felt a sense of pride in the beautiful sword; she would not see it damaged. She placed Hisa outside where she would carve her circle and pile her ash.

"This will be goodbye."

"Fare thee well," Hisa called.

Donya plunged her fingers into the rock—it gave easily—she was at full strength these past weeks. She scraped the circle into its surface. A wave broke at the bottom of the rock she perched on and sea water misted in all directions. Nothing stayed dry but there was a high spot at the center of her circle. She poured the ash at the highest point. The circle began to charge.

She woke up the sword. It came to life almost instantly in her hand. It was aging, so this was appropriate. She wondered if it became excited that they would be going to where Scarlet lived. Probably. She always got the feeling that the sword wanted to be at the human's side.

She spoke a word of power and slowly dipped the sword into the pool of water in her circle. "Bring me to Scarlet Josephine Burke."

A ripple rolled through the water around the sword. Shadow spilled from the sword, pooling on the surface of the water. It moved slowly to Donya's feet. She wondered at the difference from the last casting—where was the fire to balance out the spring water she had used? The shadow climbed her legs. It was warm, with a feeling on her rocky skin not unlike that of the silk kimono she had felt between her fingers moments before.

There was a knowing that something rested wrong. She scanned the circle and around her, noting a hummock by Hisa. The pine branch when she set Hisa down, she set the branch down. Donya forgot to eat it. What would happen? Usually, when you botched a spell like this nothing happened. But the sword pushed through, puddling out power.

"Stop, I command you to stop," Donya said, gripping the hilt of the sword with both hands. "We will do this again in a moment. Do not expend energy on a failed spell." Both Donya and the sword were at full strength. She tried to lift it from the pool of water but found the sword would not budge.

The sword spilled more shadow. It climbed her, up her waist up her chest. What would happen? Could the sword move her all on its own without the link to green living things that the pine would have added? The ash of death, the green of life.

This wasn't going to end well.

Donya grunted and pulled on the sword. It shouldn't be able to hold itself in the water like this. Naming a sword would allow you more control. It was such a young sword; she hadn't thought about giving it a name yet. Or heard if it used a name for itself. If she knew its name, she could call it and put a stop to this rebellion.

The sword held fast. She felt the rock between her feet crumble slightly at the force she exerted by digging back with her heels.

The shadow went over her head. She waited. What would happen now? Her hands were still on the sword. It could be best to wait. Perhaps it was the youth of the sword, it needed to rebel. As she had when she started traveling. Darkness never bothered her, but she did need to get to California. Perhaps using this spell again had been hasty. A plane ticket seemed better and better every moment.

Another presence pulsed in the darkness with her. She could feel the shadow wrap around it. A familiar presence emanating heat and pressure. The sword had done it. Scarlet was there.

The shadow slinked away, falling into the tide pool and the ocean. The sword glistened in the starlight.

Donya was surprised to see she stood in the same spot. Scarlet stood next to her, dressed in jeans and a white button-up top. She had a purse and a small satchel. Her keys dangled from her hand. She blinked a few times.

"What, what happened?" Scarlet asked, sinking onto the rocky shore.

"That is what I would like to know," Donya said, pulling up the sword and giving it a good shake.

CHAPTER 9

SCARLET

Scarlet's forehead scrunched up and she tried to relax it as she spoke into the phone. "Yes sorry, I don't know what happened. Maybe two days, with the weekend I am sure it will be enough time. I could work another day next week to make up for it," Scarlet said into her phone. She paused to listen to Khloe's response. It was all positive, but she could barely pay attention, her eyes kept wandering to the dark shops around them. "Yes, I'm sure that's it. Thank you again. See you next week," She managed to say when the line went quiet.

Donya sat silently watching. She had replaced the sword in its scabbard that hung on her back, and she carried a small stone.

Scarlet stayed quiet for a few more moments. She was thankful that Donya had the presence to allow her a bit of time to recover herself. They had walked in from the rocky shoreline and sat at the chairs of a closed ice cream shop. She knew this because there was a cute cartoon of an ice cream cone on the sign. She couldn't read the kanji. She blinked and rubbed at her temples. "I'm lucky I have an easy-going boss. She thinks my stomach is acting up because of nerves. Nerves for my wedding that is happening in nine days, Donya. Nine days."

"Less. You are across the dateline. Eight days."

"God, I want to throw this cell phone on the ground and smash it," Scarlet's face and neck heated. Her stomach did honestly hurt. Would this be what canceled her wedding? It seemed likely.

"Interesting, you don't seem that upset."

"I am," Scarlet snapped. She knew Donya wouldn't care about being snapped at, but she added more gently, "but it would be nice to let my rage out. Probably healthier too."

"Keep the emotion, we could use your power. Anger is excellent fuel for fire."

Scarlet knew the troll was correct. "Ugh. What are we going to do now? How can I get back to the US? I only have four days."

"Four days?"

"Yes, I need to work on Monday."

"Work is no longer a necessity for you. Did not Grazia leave you, her fortune?"

"That is tied up in legal terribleness, and I do have access to her home at least but all the stuff in it is soaked in magic. I can't even sell any of the gold off. It's all enchanted. There is a seal on everything. Who knows what I could unleash." Scarlet focused on a spirit ambling along the sidewalk across the street. It bore the skin and shell of a turtle, but it had a birdlike beak and it walked on its hind legs.

"But soon you will be very wealthy."

"If I don't go to Italian jail. There are still a few investigators in Rome that think I murdered her and forced her to change her will."

"Not in that order, I am sure."

"God damn it, enough of your sass,". Scarlet raised her voice and the turtle spirit glanced over at them. If she wasn't mistaken, he appeared afraid of them. That seemed silly to her, but maybe Donya could be scary even to other monsters.

"To answer your questions, as I must do, I can get you a fake passport very quickly. We will fly to California in at most three days."

"This just keeps getting better," Scarlet said, putting her face into her hands. Tears pricked at her eyes, but she didn't actually feel like crying.

"Will you be calling your intended next?"

"He won't realize I'm not around for a while. He's at work. I'll wait till he gets out. Then he won't worry as much," She said, pushing the calling card back across the table.

Donya nodded.

"Are you judging me?" Scarlet asked as she dropped her head even lower into now folded arms.

"No, who am I to judge? But Hisa said a few comments you might not want to hear." Donya flicked the small stone next to her. "Now you must tell me what happened with your singer and the sword."

Scarlet was relieved she hadn't been in the middle of a shower when she magically transported to Japan. No, she had her wallet, her new cellphone, and was dressed appropriately. She even slept well the night before. Donya procured train tickets and now they traveled at three hundred miles an hour to a city on the western side of Japan. She was impressed with the troll's Japanese. Scarlet knew Donya liked language even though the troll didn't speak much.

They took a bus to the Shinkansen. Scarlet appreciated how everything looked shiny and new around her. She took the window seat on the high-speed train to help shelter Donya from any sunlight that might come through. The countryside flying by glowed almost too green. It was very early morning. She needed to call Juan, he would work late today but he'd get home before they arrived in Fukuoka. And her car would still be in the parking spot.

"What is that?" Scarlet asked Donya while pointing.

Donya leaned over her. Scarlet noted that Donya smelled much better than the first time she had smelled her. More like dirt and rocks.

"My eyes are not as good as yours. They are not as good as even a normal human's eyes. But it looks like a flock. Can you describe one to me?"

"They are flying rather quickly. Swirling around. I am trying to pick out one. They have a red face."

"Maybe they are tengu? I met one when I arrived here. Don't worry, they are harmless to humans."

"There must be a hundred of them. We are getting closer. I wonder why they have such a long nose."

"The better to sniff out evil. They are protectors of the mountains," Donya said.

"Maybe we could get one to sniff out Mars." They passed the flock of tengu and soon they would be a blur in the distance.

Donya didn't keep her eyes out the window, instead watching Scarlet. "Do you have any word on his body?"

"I guess it's good that I can tell you in person. I got a call yesterday. The PI said he woke up. He woke up and left a convalescent hospital."

Donya remained silent.

Scarlet felt bad. She should have told her right away. But she had been in shock at the circumstance she found herself in. They'd only been back together a few hours. And what could they do from over here?

"Where did he go after he left?" Donya whispered.

Scarlet was taken aback by how quiet the troll had gone. She turned to face her. Donya's skin lost some of its gray color and even seemed smoother. A shiver ran up Scarlet's spine at the sight, and she let her protective shield roll out over the two of them.

"I don't know. That PI wouldn't tell me. Wanted more money, and he deduced that I wasn't related to Mars. I think he might have investigated me. I don't look great on paper right now. It's weird to be caught up in so many seedy dealings," Scarlet said. Continuing to watch her magical ally who did not move.

Minutes ticked by. Donya didn't blink. Scarlet hadn't stared at her or any other magical being lately. And after all this time she finally received an answer to a question she had thought upon first seeing the troll. How she appeared to other people.

Her vision allowed her to see a spell, a spell she had read about; it was a glamour. Glamours were a spell, but they worked especially well on humans because humans held preconceived notions of how the world worked. In this case of how others should look.

Donya had deep brown eyes and hair. Her skin was a pale sickly tan, like someone with a severe vitamin D deficiency. Her nose was smaller than her troll nose. Her hair still stuck up, but it appeared to be shiny as with gel. And she seemed young. Perhaps about fifteen. Her teeth were bright white and perfectly square. Her lips were thin and plum in color.

Scarlet blinked and the image faded. Donya was once again a gray troll whose arms were too long, with hair the color of raisins. Donya's mouth hung a bit open. Scarlet had not noticed how sharp her teeth were before, and that they did not appear to be made of stone like her skin.

Scarlet felt impatient with the silent statue act. "What are your teeth made of?"

Donya blinked. Once then twice. Her mouth closed and she brought her hand up to her lips. "Diamond, all troll teeth are diamond. We can bite through anything."

"Good to know. Now are you going to tell me what thought you got lost in?"

"No, it is too troubling."

They arrived in Fukuoka and were blessed with a late summer rainstorm. The clouds lay thick and covered the sun. So, Donya could venture out into the city. They hailed a cab and Donya handed him an address.

Scarlet wanted to ask Donya a few questions, but as Donya had explained to her, they needed to start being more careful. Who knew what Mars was up to.

Juan took the news of her being in Japan with a long silence. Scarlet assured him that they would be coming home in a conventional airplane. He asked her to go to a consulate to get a real passport. But how could she explain how she had entered the country? There wouldn't be any record of a flight. If an official checked into her even a tiny bit, she could end up in jail. Donya traveled all over the place with fake papers.

They drove away from the bustling city and out into the suburbs. The houses all wore blue tile roofs, and many had sweet little gardens. The taxi slowed and Scarlet could see glimpses into the townspeople's lives. Here a row of white sheets hanging on a line. There a small pool with a very young child jumping in it. In another yard perched an elderly man with a teacup balanced in his hands.

They pulled into a small supermarket parking lot. Donya got out, apparently ready to stand in the rain in a very specific spot in the parking lot. "Let me do all the talking," Donya said.

"Um, if we are going to stand here for a very long time I need an umbrella."

They went inside and bought a large black umbrella, one they could both stand under.

Back outside it was half an hour before a young man approached them with a couple of quick bows. He spoke to Donya in quiet Japanese. Scarlet wouldn't be a part of this conversation. She didn't understand anything they said. They walked a few blocks and up to a house.

Scarlet couldn't see much that set it apart from any other houses in the area. A garden in the front with vegetables was perhaps too perfect. A row of green onions, a row of carrots, and one tomato plant that grew up onto a trellis. A fat red tomato hung close enough for Scarlet to take a bite if she wanted. Raindrops speckled the plants like jewels.

The young man unlocked the front door with a keypad. Scarlet followed Donya inside, kicking off her shoes as the troll did in the white-tiled entryway.

The young man asked something.

"He wants to know if you would like the guest slippers?" Donya translated.

"Oh, no thanks," Scarlet said as she followed the other two down the hall. Donya took no guest slippers either.

They passed a small living space and a kitchen but continued to a room that flickered.

Inside the room sat monitor after monitor. Computers stacked on top of each other. Everything hummed with the sound of electricity and the room was too warm despite a window air conditioner unit that blew its damnedest in the blind-shaded window.

Now that the young man was still and seated, Scarlet studied him. He was as small as Donya. At first, Scarlet thought he could be human. But she saw movement in the seat of his chair. It looked like he wore a fuzzy belt. He leaned over to turn on yet another machine. The fuzzy belt twitched again, and she realized as he turned to sit back in his chair that it was a tail, the way it clung made her think of something prehensile.

He wasn't an unhandsome man, only pale from being indoors.

Donya explained what she wanted. He nodded his head and typed.

He loaded a file of a perfect US passport. Scarlet felt very uncomfortable. Searching for Mar's body had been necessary, even a public service. But this, well this would be breaking the law for her own gain.

Donya and the man seemed to be having a bit of an argument.

Then Donya turned to her. "You cannot use your real name, but would you like to keep your first name? It will make traveling and responding to others less confusing. It does mean giving this man your first name though."

Names. Donya didn't want Scarlet to give her name to anyone. And after Scarlet's interaction with that PI, she began to think that was a good rule even for humans.

"I think it's a good idea, have him spell it with two Ts," Scarlet said. A common enough mistake, even a few of her official documents had come with it.

Donya turned back to the man, and they spoke in quick short sentences. Eventually, the man stood up indicating that she should follow him. Scarlet did.

There was a makeshift photo booth. Scarlet pulled her hair forward and fluffed it.

She smiled and he snapped a few photos. They appeared on a screen instantly.

Donya tapped the worst one. The one where Scarlet half blinked.

Scarlet opened her mouth to protest, but Donya cut her off, "it will look more official if it is unfortunate."

Scarlet could not argue with this. They walked back into the other room. The man typed at a keyboard and again presented the screen to Scarlet.

"What would you like your fake last name to be?"

The list wasn't great. He included: Doe, Obama, Bloorier, Smith, Trevino, and a few others.

"Scarlet Trevino has a nice ring."

"Do you know what it means?" Donya asked.

"It means something?"

Donya nodded. "It means living on a boundary."

CHAPTER 10
DONYA

It would take nearly twenty-four hours to properly fake the document. The forger would call her on the burner phone he'd given her when it was done. The cost of the document came to nearly double what funds she had left. Thankfully he took one payment and expected the rest on completion. She needed more money. It was easier to come by funds when she used to eat humans. Although much of the meat tasted sweet, seeds were usually better and didn't come with the nasty side effect of making her even more sensitive to the purifying light of the sun.

Scarlet managed to get a room at a hotel for them with her credit card.

The rain continued drizzling, wetting the streets and keeping the heat of summer at bay. They sat at a ramen bar, Hisa the river stone safely tucked in Donya's pocket, all too happy about the interesting turn of events. Scarlet slurped noodles while Donya ate a bowl of natto over rice. It tasted surprisingly good—warm and slippery and satisfying.

"How did you know I would like this?" Donya asked.

"It's all seeds, do you think you would like it better if the seeds were raw?" Scarlet asked.

Donya eyed the human. Scarlet's eyes shone in the low light. Red lanterns hung over her. The human's eyes never seemed still even when she watched an object. The way the iris gleamed and picked up the light was eerie to the troll. Donya had cast the spell to alter those eyes, but they took to it a bit too well. "I am not sure, they would keep me full longer, but the heat in these grains satisfy something I have missed."

Donya noticed a subtle shiver that ran up Scarlet's back.

The man serving the ramen walked over to the other end of the bar. Donya watched Scarlet watch him. When he walked out of earshot she said, "is that something warm people meat?"

Donya heard a muffled noise from her pocket.

"Perhaps."

Donya did not mean to bring up eating humans. Donya herself hadn't realized what she meant as she spoke. Speaking was difficult, trolls were meant to listen and smell. A conversation involves listening and speaking thoughtfully. Scarlet picked out meaning even between words like most humans.

Scarlet continued to eat. Her appetite was not diminished. Donya had forgotten to feed her lunch. Blue circles formed under her eyes from lack of sleep, but she seemed refreshed with the food.

The man behind the bar wandered over to them again.

"I hope I can sleep in the room, I'm all off schedule. I should be waking up soon," Scarlet said, turning slightly to Donya.

"No coffee for you," interrupted the man behind the bar.

"No, no coffee," Scarlet said with a smile.

"Sake, that will help. Here, on the house." The man put a ceramic cup in front of Scarlet.

Donya watched the transaction between the humans. It was good she didn't eat them anymore. They could be helpful like this one.

"I'll take a glass as well," Donya said.

The man gave a sharp nod and filled a glass for her. She sipped it as she thought. How would she raise funds for their tickets without killing or stealing? The sale of relics brought in good money. Things she found that the stones told her about, or she came across digging. It had never been purposeful, mostly happy accidents. She could go out digging tonight, try to find a valuable lost object. The stones would help her, and since humans had lived here for a very long time there were bound to be a few things about that she could sell for a nice profit.

Donya smiled to herself. Not eating humans felt easier and easier.

⧉⧉

The earth yielded to her as she dug deep, large stones moved for her yelling encouragement.

"Another handbreadth down and to the left," Hisa said. She had taken on communications with the quartz-laced stone that inhabited this area.

Donya moved the wet soil, snapping a thick tree root. Her hands pushed and pulled the soil.

"Gently or you will destroy that which you seek," came advice from her right.

"What?" Donya said as her pinky finger struck soft cool metal.

"Oh no, this isn't good. It's a tengu. Be careful, they won't like you," Hisa said.

Donya kept to her task, perhaps ignoring the tengu would cause it to go away. She pulled a small gold statue from the earth. It was exquisite. A depiction of the sun goddess from this land. It had been buried hundreds of years ago during the warring states period, a bloody time she heard about even on her mountain. Whoever buried her did not live to come back to their treasure.

"Hisa my friend, could you send out a message? I must ensure this statue is treated properly. I cannot go to a reputable art dealer. But is there someone who can be quick and discreet? Ask the stones." The cloud cover dissipated, and she needed to be back to the hotel before dawn. Donya wanted to show the tengu a small display of her power, so she leapt off the bottom of the hole she had dug. The statue had dwelt deeper than a coffin would be placed. She landed next to the tengu.

This one had an extremely long nose, and his red skin dulled as with age. He wore a wooden mask pushed up on his head. She bowed slightly in greeting to him. A show of respect was also a show of strength.

"You will sell a sacred object?" he asked.

"Yes. I could give her to you if you have human coin."

"I have no coin."

"Then this is where we part ways. Farewell."

"I have something else you want."

Donya paused. She had heard of other treasure buried, none worth as much as this, but she would trade. "What is it you have?" Donya asked.

"Information."

"I can get information. I have allies here."

The tengu cocked his head like a confused bird.

"Good one," Hisa said. The tengu would not be able to hear her, they were of the air even if they guarded the mountains.

"Give me an exact location of the woman I seek and you can have this golden goddess." This would be a generous trade. She could see that the tengu wanted the statue.

Donya waited. Finally, the tengu said, "this brings you no goodwill. You have made a mistake." His wings flapped with a wet sound like the feathers could barely fly.

"I think we better hurry, you need to leave Japan," Hisa said as Donya tucked her back in her pocket.

Donya did not wait to see which direction he flew. She took off toward the sleeping city in complete agreement with the river stone.

⤜⤛

They were seated on an express train to Tokyo. It was safer to travel by train in Donya's opinion. She had paid the forger, even given him extra, and he bought them these tickets and plane tickets to San Francisco. That plane left at midnight tomorrow night.

Scarlet sat wide awake in the seat next to her peering out at the nightscape traveling by them.

A woman sat near them. But she listened to music on big headphones and Donya could hear them buzzing as the woman kept her eyes on a tablet before her. Donya liked the woman's perfume, its notes mingled well with her scent and her clothing detergent.

"I have been meaning to speak about your eyes," Donya said.

"I think they are mostly stable now. At first, I felt like my vision shifted every day, and I could see different aspects of reality. For the first few months, it could be disorienting. Not everything they did stuck. For a few weeks, I could look at a picture or text and be able to see it in my mind's eye perfectly any time I wanted, but not anymore. One that did mostly stick is reading emotions," Scarlet paused like she was finished speaking on the subject.

"Please elaborate."

"It's not that important. It worked best with liars—I could just tell when someone lied. It was like the shadows on their face got extra dark. Totally awkward, I never knew what to do about the situation. The most helpful thing they can do now is zooming in."

"Again, elaborate," Donya said, starting to get irritated. Spending time around humans was exhausting. "If I stare at something stationary in the distance or even something small, it sort of comes into focus better than it should. Makes my job way easier. I don't even need to look through my microscope."

"I suppose that is a bonus."

"Yep, most of the things I can do with them are a bonus. I should try to think of them more positively. The one thing that still bothers me is the few times when my eyes lose focus. Like completely. It only lasts a couple seconds. I can't tell if there's any correlation with an event. It seems random."

"It is an unstable spell." All of these extra abilities made sense in the way magic worked. Donya wanted Scarlet to see the world more clearly, to not be confounded by the dark in that spell. And yet, she got the feeling Scarlet was hiding something from her. "What can you see in the countryside?" Donya asked, watching the night speed by. Japan contained a wealth of spirits and creatures. It surprised Donya, as she had seen fewer in the human realm where she normally lived in the last few hundred years, but here the numbers appeared even higher than in her youth. Donya breathed deeply as Scarlet looked out the window.

"I keep seeing these beaked turtles that stand on two feet. Hmmm, there was a flying eyeball a few towns back. Right now, I see wil-o-the-wisps fire. Would they be called that here? I have been studying Grazia's books."

"Occasionally what humans call us is what we call ourselves. I'm not sure. I have seen one tonight."

"I counted around eight so far."

Donya nodded. Scarlet's vision was impressive. The spell would wear off one day and she would only have her second sight left, but for now, these extra abilities were a fantastic boon. Scarlet's smell did have the faint hint of magic about it. Normally Donya smelled it only after a strong casting was done, but if she picked apart Scarlet's smell, she got it now, when she did not in their earlier meetings.

"Focus your eyes and enact one of your new abilities," she instructed Scarlet.

Scarlet did not turn her head, "Okay."

Yes, Donya was sure of it now, she could smell the spell activating. Magic smelled indescribable, but if she tried to think of anything it was somewhere between an apple and citrus. When it spoiled it was foul, also beyond description. Donya sighed, Scarlet would be more noticeable to other creatures now with the scent of magic on her all of the time.

Donya wondered at the blurring. Perhaps it wasn't that her eyesight blurred, but more like her mind could not make sense of what she saw. Donya pondered the idea. "For now, keep your eyes open and your shield extended. You don't have to weaken it for me. Remember, it doesn't bother me anymore."

"Okay, I forgot. It bothers Ariel. So, I try to keep it down as much as possible."

Scarlet let out her shield. It wrapped over Donya hot and pleasant. Scarlet tended to mix her magical natures. Using both fire and the shield at the same moment. There was no harm in it and Donya feared that everything she and the alchemist tried to teach Scarlet would overwhelm her eventually. "Keep your eyes open for now, we need every advantage we can get. You can sleep on the plane."

"Sure, Juan should be waking up. I think I'm going to message him real quick, maybe call. It's nice that this train has free Wi-Fi."

Donya nodded and gazed past Scarlet to the night scenery again, mostly trees and fields, occasionally a town. The moon was out, she let her eyes drift up to the pale face. She hadn't planned on leaving Japan empty-handed, she'd believed she would find Nera here. Find her and apologize, and then they would leave together. Donya surprised herself with the end of the thought. When did just a simple apology morph into more? She wasn't sure, but Donya knew what she wanted.

CHAPTER 11

SCARLET

"I'm just glad you both will arrive so soon," Juan said. "Give Donya my thanks for pulling it off."

"Will do babe." Scarlet smiled out into the night as it moved past her. At Donya's insistence, she was practicing with her eyes. Perched in a colossal tree, Scarlet picked out a large creature, almost bear-sized but with large rabbit-like ears. "I'm stoked that my flight will be arriving in SFO before it was scheduled to take off in Tokyo. It's like I'm gaining time."

"We will have to thank the international date line too," Juan joked. He always joked more when he was relieved.

"So how are things going with your sister's dresses?" Scarlet asked although she didn't want to. But something was wrong with Bertha's dress. Lettie had let the information slip to Scarlet in a message about the ranunculus used in the corsages.

"Lettie's is ready to go, but Bertha had to order another one."

90

Scarlet let the silence stretch; she'd made this call over free Wi-Fi, not Donya's calling card. "Did she get the right one?"

"She said she did, and the store rushed the shipment, they promised it would be here on time."

Scarlet had given her bridesmaids three different dress designs from the same collection. Tessa, Scarlet's sister, and Elise ordered their dresses within a week of Scarlet letting them know her choices. But neither Lettie nor Juan could ever confirm that Bertha had ordered hers, she might have just forgotten. It crossed Scarlet's mind that she ordered a dress, but no one saw it because it never fit. Bertha might have ordered it small thinking she would lose weight. Brides sometimes did that with their wedding dresses, Scarlet received a long lecture from her seamstress not to do this. Scarlet didn't see why Bertha's appearance mattered this much to her. It wasn't her wedding day. Scarlet thought she should just be happy that the dress wasn't ugly.

"Well as long as it's here and mostly fits. Anything else going wrong with the wedding?" Scarlet asked and instantly regretted how pissy she sounded.

"No, don't worry, it's going to be perfect, one of the best days of our lives."

Scarlet took a deep breath. "I know, I love you. Is Ariel still asleep?" It was early evening in Japan but very early morning in California.

"Love you too, yep, well I think, the water hasn't moved and the remote doesn't wiggle for movie time."

"Good, you sound tired. One more question and I'll let you go get ready for work. Have you heard that song anymore?"

"Nope." Juan yawned the answer.

"Go get ready for work, love you." Scarlet felt a weight lift from her shoulders, he hadn't heard the weird song since the night with the sword. Maybe she had managed to get rid of the singer with the shadow that shot into the sky. That would be lucky.

"Love you too, I could talk longer," Juan weakly protested.

"No, you can't, you said you have that early meeting. I'll call you again later."

"Sure, sure."

Scarlet felt bloated. Donya took her shopping and all the clothes here were cut small. Scarlet needed to buy everything extra-large, but she kept her irritation to herself, thankful for the change of clothes, and that Donya didn't insist on designer. Donya had a thing for Prada, and they were getting on a train to Tokyo. She was sure all the designers kept shop there. They purchased two small travel bags too. It would seem suspicious if they entered a transpacific flight with a purse and two tiny backpacks between them.

A glint of light caught Scarlet's eye as she observed a distant hill. There was a waterfall. It glittered in the moonlight. She wished she could see it during the day. Colors at night were strange to her still, the sky was purple, and the stars flickered in blues, yellows, and reds. Even the moon looked different—more golden than the silver everyone else saw.

Something moved in the waterfall.

She'd seen her once in person, for maybe a minute before Scarlet was transported to another realm.

Scarlet viewed her again in visions from the Kraken.

A blue woman. With black hair. Beautiful and blinded.

Nera.

Scarlet did not take her eyes off the woman bathing in the waterfall. She wanted her eyes to obey her. To focus on the woman. But she didn't know how to start them doing it. She could fix her gaze and hoped it worked before they passed the scene, which would happen quickly in this train. Without turning she shook Donya, who sat next to her motionless.

"Do you see her?" Scarlet asked breathlessly and a bit too loud. It wasn't that late, but others slept with eye covers on. In her peripheral vision, she saw a passenger twitch in their seat.

Donya leaned over Scarlet. Again, Scarlet smelled her earthy scent. "No, what do you see?"

"There, there," Scarlet said pointing. She wanted Donya to say Nera's name. To see her.

"As I said before my eyes are not strong."

Scarlet's eyes took that moment to zoom in. It was Nera. She could see her shut eyes and the old scars of stitches. The woman frolicked fully nude, jumping in and out of the water. Throwing sprays into the air so that they caught the moonlight casting tiny violet rainbows.

They were getting closer. Soon the train would be past.

"What is the next place this thing stops at?" Scarlet asked.

"Kyoto."

Scarlet continued to point. "You really can't see her?"

"I can see a waterfall, I think. That hill is very distant."

"It's Nera."

⤙⤚

The next half an hour had been tense. The express train had more stops than the Shinkansen, but not that many more. Donya needed to wait. Then, of course, no trains headed in the correct direction for over an hour. Donya hailed a cab. The first one would not leave the city.

The second one was fine with it, however, the cab driver seemed concerned. They didn't pry. Prying seemed culturally inaccessible here, which worked for Scarlet and Donya.

They made it to the closest town. Donya asked to be dropped off at the best bathhouse. The cabby didn't know that information, but she found one that stayed open almost all night. They usually stayed open late so people could bathe after work.

"Stay here, take a bath, relax," Donya instructed.

"Sure, take as long as you need," Scarlet said.

Donya ran down the street before Scarlet even got into the bath-house.

Scarlet fumbled through the transaction, but she got it across that she wanted a bath. The woman gave her a locker key for her two pieces of luggage, purse, and clothes. Inside the locker, two towels waited for her. She undressed and wrapped herself up.

The place was pretty empty. Two older women sat in a large pink water bath, the bathing area continued outdoors with what looked like barrels and a large rock-lined pool. She could hear people speaking softly. She didn't need a bath but wouldn't refuse one while she waited. She hoped Donya found Nera soon and they both came back for her.

She started in the shower stalls, where you sat on a bucket and soaped up. Scarlet scrubbed at herself, lathering up with liquid soap from a dispenser. It smelled like strawberries. Everything here smelled like strawberries she realized. And not fake ones—real ones.

After she rinsed off, she walked over to the pink pool. Whole hulled strawberries floated around in the pink water. She waded in and a woman with a white bun on her head watched her intently. Scarlet's hair wasn't up, it would get wet but that was fine. She didn't care. It fell past her shoulders to her mid back now. Long and red, she babied it for the wedding with warm oil treatments and expensive conditioner. One soak in warm water wouldn't cause it to split and all break off.

She relaxed into the warm water but couldn't get comfortable. This tub was made for sitting. She wished she had a book to read while she waited—something funny.

She got up and went to the outside portion, modestly covering herself with a towel as she walked. There had been three women around her age outside, they were all getting up to leave as she walked out. She got in one of the barrels, water overflowed the top, and a spigot of warm water ran into the barrel, so the barrel kept fresh and warm. The night air was warm as well.

Scarlet relaxed and gazing up at the sky she noticed one of those long-nosed red-faced men flying above her. She instinctively slinked lower into the water. Donya said they protected the mountains, but she didn't like them. They looked scary, although that was probably to help them protect the mountain, she mused. What were they called again, she wondered? It had been a long few days, she couldn't keep everything that had happened straight in her head. She couldn't even decide what warranted worrying about. Probably nothing, that seemed a very Zen approach. She would try to keep that in mind while she was in Japan.

No worries, just Zen.

She tilted her head back and her eyes closed.

She must have fallen asleep because she'd been alone and now she heard giggling.

Scarlet's eyes popped open. Nera stood over Scarlet, her eyes blind, but she still produced a big smile. Nera's hand dipped into the pool of water Scarlet soaked in.

"Oh yes, it is the spell. How strange, how strange. And so many connections, too many," Nera said.

Scarlet felt startled by everything about the woman. Her height was above average, her voice sounded perfect, and she was beautiful. Behind Nera, Donya stood in a dark corner. The troll looked strange to Scarlet, but she couldn't place why. It could be the small smile that turned up the troll's gray lips.

"What can be done about it?" Donya asked

"I can't say now," Nera responded.

"Ummm I'll get out and we can go," Scarlet said, making to stand up.

"No no, sit in the water. Here I will get in with you," Nera said, letting the white cotton towel she'd wrapped around her body drop to the ground as she proceeded to hop into the barrel.

Scarlet hugged her knees in the now cramped space. And somehow Nera snaked around her. She reminded Scarlet of a river otter all supple and slick. Scarlet's eyes landed on Donya, for some help. The look on the troll's face was unusual. Strong feelings played across her gray features. Scarlet thought the little troll had feelings before, but they just didn't seem to have a lot of force behind them. That was not the case now, Donya had feelings and that feeling was jealousy.

Scarlet did not want to be in this situation.

"The dream. On repeat like a broken record. Over and over," Nera said. "The Kraken knows we are here, how fun."

"Donya, what is she talking about?" Scarlet asked. Nera poked at her knee, then at her shoulder.

"I told her of our dreams," Donya said.

Suddenly Scarlet felt a strong emotion too. Anger.

"Oh, ow ow," Nera yelped and leapt from the tub.

"I'm sorry, I didn't mean to." Scarlet stood, reeling in her shield. She always lost control when she got mad. It hadn't extended much beyond her skin, but Nera brushed her fingers on Scarlet's back while Donya spoke.

Nera sucked on her fingertips. When she pulled them from her mouth Scarlet got a better view, they seemed fine. It had only been a small singe.

Donya still dwelt in the same spot.

Scarlet grabbed her towel. "You dragged your sorry ass all over the world and the first thing you did when you found Nera was tell her about the dream." She managed not to yell, but her voice was much too loud for the late hour.

Donya startled, mouth dropping open, but her body stayed still.

"Do not be angry at my rock, she said sorry," Nera said, waving her hands.

Scarlet looked at the troll, then at the blue woman, then back at the troll. "Just sorry."

"Yes, and that she would stay with me forever and ever if I want."

"Sorry I lost my temper, I guess," Scarlet said. She felt deflated but still annoyed. Donya probably didn't even understand her feelings about Nera, of course, their first meeting wouldn't go like a scene from a movie. It took her a moment to process what Nera had said. "Are you not coming back to California with me?"

"You can understand Nera? She is not a puzzle to you?" Donya asked.

"A puzzle, sorta, but read between the lines," Scarlet said. They all walked inside past the strawberry pool. The older woman with the bun sat now in a smaller bath. She stared more openly at the trio. Nera was still naked, her towel draped over her shoulder.

"We will all go," Nera cooed.

CHAPTER 12

DONYA

"I am worried. Attempting the spell again could be a mistake," Donya said to Nera.

"No, you only need to follow what you learned, it will be wonderful," Nera said. She held the pine branch, the night air around her did not stir with sound or wind.

Donya scraped up the flecks of ash she needed. This remained the simplest course of action, almost the only course of action if they all wanted to stay together. They didn't have enough time to get another fake passport. They needed the one Nera already had on the Fin and Tonic. "We require water, come." Donya extended her hand. Nera let her warm fingers feather over Donya's palm and then up her wrist before she shifted directions with her palm and held Donya's hand. They ran through the night together. Nera's grace kept their hands intertwined as she skipped and ran by the troll's side.

They arrived at the waterfall where Scarlet first spotted Nera. Donya felt this water would be best to bring them to the Fin and Tonic. Perhaps this water could fix all of Donya's problems if she knew how to use it. Donya often felt this, that the key to her happiness and prosperity lay right in front of her but she did not know how to grasp it.

"You are very romantic, my dear one," Nera said breathlessly, squeezing Donya's hand.

Donya stooped to collect the water and studied Nera in the moonlight. She wanted this night to go on forever. And it felt like it would. Nera frolicked around a grassy area. The grass boasted tufts of setting seed, which swayed each time she passed one.

Donya didn't want to interrupt but they needed to move while the night stayed with them. "Nera I will have you scatter the water if you would."

"Of course."

Donya trenched her circle and piled up the ash at the center, Nera sprinkled the water, and Donya ate her pine branch trying to chew slowly, remembering the last time she did this. The sword on her back awoke instantly when she pulled it. Nera walked up behind her lightly placing her hands on Donya's shoulders.

"Take us to the Fin and Tonic," Donya said, driving the sword into the circle. She hoped the landing would be smoother than last time.

The sword waited not even the length of one of Nera's heartbeats. Then Donya landed in almost the same place as last time—lighter this time. Her feet did not drive through the bottom of the expensive yacht. Nera's hands were still warm on her shoulders. She wondered at this place where they landed. It sat near the engine, she could smell the heat and metal. A landing on the upper deck would have been preferable both times. Why did the spell take her here? Would it be considered the ship's belly or heart? Either way, it was a vital area, and it felt as though the sword decided this location.

Donya scented the air, no fresh smells, save the wood used to board the hole under her. Nera stayed quiet, listening.

"We are alone," Donya said.

Nera trilled and danced in front of her. "I will get my things."

Nera packed a large duffle bag with expensive gowns and her passport. She pointed out a safe to Donya and asked her to pull it open. Donya complied. Nera's circlet sat inside—along with a large amount of cash and a handful of jewels. Nera scooped it all into her duffle bag.

One of the rubies yelled about the rough treatment, it seemed to Donya to have a French accent.

That was all much easier than finding buried treasure and then hawking that treasure to the nearest fence. She had been severely underpaid for the golden goddess statue. The shopkeeper gave every penny they could scrounge up though.

On the deck Donya inhaled the briny salt air. Humans revealed a few boats away. Laughter rippled in the air and the sound of glasses clinking could be heard. A celebration. Donya wanted to celebrate her reunion with Nera. But she didn't know how. Perhaps food and wine would work. Nera moved around purposefully seeking something else on the ship. She went into the kitchen. Donya followed her. Donya picked up an unopened bottle of wine, from 1947, a Chateau Cheval Blanc. Nera hadn't lied to Scarlet; Donya almost immediately made her awkward apology. But she didn't say anything about staying together forever. However, the more she thought of it, that was what she wanted to say, then and now. Perhaps Nera understood her more than she understood herself.

"I found it!" Nera said, holding up a jar.

It did not take good eyesight to see the dark magic emanating from the jar.

"Nera what is that?" Donya asked.

Nera popped open the jar without an explanation. She pulled out a set of eyes. Their irises shone golden in the dim light and contained diamond-shaped pupils that dilated as if in fear.

Donya watched as her nymph popped the eyes in one by one. They were not human. Donya inhaled; there was a sharp tang in the air, perhaps they came from a cat, a large one but not a lion or tiger.

"Nera, who got those for you?"

"He got me lots," she said, blinking her new eyes, that fully functioned at once. The pupils constricted as she gazed at Donya. "It is lovely to see you again."

Donya moved closer and inspected inside the opaque earthenware jar. There floated more eyeballs. The pairs were tied together by their optical nerves making it easier for Nera to grab a matched set.

"He, as in the owner of this boat? Quickly Nera, we must be away from here," Donya said, grabbing Nera's arm and pulling her up to the upper deck. Nera clutched at her jar and Donya tossed the bottle of wine into the duffle bag and hefted it over her shoulder. She thought about leaving the jewels and money behind, but couldn't quite bring herself to do it. Inside, a small part of her wanted to punish this man who'd spent time with Nera. Keeping the money was the least she could do, the most was eat him. Eating him could be difficult if he was some sort of dark magician.

They hopped onto the dock. And then they ran. Nera was much faster than Donya and she kept swinging her arms and laughing. Soon Donya smiled too. Donya did not like the smell of those eyes. They smelled sour like fear, it clashed with Nera's scent. She vowed right then to find Nera's true eyes, find them, and return Nera's sight forever. Heldrig would not have destroyed them, of that Donya was sure.

Donya felt a miniscule part of her protest that if she did that Nera would be even more able to run around the world, away from her. Donya did not listen to that small mean part.

They stopped in a field of sunflowers. Their gold petals were closed slightly for the night. As night came to an end they would turn to the east pursuing dawn's first light.

Nera began to dance between the heavy-headed plants, she hummed a tune and Donya watched as the heads of the sunflowers perked up. Donya thought Nera was like sunlight, all happiness and warmth. Donya continued to smile. They needed to return, but Scarlet would be safe in that all-night gaming cafe they'd left her in.

Hisa watched over her. Donya relaxed back in the flowers. The sky sparkled full of stars, she smiled up at the tiny points of light, distant suns that did not turn her to stone.

Nera came into view. "Why are you not looking at me?"

"I am listening to you, and feeling," Donya responded. She inhaled deeply. Nera's scent intertwined with the bright scent of the sleeping sunflowers. Donya licked her lips to see if even the air tasted sweet.

"Feeling?" Nera asked. Her voice rose at the end of the word.

Donya closed her eyes. Yes, she was feeling happy. Giddy happiness, she could almost giggle. "I am happy."

"Does this make you happier?"

Donya felt soft lips brush the tip of her nose then alight on her mouth, and a warm body pressed on top of hers. The smell of sunflowers disappeared, everything disappeared but Nera. Yes, this made her very happy. She kept her eyes closed and raised her hands letting them rove over Nera's hips and lower back. She did not want to open her eyes, it could be too much like before when Nera held her down at the bottom of the river in Italy—when Donya could not move.

Donya returned the kiss slowly. Nera pulled back. Donya opened her eyes as Nera finished tugging the dress off the top of her head. It was not like before, everything felt soft and warm. Donya let her hand rest on Nera's hip moving slowly and carefully. Nera pushed her hands under Donya's dress and began to drag it up, she was not slow or careful. Donya let her do as she willed. And when nothing but air came between them Donya used her superior strength to roll Nera under her. Then Donya kissed her hard.

CHAPTER 13

SCARLET

Scarlet woke up in a daze. Donya had left her at a gaming cafe, but her screen was dark in front of her. Scarlet found the gentle tapping of keys and clicks of high-speed mice soothing and fell asleep. She wanted to fall back asleep even now.

Bzzzz

It was her phone that woke her, humming against her leg. Scarlet scrambled to get it out of her pocket. She blinked at the bright screen in the dark. It was Juan. She'd emailed him before she fell asleep, but she had no service. She wasn't sure how the call connected.

"Hello," she whispered.

"Hey, I finished your list. And I have bad news."

Scarlet didn't respond, just nodded her head still half asleep.

Juan continued, probably guessing her silence was quiet consternation. "The venue booked the second ballroom."

Scarlet's heart sank. She'd asked them to put it in writing that her wedding could have the second ballroom as a backup space for the ceremony. But they wouldn't, explaining they never booked two events because their staff couldn't handle it. The ceremony space was out on a lovely wooden deck boarding golden sand and a blue ocean, but if it rained it would be a damp wooden deck by the kelp-covered beach and gray frothing waves.

She doubted the hotel suddenly employed more competent staff, which meant not only would the weather possibly ruin the ceremony, but all other aspects of her wedding would probably be ruined too.

"Why can't all this happen to anyone else?" Scarlet wailed. Then she sobbed.

Juan said something but Scarlet couldn't hear. Very politely the young man from the front desk came around with a box of tissue. He nodded solemnly. Absently Scarlet wondered how often gamers burst into tears.

No one scolded her but she felt like she would die from embarrassment if she stayed once the tears dried.

"Let me call you back," She said to Juan.

"Alright, I love you. And don't stress about it too much, the chance of rain has fallen by twenty percent or so."

"I love you too," Scarlet whispered.

She gathered her bags, swept a small rock Donya had left by her keyboard into her purse, and made it out the door. No one noticed as she departed, all eyes stayed fixed on bright screens. A bakery across the street opened its doors, they placed a small table outside and a cute chalk sign advertising hot drinks and pastries.

That's what she needed—food and caffeine. Yes, the venue booking was terrible, a major blow for any wedding. But honestly, she had much bigger fish to fry right now. The universe could have thrown her a bone and let her have an easy wedding.

But that wasn't how life went. Tragedies came in threes supposedly. Scarlet ticked off her big upsets of late, the weird song, the sudden transport to Japan, and now the last tragedy—her wedding day would get rained out and probably the hotel would mess up other important parts of her wedding. Perhaps they would drop her wedding cake or overbook the rooms. Scarlet sniffed a bit and wiped at her face, opening the door to the cafe.

The workers seemed startled. Maybe they weren't open yet, but no one said anything. Scarlet perused the cases. The pastries looked amazing, she spent almost ten minutes studying all the different breads. But how was she going to ask for one? She couldn't read the signs. And she didn't have any cash, only her credit card. But it did work, she'd used it the first day she arrived.

Finally, an elderly woman said, "Melonpan," and pointed to the bread Scarlet stared at the most intently.

"Yes, please," Scarlet said, nodding vigorously. The bread reminded her of the breads Juan's mother would bring over. She thought those were called concha. It had a similar pattern on top. The woman picked it up. And Scarlet took a few steps over and pointed to one with chocolate oozing out of it.

"Chocolate cornetto," the woman picked one up with tongs and placed them both in a pink paper bag.

Scarlet managed to order a cup of dark green tea and thankfully her credit card once again worked. She sat outside to wait for Donya's arrival. She picked the table the farthest from the cafe window, realizing now how much more private the internet cafe had been.

The melonpan tasted lightly sweet, she ate the whole thing in a few bites. The carbs worked their magic on her blood sugar, and she felt calmer when the sword appeared in her right hand. Scarlet opened her hand so that the double would disintegrate. Hopefully, that meant Donya would appear shortly.

Scarlet checked the sky as she began to eat her second pastry, the chocolate a pleasant deep blend that wasn't too bitter. The sky showed signs that dawn would break any moment. Scarlet's shield barely worked against sunlight, they tested it on the train ride to Fukuoka. Scarlet couldn't make her shield opaque. And given Scarlet's other nature of fire the troll said it would be hard for her to block heat and fire. Donya explained earth blocked fire, as did water but less effectively unless it quenched the source. Donya thought if Scarlet practiced with the sword maybe she would change the nature of her shield. There had been many mentions of practice on Donya's part in the last few days.

Scarlet wasn't in a good mood yet. But still, she checked her phone. It stayed connected to Wi-Fi all night. Maybe she had messages from one of her bridesmaids. A report of events going as planned, or maybe even a price drop on airfare, she still hoped something good could happen.

There were a lot of messages and emails, many could be ignored. Her sister, Lettie, and two from her mother needed attention though. Lettie and Tessa asked questions about the bachelorette night. Scarlet thanked the gods it hadn't been this weekend. Both messages from her mother nattered about the incoming rain. Neither message contained any helpful suggestions about what to do, just general panic.

One other message caught Scarlet's eye. Truly, she would have ignored it but the subject line did a little wiggle at her courtesy of her extra special eyesight. Her eyes did the same thing to text in Grazia's books, especially the *Liber Unguium*, one of the first books she sent home with Scarlet. When it happened, she would often know the meanings of words without needing to translate them. This message was from Trun, her neighbor, subject line, "weirdo lady." Scarlet clicked on it and was taken aback by the long email. A young woman came by his apartment asking questions about her. At first, Trun thought it was one of Scarlet's friends or bridesmaids. And he'd answered, thinking they were planning a surprise before the wedding. But then she asked a few odd questions and when he asked her name and why she wanted to know, she became cagey.

But he worked at the DMV. And he'd recorded her license plate info.

He didn't say he illegally searched for her, but it was heavily implied. The car's license belonged to a business, a private investigative firm called Morgan and Associates.

Scarlet thought maybe the rule of three didn't apply to her. Another problem rearing its ugly head. Guy Morgan, her PI, who didn't find Mars' body, and seemed to be going off the rails. She wanted to tell Donya to eat him when they got to California. Serve him right. He was supposed to work for her, not against her.

Scarlet let out a yelp, as from the thin air to her left Donya and Nera stepped forward. It seemed like they came out of a bush, but Scarlet could see the shimmering air all around them. And behind them, a dark green grass swayed, as she looked through space to the place they'd been before.

The space behind them closed up like a zipper. But a line lingered winking darkly before dissipating. Like the sword cut through and now the world needed to mend itself. Scarlet didn't like it. Donya had told her she altered an old spell she knew, she blamed that on Scarlet's sudden transport. Scarlet remembered a short chapter about the dangers of altering a spell or circle; those words had leapt at Scarlet, allowing her to read through it quickly. Now that Scarlet thought about it Donya seemed to wing a lot of the magic she performed. Perhaps it was more normal for a troll, or perhaps Donya took unnecessary risks to reach her goals.

"What has happened?" Nera asked Scarlet.

Scarlet blinked a few times, she had been preparing to start lecturing Donya. Scarlet thought she must look awful. Well, she always did after she cried. Her face got all blotchy, and she teetered on the verge of tears again within seconds of Nera's question.

"Donya, go in and get us more bread, this will take a while," Scarlet said, her voice breaking.

Donya made no protest, only turned to the cafe doors with a smile. Scarlet couldn't help but feel bitter that the troll seemed happier than her before her wedding day. Scarlet wiped at her face and decided not to ask Donya to maybe eat a few people from the wedding venue and that PI.

CHAPTER 14

DONYA

Donya felt dazed. Dawn approached; she could smell it in the air. The best hours of her life had passed, and now she took orders like a puppy.

Nera wrapped herself around Donya as she sat in the chair beside hers. Nera and Scarlet continued to converse energetically. But Donya let her mind replay and consider the last few hours. The spell felt downright easy to do. Donya couldn't even lament the time she messed up. That blunder brought her Nera. And Scarlet seemed better for the distraction. She bore a pale and worn continence when she arrived and now Scarlet's eyes were bright again. She wanted to ask the human questions. Now that Donya had tasted romance, she wondered how to keep it. Scarlet managed to keep Juan, there must be a strategy or technique.

Donya would like to stay with Nera.

Donya was warmed to see Nera's concern for the human.

"And now a storm is supposed to arrive the day before my wedding!" Scarlet said, gesturing to the air around her.

Donya did not understand what upset Scarlet.

Nera fluttered her hands. "We can call the water away. It will be easy."

Donya also didn't understand Nera's intense reaction.

Scarlet peeked up at Nera with shining red-rimmed eyes. "We can? Just like that?"

"Yes, it will be easy for me, I can ask the water in the rain clouds. But even you can do it. You have your shield, you could make it so the rain does not touch," Nera said.

"I hadn't thought of trying that. We tried to use it on sunlight for Donya, but it only kinda works. But I guess water would be different, but storms mean wind too. It's going to be awful, I just know." Scarlet paused then blinked at Nera. "Oh my god you have eyes, how, where did you get them?"

"We got many things all from the boat." Nera shook her bag and the contents spilled onto the pavement. The jar of eyeballs rolled across the cement stopping by a potted plant.

Donya moved quickly to keep Scarlet from reaching for the jar, knowing her power she would incinerate the whole thing. "Nera please keep these tucked away," Donya said, while listening to the ruby from the boat, it had clattered to Scarlet's foot and was full of things to say.

"So serious," Nera pouted. "I thought you would be happier longer after."

"After what?" Scarlet asked as she picked up the ruby. "Is this real?"

"After the—" Nera started to say. But Donya grabbed her hand.

"It is real." Donya had explained she wanted to keep their relations between them for now. Not out of embarrassment, it just felt nice to have a love affair. Donya collected the stones and placed them back in the bag. Several whined at the poor treatment, the ruby gushed about how warm Scarlet's hand felt.

Nera unbuttoned her dress. "Time to change."

"No, not time to change." Scarlet scanned the street, which was mostly dead, but a few cars passed up at the intersection.

"But it is morning?" Nera said.

"We will change at the train station. We need to get there before the sun really comes up. Remember Donya can't take the sunlight," Scarlet said. As if to hurry them along, she tipped back her paper cup of what smelled to Donya like tea and finished the whole thing.

"Oh yes," Nera said, smiling radiantly.

"Come," Donya said, sweeping up the heavy duffle bag.

"One moment, I must clean." Nera jumped up.

Donya listened, intrigued by the language Nera spoke as she quickly uttered a few words and used the morning dew on the bush to wipe away the trace smell of magic left by their movement with the sword. This was what she used to avoid detection. It looked simple, but Donya could sense it took great control. When Nera finished, she winked at Donya with her new eyes.

Scarlet dragged their two luggage's after her and limped on her bad foot. Donya was thankful they did have a few spare clothes. She realized she still stank of magic, she would need to throw these clothes away, preferably soon. That would keep anyone on their trail confused. They should divide up the money between the bags, presenting a less suspicious front to authorities. Donya would have to keep more of the foreign bills as her passport boasted many stamps. Scarlet's stayed relatively empty, it appeared to be a couple of years old but mostly unused. But Nera seemed the most well-traveled of them all. Donya would pick her up a cute purse at the airport to carry the gems. The gems would enjoy it and Nera deserved nice things.

The sky turned pink and then blue; the sun rose in the east. They rushed the few blocks to the large train station. Upon entering it Donya stopped to put on a light coat. The day would be hot, but she liked to stay covered if she was not sleeping in deep shadow, in case the sun's rays caught her at an angle. A little exposure wouldn't bother her now but even if she never ate another person full daylight would probably be out for her.

She readjusted the sword strapped to her back. Its short blade ran the length of her spine. It stayed awake. And not tired, the sword's growth pleased her. This close to Scarlet, Donya felt sure the sword would push itself even farther. Perhaps she could find a few moments to train with it once they got to Tokyo, or better yet get Scarlet to train with it.

Getting three tickets for the next train to Tokyo took only a few moments. They had a choice of Shinkansen or one of the slower lines. The slower line left earlier but they arrived around the same time. She opted for that one so Nera could see more of the lush green countryside. Nera held out her hand for the tickets and Donya placed them in her upturned palm letting her fingers linger on the soft skin. Donya wanted to appreciate every moment like this.

Scarlet kept glancing from Nera to Donya. And occasionally lingering on Nera's yellow eyes. She would squint at them. Donya wondered which of her new abilities she used. Was she counting something, or seeing them more closely, or perhaps studying the spellwork that held them together? Donya would be interested to know that. She may have to ask Scarlet to inspect the eyes in the jar.

They made their way to the platform, Donya noted and felt thankful for the shade as the sun climbed higher into the sky. Scarlet stepped away to get drinks from the vending machines. Donya thought Scarlet tried to give her more time alone with Nera. Scarlet did understand relationships, Donya concluded. She needed to think of all the things she could ask the human. Perhaps a recounting of what Juan had done to woo Scarlet. Real examples of romance would be a good place to start.

Donya took a step closer to Nera. Now that they were alone Donya could not think of anything to say. She wanted to ask about Nera's travels. But Donya did not want to hear about Nera's lovers, not yet. Eventually, Donya would want to hear about it all.

The train came rolling up. It possessed a flat engine, not pointed and sleek like the newer trains. Donya liked it immediately. She turned to find Scarlet; the train wouldn't pause long.

Scarlet's eyes glared at the sky.

Donya could hear the train doors squealing open even over the sound of the metallic breaks, and she smelled cedar, so much cedar she thought it would be similar to a ramble through a forest. She turned, on top of the nearest passenger car a dozen tengu roosted, standing with their wings folded back. Half of their number held antique round mirrors.

Nera's cat eyes widened with fear.

"Evil," shouted a tengu taking wing into the blue sky.

"Evil," responded the others. Several of them held up shining mirrors.

"Pull the sword!" Scarlet yelled from across the platform.

Donya could feel Scarlet's fear. Scarlet's shield went up and around herself. It pushed out in a hot wave. Donya didn't think the shield would be able to go around Nera without hurting her. Maybe Scarlet had the same thought because the shield stopped shy of Donya and Nera.

The tengu moved with great speed, wings flapping and legs pushing off. Donya whipped out the sword, not knowing what would happen. A knee drove into her rock-hard back. The sword clattered from her hand. She turned and bit at the hand that clamped on her arm. Her teeth cleaved through the flesh. Blood spurted into her mouth warming her tongue with its salt and heat. For a moment she was free.

Nera struggled with a tengu, clawing at its outstretched arms. Scarlet stumbled but reached the sword.

More arms ensnared Donya. They lifted her. She was very heavy. Scarlet managed to burn a tengu at Donya's right and shatter the mirror he held. Donya's feet left the ground. This was not how she wanted to be flying today. Donya kicked and bit, her joints could bend farther back if need be and she used this to manage to get a fist connected with another tengu. Bones broke, even shattered. But still, other hands clutched at her.

There was another human on the platform, a big tengu beat his wings at the stranger. The tengu did not injure any of the humans, even Nera seemed safe. For a moment Donya felt hope flicker to life, then Nera shrieked at the top of her lungs. But Donya could not make out the words over the flap of thick wings.

Several tengu hovered in front of Donya. The mirrors, she realized their purpose too late. They redirected the sun's rays, concentrating them on Donya's chest.

Then everything went hot and bright.

CHAPTER 15

SCARLET

Donya turned to stone. It happened right in front of Scarlet. It took four tengu to lift her into the sky past the protective shade. Another set of them circled up higher using mirrors with age spots around the edge to send sunlight right at Donya's heart. Then they dropped her stone body. Surely Donya would shatter on the cement platform below. Scarlet scrambled, managing to point the sword at the ground thinking of the other night and the shadow. "Do something," Scarlet commanded the sword. Shadow puddled out of the sword moving like oil on water catching Donya before she stuck the hard surface below. The sculpture that had been Donya disappeared into darkness and the shadow puddle shrank and seeped into the earth.

Scarlet wasn't positive she had helped. Surely what happened was better than Donya breaking into a million pieces.

The tengu disappeared too, up into the sky. Scarlet watched as they went, afraid they would come back for her or Nera. They did seem interested in Nera. Scarlet heard one of them ask her to come with them, but Nera hissed at it. One of their number appeared quite dead, he was carried away. Scarlet remembered Donya landed a punch on that one. Two other tengu were missing limbs.

Scarlet made her way over to Nera. Nera's dress bore a large tear up her ribcage and she held a red foot in trembling hands. That explained one of the missing limbs. Scarlet's temple hurt and her knee. Several other people lay on the ground covering their heads. A police officer ran up the platform.

Scarlet did not want to be questioned by the police. Her documents were fake. Scarlet tucked the sword under her arm and stumbled to Nera. The sword chose that moment to feel heavier and Scarlet almost dropped it.

People milled around in the doors of the train, looking to see what happened. The whole incident only lasted a minute or two. Scarlet collected all of their luggage haphazardly, gasping at how heavy the duffle bag was. They rushed to an open door on the train. The seats were half full. They took two on the far side away from the commotion.

Nera hummed a frantic tune. The sleeve of her dress wouldn't stay up.

"Go to the bathroom and change," Scarlet instructed as she shoved the heavy sword into the already heavy duffle bag, covering it with clothing.

"Change? I can't change. I ruin everything. Even when I do not use the circlet. Even with no father, everything's ruined," Nera said around tears that spilled over her cheeks.

Scarlet noticed the tears left blue streaks, so she waved her hands frantically, not good at comforting even those she was close to. "I meant change clothes. Like you wanted to earlier. Put on a pretty new dress. We will fix this."

"I know, yes the pink one."

Scarlet sat, her heart hammering in her chest. She peered out the window. The tengu were not gone, they circled high in the sky. She let her eyes relax trying to see the glamour they wore for normal people. They looked like a bird of prey wheeling in the morning air.

She wondered how long they would be stuck there. Would the police come on to the train to get witness statements? She and Nera would have to get their story straight. Perhaps they boarded before the 'birds' did anything.

Nera tottered back to their seats, a neon pink evening dress on, with ballet flats. The dress opened to her navel. Now the cops would notice them for sure if they came into the train.

To Scarlet's surprise, the train started moving, and Scarlet could feel something move with them. It was similar to when she felt Donya move continents. Scarlet could feel the troll's presence, it stayed with them as they moved down the track. Scarlet relaxed feeling like her luck was finally turning around, even if she did just break a mirror. No cops came into their train car, Scarlet recalled the Japanese liked to stay on schedule.

Three hours and three minutes later they arrived in Tokyo. It was morning still. The day grew hot and humid. They had hours before they needed to be at the airport.

"First thing is food," Nera said stepping out of the train.

"Food?" Scarlet asked. Didn't they need to find onyx and wool of a black lamb? That was what Nera had said on the train.

"Yes, you are tired. The sword is tired. You need fuel, you are much smaller than the last time I saw you."

"That is on purpose, really I don't need fuel."

"You do, with cinnamon, such a warmth and good for grounding," Nera sang into the air. Then she sniffed loudly.

"Nera, we are going to get lost. Tokyo is too big to wander around," Scarlet hissed. They were already out of the train station. The buildings towered around Scarlet but in the sunlight that made it to the street Scarlet could see the Ged swirling thick on the ground.

"I can go wherever I want. You can too, it will be fine. You saved Donya."

Scarlet wasn't sure if she agreed. It hadn't felt like a rescue, it felt like a last-ditch effort. But when Scarlet told Nera of the feeling she got, that Donya traveled with them, the woman jumped up and down with delight. Then Nera began making plans, asking Scarlet how many spells she had completed, and strangely how many dead birds she had seen lately.

Scarlet dragged her feet. Her eyes itched from exhaustion and the horrifying realization that everything in her life tumbled out of control again, and even though she was more proactive she couldn't stop this downward slide into chaos.

Nera led Scarlet to a curry shop and ordered food on a video game-like machine. She handed Scarlet an orange ticket.

Scarlet let herself be led to a bench in the sunlight. She didn't have a lot of choices at this point. They made it to Tokyo, they needed to get on the plane and get back to California. It was the only thing to do. And when they arrived a mess would be waiting for her, Mars stalking them from the shadows. He probably controlled the song, her wedding, which she should just call off, and maybe even an over-ambitious PI digging into her business.

Scarlet was exhausted and increasingly frantic, but she wasn't weak. She made a tiny shield in the sunlight and pushed around a few shimmering Ged in the windowsill. She created this exercise before, turning a minuscule ball of shining free magic into a game of Pong between two shields. The Ged didn't react like sunlight, it did not pass through her shield. Once she managed to trap the Ged, if you squeezed it hard, it split like an atom, turning into colorful sparkles. The Ged could not pass through her shield, but it could pass into other things. Nera set down a glass of cool water near Scarlet's right hand.

Scarlet let her pong paddle miss and the Ged went bouncing against the glass of clear water. Scarlet moved the paddle and pushed the particle into the water. It sparkled in the glass. If Donya was here Scarlet would point out that she did practice some. However, the more she thought of it she admitted she did not do it enough.

Scarlet's stomach rumbled. Nera was right, she did need a hot meal. And the scent in this place was making her dizzy with hunger. After she ate the first curry plate she might need to order dessert.

"Do me a favor and drink this water," Scarlet said, handing Nera the glass.

Once Scarlet ate a chunk of chocolate she'd pushed Ged into. Nothing happened. But she wasn't a magical being. Donya had spoken to her before about the different types of seeds, how they filled her not just with physical substance, but with magical potential too.

Nera, thinking nothing of it, brought the glass to her lips and took a sip. She cocked her head to the side as she pulled away and swallowed. Then tipped the glass to her mouth again, consuming every drop in the glass in a long pull. Scarlet noticed another customer at the bar watching the scene. It was strange to see a beautiful woman chug water like a beer.

"You were thirsty," Scarlet said louder than she needed.

Nera tipped the glass looking through the thick bottom. "Tell me what you did."

CHAPTER 16

DONYA

The heat and light vanished quickly. Donya thought it would always be like that—burning as a stone. Similar to what humans thought of as hell. As suddenly as the heat and light had begun, they vanished. She sat in shadow, her mind active. Would this be her eternity? She suspected eventually she would go mad, but for now, she felt content enough.

She had completed her quest and found fair Nera, made her apology, and then enjoyed a wonderful part of a night. If she parsed out running with Nera through the night and their time in the flower field over the centuries, perhaps she could keep the madness at bay. If she recalled even farther back to Italy she held more memories of Nera. She could live in those memories. Trolls had excellent memories. This wasn't that unlike being in her cave, although the void's darkness was more complete. Her eyes detected nothing. Her nose was blind as well, but she could feel her body.

She tried to move, but indeed she could not. Her body was locked in stone. It reminded her of Florence, when Nera had bound her. That had been such a horrid memory until only a few hours ago. Now that recollection was dark and not something Donya would regularly replay, but it contained Nera. Thinking of it made her immovable state less dreadful.

A few questions still nagged at her. What would Nera and Scarlet do now? How would they fair with her out of the picture forever? It felt like a surety to Donya that the tengu targeted her alone. They were protectors, and she a predator. Not any longer, but that hardly mattered.

Perhaps hours passed, and Donya recalled Nera's smell like clean water. One scent did mar the purity of her smell, it was the blood magic used on those eyes—so coppery. She never got around to asking Nera if she kept the charm Donya gave her. It had been a gift from Donya's grandmother. She hoped Nera wore it still. Nera could use it as a memento if she was ever inclined to think about Donya.

Nera called Donya her rock, and now Donya truly was.

The kimonos sat in the luggage. She hoped Scarlet found the one meant for her. Donya recalled the smell and feel of the lovely silk. Perhaps Nera would wear the one Donya had bought for herself. The black silk would complement Nera's equally black hair.

Donya could still feel her body, perhaps eventually her smell would return. She wondered if in a hundred years, she would feel moss growing on the parts of her that faced north. A tingle ran through her palm. She felt the shadow of her sword appear. Scarlet was using it out in the real world.

She pictured the last things she had seen as the tengu lifted her into the morning sky. They had gotten her rather high. Donya wondered at them, setting her down again gently. Why would they do that? They wouldn't do that.

The burning had stopped as suddenly as it began because the tengu dropped her. And her stone visage shattered.

If that was it, she was surprised her consciousness was left at all. Donya wanted to sigh but could not inhale to do so.

She could still feel the sword, it grew warm in her hand and buzzed slightly. How nice, she thought, something to break up the monotony of eternity.

CHAPTER 17

SCARLET

Scarlet and Nera ended up in Akihabara. Possibly the brightest and most confusing section of Tokyo, every structure appeared to be a storefront. And people wandered around with cat ears that looked so real Scarlet could not tell if they were spirits or humans. A woman with nine fox tails and whiskers winked at Scarlet, and Nera gave the woman a smile that looked more like someone baring their teeth. Which caused the fox woman to laugh, and Scarlet to wonder what that was all about.

Scarlet got Nera to explain a few things to her after they finished their lunch and walked in the sunshine. She could understand the herbs and leaves Nera collected. Even an earthenware plate Nera purchased, at a ceramics shop. But now they moved back and forth between brightly lit, very crowded stores as Nera inspected anime figurines in each. Nera kept picking up figurines of every size, messing around with them, and putting them back. Then she saw one behind a glass case, it was smaller than a Barbie but only by a little. Nera pressed her face to the glass until a worker came over to help her. She handed him a wad of cash and took the figurine with them.

Scarlet could dimly recall the character, it was from an old anime. She checked the tag, Hiei from *Yu Yu Hakusho*. The price was forty-two thousand yen. Scarlet tried to do the math in her head. She thought Nera had just spent around four hundred dollars on a doll. Then Nera went into another shop; she didn't spend much time deciding on the next figurine. It was a very busty scantily clad blue-skinned woman. Scarlet did not recognize this character. They were almost out the door when Nera saw another toy she wanted, a redhead.

Scarlet finally understood. The dolls represented herself, Donya, and Nera. The last character was Ezra Scarlet from *Fairy Tail*. She was priced much more reasonably at thirty-six hundred yen. And she came with a sword. The sword looked nothing like Scarlet's but maybe that wouldn't matter.

"What are these for?" Scarlet asked Nera.

Nera's eyes appeared more focused. She gazed down at Scarlet. "Protection," she said as her brow furrowed.

"Who do we need protection from?"

"Many others, but mostly the one."

"Which one?" Scarlet asked. She could see why Donya said Nera was hard to understand.

"I will answer, but I need you to try on this dress." She pointed up at a dress in a window.

Scarlet couldn't believe her eyes. It was beautiful, all cream and red, but cut to show all of her decolletage. "I can't put that on. It won't even fit."

"It will." Nera tugged her arm.

Scarlet thanked her lucky stars that no one she knew would ever see her in it. "Fine, but don't forget to answer my question."

"All will be clear in time," Nera whispered, clutching the bag with the three figurines to her chest dramatically.

Nera glanced back at Scarlet who she towed into the store that absolutely burst with dresses. She pointed up at the dress in the window and then at Scarlet.

"Hihi," said a shopkeeper with a feline grin. She wore a peach yukata with big blue morning glories on it and a blue sash.

"But where will I try it on?" Scarlet squeaked.

"Over here miss," said another shopkeeper, this one dressed as an old-fashioned French maid, with a black dress puffed out at the knee and a lacy apron.

Scarlet was ushered into a curtained dressing room in no time. The maid went with her.

"There are many buttons, I will assist," the maid said. She was taller than Scarlet but very slender.

Scarlet nodded. She took off her new pants and blue tank top then wiggled into the outfit. She thought there was no way it could close. But then the maid undid ties and eye hooks. The dress was short and frilly. Only hitting Scarlet mid-thigh. She thought it would be scratchy, but it felt soft against her skin. It finally dawned on her that it was very similar to the outfit the red-headed doll wore. All cream and red. Scarlet studied herself. She couldn't believe what her boobs looked like. She worried that her cleavage would strangle her. Her white bra showed through the outfit and the straps were in the way as the puffy cap sleeves rested on her shoulder.

The maid saw her looking. "We can fix." She gave a quick command through the curtain, then pulled a measuring tape from a deep pocket.

Scarlet took a breath and checked her watch. It was three pm now. They needed to be at the airport by ten, earlier would be better though as they needed to buy Nera a ticket. There would be one spare seat on the plane. Donya would not be checking in, if Nera got a standby ticket she would get the spot. Originally Scarlet had tried to get Nera to go to the airport first thing, so they could wait out the day there. But Nera insisted they do this spell first. She kept saying the sky was too dangerous a place. Scarlet believed her, recalling the spell Nera had helped launch at her on the airplane from Rome back to California.

Something came through the curtain and then the buttons in the back of the outfit were being opened and Scarlet realized how tight the outfit gripped her. She took a big relieved breath. Then the maid undid her bra and put what felt a bit like a corset around her. It was nude and plunged deep but did conceal her nipples.

"Bend over please," the maid instructed.

Scarlet remembered the move from her dress fittings. She leaned forward and jiggled. One breast fell out. And she stood up. The maid was unaffected, pulling at the cup to cover her nipple.

"It is the largest, I think I can still make it work," she yelled through the curtain and something else appeared.

"Is that tape?" Scarlet asked.

"Yes, two sides." The maid applied the tape to her skin and pressed down the corset on top of it then pulled up the dress and rebuttoned and tied it into place.

After that, no amount of moving or jiggling caused anything to pop out.

When she stepped from the dressing room a pair of red boots waited for her. The boots matched the dress perfectly. Scarlet regarded the mirror. It was all quite a style; she didn't know what style though. Perhaps a slutty warrior marshmallow princess she thought. The two shopkeepers clapped. Nera joined in clapping and spinning around. Two other customers nodded and started pointing at the dresses they wanted. Nera came in close and bounced one of Scarlet's breasts.

Scarlet wasn't that busty, but she realized she did have the largest ones in the room. The corset pulled in her waist too. And that tape, she needed to remember that for the wedding.

Nera counted out yen from the duffle bag she kept over her arm. The French maid put the clothes Scarlet had walked in wearing into a bag and handed it to her. "Have fun," she said. "Oh, and it is okay to tell the tourists no, you don't want to take pictures if they bother you."

"Sure," Scarlet said, feeling very confused but not as embarrassed as she thought she would be in the dress.

Nera locked arms with Scarlet's as they walked out. Scarlet felt funny dragging the luggage behind her all dolled up like this.

"Stop," Nera said.

Scarlet stopped in her tracks. Nera reached forward and dug into Scarlet's purse. She came out with Scarlet's phone.

"Smile," Nera said, holding up two fingers as they had seen other young women doing in the streets.

"Now isn't the time for that." Scarlet put up a hand but in a flat warding way.

"Your love would want to see you looking so beautiful, you must send him an image. Smile."

Scarlet dropped her hand. Juan would want to see this, and there were no words to actually describe the outfit to him over the phone. "Fine," she muttered and tried to smile. Nera quickly snapped many photos. Scarlet hoped at least one of them would be of her smiling and not blinking.

"You still want your answer?" Nera asked.

The half-hearted smile dropped from Scarlet's face, and she nodded. She needed to know who was the threat. Or at least who Nera thought was the threat. More information was always better than less, even if the information would be terrifying.

"We need protection from the one inside my brother's body."

CHAPTER 18

DONYA

Donya felt a shift her senses were working. A glow came from the sword, one she had seen before, it sparked purple and red. The void around her never ended. But she could see her body—her black dress, tights, her leather boots. She wasn't stone, at least not now, not with the sword in her hand. She wished she had taken the time to change at the cafe when she'd thought of throwing out this outfit. The tights bore a hole in them, but she suspected that arose during the struggle. She could smell the cedar scent of those tengu in her nose.

If Scarlet wielded the sword did that mean she and Nera were in trouble?

The dark void felt like nothing, but that changed. It felt like water. She opened her mouth and got a hint of salt.

Donya waited intrigued but also suspicious. Of course, she could not have spoken to a troll that turned to stone, but this didn't feel right. The old stories of being turned to stone. They mentioned one would feel the heat. Or the burning cold. There'd been no mention of water.

She moved her hand with the sword. The water was as black as the void. Donya started to swim.

Time passed but Donya couldn't tell how much. Trolls were terrible with time, they could sleep for months or years and have no idea. Donya stopped swimming. Not that she felt tired, but she let herself sink. And sink, and sink. Then her feet struck the bottom. Sand kicked up in the pale light of her sword.

The scene changed, kelp grew up around her, and light trickled down through the water column.

It was the dream. The same dream that she and Scarlet experienced on many nights. The dream that Nera helped make but was unaware of after the fact. Donya couldn't believe it. Maybe just maybe she hadn't been turned to stone. What happened then? Was this her real body or a dream body?

She nipped her pinky. It did not hurt, no this couldn't be her real body, but her spirit. She started swimming through the kelp, riding the high the moment of hope gave her. Letting her senses out to see if she could find Scarlet. Maybe that was why everything changed. Maybe Scarlet entered the dream. Maybe Nera too, now that she knew she could.

Would it be too much to ask for more time with Nera? With Scarlet too? She'd grown fond of the human. They could go to California like planned and she could finally see the baby kraken Scarlet spoke of. Donya cracked a wide smile.

There. Over there. She could sense them.

The scene changed again, and the water drained away. Good, she would be able to call out to them in the desert that the sea became.

The mud dried out quickly and Donya ran over it. Knowing that soon the seal constructed by Grazia and the Kraken would appear.

"And what are you smiling for?"

Donya stopped cold. She told Scarlet nothing dwelt in this dream. No one to hurt them.

Donya turned to the sound of the voice. A voice she didn't recognize.

She knew the body though. Mars stood before her. His clothing style had changed—no dark colors. He stood in white pants and a baby blue button-down top. His body seemed still young and coltish, but the outfit and the posture were different.

Donya no longer smiled.

She clutched the sword. "Who are you? Not the original soul for that body." It couldn't be the real Mars.

"I kept a name, but locked away for eons I can't recall it," he said, his voice booming like thunder from the small body.

Donya felt the sound reverberate through her heels. Who could this be? She must keep him talking, but she wasn't adept in conversational maneuvering. Another question perhaps, any question. He said locked away—she would follow that. "If you can't recall your name, can you recall what imprisoned you?"

He cocked his head like a bird would and brushed at his leg. "I do remember that. Those with eyes. I was too beautiful, my priests cut out their eyes to be around me. But not all wanted to cut out their eyes. They covered me instead."

Donya tried to recall any story she had heard like this. Most living things needed eyes, it did not shorten the list much to say those with eyes. Perhaps it didn't matter who this was as long as it wasn't Mars. She would keep the questions coming. "What do you want with me?"

"Nothing. Nothing at all. This place, when you are here, I can feel the one I want." His bright eyes wandered into the distance.

His gaze went the way that Nera and Scarlet were. Which one did he want? It must be Scarlet. She possessed special eyes, but Nera didn't have eyes, she was similar to his old priests. Donya ground her teeth.

The one in Mars's body raised a hand, thunder clapped, and Donya saw lightning in the young man's eyes.

He moved her or perhaps shifted the whole dream, he stood to her left and Nera and Scarlet stood to her right. In Mars's body, he would have control over the dream space.

Scarlet blinked, took a step back, then pointed the sword at Mars. Scarlet did that a lot, Donya realized, striking first and asking questions later. Donya could smell something on Scarlet though. Fear. The human previously did not smell so strongly of fear. Whoever this person was, they were stronger than anything Donya had ever felt, so perhaps the fear was warranted.

"Wait, it is not Mars," Donya almost yelled. She took two steps, positioning herself between the intruder and the only living beings she cared about.

"It is not," Nera said, holding up her hands to her cheeks. She took a step forward gripping Donya's hand. "How are you in brother's body?"

"Brother? That is why I have memories of you. Of your power," he boomed.

Nera touched the circlet on her head. "Power," she whispered but her voice carried in the still air.

"You didn't answer the question. How are you in Mar's body?" Scarlet demanded.

The man glared at her—his eyes narrowed. "After the ones like you waited till, I flew the sky, they hid my body. I could not land, but they dragged me from the heights and tied my essence to tree roots. Those trees, even when one died another would spring up. The roots tangled around a talisman I could not break. But then a machine came, it ripped out the tree's roots and cracked the old talisman. Yet my body is lost. There were no vessels. I wandered and wandered. The land changed as I wandered. I could not fly, how can I be a sky god who cannot fly? Then I found this body, sleeping. It called to me."

Donya hissed. He was a god.

"Can you fly now?" Nera asked.

"Not alone." He stepped forward.

Scarlet reacted by stepping past Donya. An arc of flame swept forward from the sword. Donya watched as the man held off the flames with only a raised hand. He moved toward Nera.

Nera did not try to flee, instead letting go of Donya's hand. Nera opened her arms, dancing in a circle toward the sky god.

Donya would not lose her again. She slashed with her sword, and an arc of shadow went flying at the man. It rose dark and dense, but Donya noted that the sword dragged as though tired. These attacks were not as strong as they could be.

He dodged the shadow and grabbed Nera around the waist.

His body morphed, transforming into a great gold and green bird. His massive talons wrapped around Nera and with a beat of his wings, he launched into the dry air.

Nera caught in his claws, but also not in his claws. As one Nera still stood before Donya.

Scarlet looked as shocked as Donya felt. "Nera?"

"Remember, he has the doll?" Nera giggled and twirled again, this time back to Donya. She placed her hands on Donya's lowered arms.

Scarlet squinted into the distance. "The doll is still moving just like you. And he said he couldn't fly without you."

"I am part of this dream, and that doll is my avatar. He is pulling of my energy," Nera explained. Her hands were warm on Donya's rigid arms.

Donya dropped the sword and wrapped her arms around Nera. She could smell her and feel her warmth. "How is this possible?"

"He left," Nera said into Donya's hair.

Donya could no longer feel the man wearing Mars' body. He left, they were safe.

Donya pulled back from the embrace. She wanted to see Nera. But Nera's mouth turned down at the corners and her new eyes filled with dark tears. She stroked Donya's hair.

"I need you to cut me out of this place, or he will come back and take me away," Nera said.

Cut her from this place—but if Donya did that—her heart ached at the thought. Donya would never see Nera again.

CHAPTER 19
SCARLET

Scarlet didn't avert her eyes, but she also didn't watch too closely. Nera and Donya were getting another reunion. Their relationship sure was full of drama. Scarlet longed for Juan. She would be hugging him the first chance she got.

She kept scanning the light blue horizon of the dreamscape. Making sure that god didn't come back. Scarlet knew he wasn't exaggerating or putting on a front of power. She could see the waves of magic coming off him. A sky god bound to a tree. She wondered if she could find that legend and get more information.

"No, I can't hurt you," Donya argued with Nera.

"You must pierce my hands and feet, it will hurt, but I heal quickly," Nera said, wiggling her toes. She'd taken off her shoes.

This dream went on too long, Scarlet's palms became slick with sweat and her stomach hurt. She never liked the ocean water and the kelp, but the dessert with the cracked earth was not any more pleasant. With any luck if they could take Nera out of this dream then the spell would be broken, and they would never dream it again. But one look at Donya's face told Scarlet she would never get around to doing as Nera asked. Scarlet didn't want to hurt Nera either, but if the god came back and took Nera who knew what would happen?

"Here, I'll do it," Scarlet said. She was the only one with a weapon anyway and it was barely awake, its glow dim. Donya used it a lot in the last few days, and the spell to transport her, Nera, and Donya into the dream was difficult even with Nera expertly handling it. Then the two attacks she and Donya thrust at the Sky God drained it further. She didn't even trust handing it over to Donya. It could fall asleep any second and they would lose their chance.

"Okay," Nera said, holding up her hands.

Scarlet hesitated. And Donya glared at her. Scarlet hadn't actually thought through stabbing a person.

"I will miss you," Donya finally said, seeming forlorn. Her small eyes drinking in Nera.

It dawned on Scarlet that they hadn't explained anything to Donya. They were not expecting a visitor to be here. Nera had mentioned another attack from above, but it didn't seem to be certain. Maybe Nera sounded flippant, when in reality the events she mentioned would almost unquestionably happen.

"We are going to get you out of here too," Scarlet said. "We came here to try and do that. But now the sword is all tired out. Nera, give her the charm."

Nera licked her hand. "I always kept it in my cheek or stuck to the roof of my mouth." She placed a small charm in Donya's hand. "We sprinkled it with shadow and powdered onyx."

"You turned to stone, but I caught you in what Nera says is a shadow pocket," Scarlet said, watching Nera and Donya closely.

Donya nodded once, seeming dazed. "It might work, but if it does not this will be farewell."

"If it doesn't work we will find a way," Nera said.

Nera held so much conviction that Scarlet found she believed her. Donya seemed reassured, her shoulders coming up slightly. But Scarlet had studied the troll closely the last few days. And in the shadows of her face, around her eyes, Scarlet could see she lacked faith in them. Scarlet bit the inside of her cheek, it didn't hurt but it helped. She knew she shouldn't be this defensive, she was new to this world. But still, Donya had to know they would do their best.

That brief flash of anger helped get Scarlet moving. She fixed her gaze on Nera's hands. Nera held up her palms. Scarlet placed the tip of the sword on each one. She gave a little upward pressure. Nera's delicate skin cut open easily and blue blood trickled over her hands.

Then Scarlet pressed the tip to the tops of her feet. Nera yelped on the left foot. "Sorry," Scarlet mumbled. Nera paid no attention to her though. Nera gazed at Donya.

Nera danced away from Scarlet on her wounded feet and fell into Donya's arms as she faded away. Scarlet found that this time she couldn't avert her eyes.

"We will be together again soon," Donya said, patting Nera's back as her image faded.

It was like watching a Polaroid develop in reverse. Nera became more and more transparent, only her outline existed, then she vanished.

Scarlet inspected her hands. Nera was always the force that pulled her into this place. With her gone Scarlet faded too.

Donya still stood very solid.

"I wonder when you will fade from this place?" Scarlet asked. She wanted to slap Donya out of whatever sad mental space she'd fallen into.

"I suspect I will be here till this place cracks for the last time. The sword, it is exhausted?"

"Yep, Nera said we needed to get you that charm. If we did, you would have a chance of waking soon."

"You will have to pull me from the pocket. Don't use the sword for three nights. It should be refreshed by then."

"Three nights. Got it." Fading felt itchy, she wanted to keep her mind off of it. "Nera never explained the shadow pocket."

"She is bad at explaining."

Scarlet cracked a smile. Donya must be perking up.

"It is similar to another realm; darkness is good at holding objects. All of creation starts in darkness, so you have made a pocket of that darkness. It is the best place you could have put me. I will travel with you now until you release me."

Scarlet's arms and legs itched. Another quick inspection showed she'd faded but her outline stayed intact. "What if you put something in a shadow pocket from a distance, would it still be with you?"

"No, but it is very hard to do. Aiming the shadow is not easy."

Scarlet thought of the shadow she'd shot from the sword that night in California. Juan never heard the song after that. The pocket that caught Donya went low but the one in the sky had been very similar in the way it moved, like a dark amoeba.

"We will get you out, you know," Scarlet said.

Then Donya was gone. Scarlet opened her eyes. Nera still sat across from her. The sun had set, but the summer air remained hot and humid. In the center of the circle Nera had drawn with sidewalk chalk stood two figurines. The one for herself and the one for Donya. "Where is the third one?" Scarlet asked.

Nera shrugged. "Wherever that man is." She scooped up the two remaining dolls and stood. They'd bought a small amount of gasoline in a tank. Nera picked it up, opened it, and poured it on the circle.

Scarlet barely escaped being splashed by the dangerous fluid. The secluded spot they sat at, a little stone shrine surrounded by trees, had become deserted. "What are you doing?"

Nera lit a match and threw it. "Burning it down."

❧❧

Scarlet changed into khaki shorts and a sky-blue tee when they got to the airport. There wasn't another ticket for Scarlet's flight, and they couldn't get Nera on the standby list. She watched as Nera put a water glamour on herself. Nera walked into the restroom tall and elegant and walked out short and spiky like Donya. Except to Scarlet. Who could see the spell layered over her form. It was made entirely of water.

Scarlet wanted to put the sword in the checked baggage at first, but Nera insisted it stay with them. Scarlet wore it down her back as Donya did. Nera glamoured her so that no human would notice the sword. Scarlet paid close attention as Nera wove the spell from water, whispering incantations over a bottle they bought from a vending machine.

They checked one bag with clothes in it. After security, they ate and spent money on whatever trinkets Nera fancied. Scarlet felt tired from the events of the last few days and the stone sword lay heavy on her back. Nera spoke of all the places she wanted to go in California. She wanted to see many bridges once they freed Donya. Scarlet recognized the Golden Gate, but all the others she named were new to Scarlet. Nera picked out a pair of sunglasses with shades the darkest Scarlet had ever seen, but the frame was a pink tortoiseshell pattern. They were Prada, Scarlet felt Donya would approve.

Scarlet did buy a few things. A hat that said Japan on it for Juan, and cute erasers in the shapes of snack foods. She thought Ariel would like to play with those. Then she got cookies, snacks for the flight, and two neck pillows. One time she accidentally used her credit card instead of the yen Donya provided. Scarlet did not expect to enjoy whatever travel charges she would get.

They boarded without a problem. The flight went by uneventfully and the landing in San Francisco went smoothly. Juan waited in his truck for them.

He almost leapt out of the truck as soon as Scarlet cleared the arrival doors. Scarlet ran up to him. He smelled so good. Like warm spices and his arms were strong and real. Scarlet could feel herself smiling. She wanted to cry but held it together. They held each other for a moment, Scarlet closing her eyes and rubbing her face in Juan's slightly rumpled T-shirt.

"Where are the other two?" Juan asked, scanning the area.

Scarlet hadn't filled him in on what happened to Donya. Even though she talked to him after. She didn't want him to worry even more than he already was. The sun stayed obscured by fog and the marine layer, Scarlet thought how that would have worked out well for Donya. Nera stood on the sidewalk considering a spot outside the doors.

Scarlet knew that spot. She'd intentionally avoided it. Taking doors far to the right. That was the last spot Heldrig had ever stood in.

"Nera's back there."

"Oh," Juan muttered. He knew that spot too.

They didn't really ever talk about what happened that day. Scarlet told Juan what she could see, what she could do. And he accepted it. But they didn't often talk about the darker side of all this magic stuff. He liked the nice parts, like having a magical godchild that ate ice cream and corndogs.

Scarlet couldn't even think about how to tell him all the details of what had happened in the last few days. But right now, there were more pressing matters. "I should go get her, that traffic cop is eyeing your truck," Scarlet said.

Juan squeezed her hand and took the luggage. "Okay, then I can fill you in on the wedding drama."

Scarlet winced. She should probably tell him that although the wedding stuff wasn't life and death, somehow it almost seemed worse to her than the magical songs, Sky Gods, and stone friends.

⊰⊱

"What happened to the apartment?" Scarlet asked.

Cardboard boxes littered the apartment, about ten stacked into what appeared to be a fort. Sticking out of the tops of the fort were wooden sticks, the kinds that came in a corndog.

The cat perched on top of a large KitchenAid box.

"Presents," Juan said.

"Wedding presents?" Scarlet tried to clarify.

"Yep. I started unpacking them and trying to clean up, but Ariel won't let me throw away any cardboard."

Nera remained quiet the whole car ride, she still wore her Donya glamour. Scarlet wasn't sure why.

Scarlet walked up to the fish tank, where Ariel bobbed up and down. She smiled at Scarlet but also peeked behind her at Nera. Scarlet picked Ariel up and hugged her.

When she turned around, Nera removed the sunglasses. Her eyes behind the glamour appeared not the bright clear yellow they'd been before but a dull green.

"Hi," Ariel said, waving. She put one other hand up and wiped at her eye.

Well at least she hadn't started repeating eye first thing, Scarlet thought. Look at her small ward, tactful at such a young age. Or she didn't know the right words yet—one or the other.

"Hello little one, I am Nerawen. You can call me Auntie Nera."

"Auntie, Newa," Ariel repeated.

"Awwwww," Nera squealed and spun around.

Scarlet sighed with the ease of tensions it brought to see Nera starting to act more lively again.

"Let us go watch the twilight," Nera said.

Ariel stretched out her arms and Scarlet let her pop over to Nera, who did not seem fazed when the small spirit appeared in her arms. They walked back to the balcony. It was small but fit two chairs and half a dozen struggling plants.

"You should get some sleep," Juan said.

"We should get some sleep," Scarlet corrected, noting the dark circles under Juan's eyes. How worried must he have been the last few days?

"It might be hard to rest, with all the guests."

"I doubt Nera will be hanging around the apartment."

"Really, but where will she go?" Juan asked.

"Probably everywhere."

CHAPTER 20

DONYA

How long would this place last? Donya preferred the dream to the void, especially because she could move and see and smell. But cut off from Nera, its continued persistence presented a strange situation. Her chest felt tight. The wounds Scarlet had made on Nera mirrored the wounds that Donya suspected she got at that house in Rome. Donya had found the spikes in the basement. Heldrig had enjoyed his blood magic. Donya thirsted to kill him all over again, but she had not before and would never get a chance now.

Donya wanted to get out of this place and help Nera. When Donya had resigned herself to this fate a sense of detachment colored her emotions. Now agitation snaked its way around her stony skin. If she got out there was so much waiting for her. How would Nera plan to get her out? She pressed the charm between her fingertips. The one she gave Nera that night by the river in Florence. That night when she betrayed Nera.

Donya noticed the seal forming on the ground. It materialized in the same design and size as the original casting. It came from the Kraken and Grazia. It occasionally manifested in this dream space before. But never with the golden glow that it produced right now. Grazia was known as the golden sealer at one point. Her mortal body had died, but that didn't stop her from existing.

The seal pulled at Donya's arm when Grazia and the Kraken appeared in this space. She couldn't see them, but she could feel them. Donya walked their way. Her ability to sense others continued to improve. Sensing others with magic wasn't something she needed to actively practice before. Trolls have excellent senses of smell and were not preyed on by many so there was no need for constant vigilance. Having a human partner and trying to teach her to do it made Donya more adept.

Donya smelled her new visitors before she saw them. Grazia smelled of willow leaves and rich soil, although all of this was faint in the warm air, as Grazia's form was thin and transparent. The Kraken on the other hand smelled of the lagoon she loved, cool and damp with saturated logs and old wood.

"It is nice to finally see this place. What a barren land, blood magic lacks creativity," Grazia said to the Kraken.

The Kraken appeared a touch more menacing out of her pool. Her appendages spread and swayed like feathers in water, in the air they hung in spikes. Her color shifted to a deep red. Grazia stayed young and beautiful but in this light was quite transparent.

Donya gave a small bow to both of the other women. "It is good to see you both again, I wish it resulted from better circumstances."

The Kraken lowered her chin, and a wash of purple colored her face. Donya remembered she could not speak outside of the water.

"We assumed unprecedented events when Scarlet suddenly moved across an ocean. You and young Scarlet get into the most interesting situations. What has happened now?"

Donya tried to summarize recent events; her search for Nera, accidentally relocating Scarlet, the tengu, and of course Mars and the Sky God. Donya still did not trust Grazia completely. It felt like she used Scarlet and Donya for her own gain back in Rome. Without them, she would not be young again or a shade. However, she had paid Scarlet back in worldly wealth. Although Scarlet could not access that wealth yet.

"I knew we should have been keeping a closer eye on both of you, but we have undergone dramas of late as well. A Sky God turned into a great bird. It never even occurred to me to inhabit Mar's body," Grazia said with a glint in her faded eye.

The Kraken glanced at Grazia and gave a small shake of her head.

"I do not think inhabiting that body would be good for any soul," Donya said. She thought of how the god spoke. Perhaps it was his long imprisonment, or perhaps the years of wandering, but he seemed unfocused and lost.

"Yes, the vessel for one's feelings, thoughts, and soul is important. You are right. If I became a body snatcher I would pick a much better body," Grazia laughed to herself. "In any case, it sounds like Scarlet has mostly saved you. You did not shatter when the tengu dropped you which is I am sure what they aimed for. Although it is strange. You do not have the reek of a flesh eater anymore. It is not completely gone, but I am surprised they would notice you."

"Like I said, it was a flock. Many creatures get agitated in large groups," Donya said.

The Kraken faded her color and nodded her head. She moved her hands. And for a moment Donya could see in her mind's eye a group of humans after a woman. They bore torches and yelled. The woman dove into a Venetian canal and the Kraken pulled her to a safe air pocket.

The image faded.

"It wasn't just chance that it happened now. No, you mentioned that the old god knew of Nera when you entered this place. Perhaps the tengu tried to protect Nera. They might have sensed the connection, they are of the sky," Grazia said. She scratched at the seal on the ground—changing its shape and two symbols.

The Kraken hummed a few bars. She could still sing out of the water.

Donya recalled her first night in the harbor searching for Nera. "The tengu seemed to be after me even before Nera made it to Japan. I ran into one my first night."

"Perhaps they were in league with the Sky God then," Grazia countered.

Donya remained rather proud of her ability to lay a trap, although she now accepted she lacked a talent for spotting traps. This could have been one. The harpy that led Donya to Japan in the first place also hailed from the sky.

The Kraken loved to sort through memories. Donya didn't like the feel of it, but the process did help bring clarity. Right now, it felt like Donya swam over a methane leak on the seafloor, tiny bubbles drifted over her brain too light and with a sulfurous edge.

"Oh yes, I almost forgot. We came here out of curiosity, but also to remind Scarlet to use her cards. Pity we missed her," Grazia said.

"Cards?" Donya asked, still feeling out of sorts from everything in the past few days but also the Kraken's spell.

"Yes, I gave her a few tarot cards, from one of the original decks. With her eyes, she needs to develop divination skills."

"I do recall her mentioning this, I had not realized you bequeathed her a deck."

"Partial deck. She needs to search for suitable cards to fill out the missing arcana."

Donya chided herself, she should have been more on top of Scarlet's magical training. The cards could have revealed clues to what was happening with that song that so disturbed Scarlet. Not to mention warned them about Mars's body. If one became adept at reading current events and future events many of their problems could be solved. Divination should be easy for Scarlet. Eventually, she would be able to see through to the story fate wove. Many events in one's life were changeable at least in small ways. And that which could not change, then your reaction to the inevitable counted. It would take years to perfect. But even a little help would be welcome now.

Donya felt strange. Even with her body locked in stone and her essence here she kept wanting to make plans for the future. Was this hope? Trolls were not hopeful, and it was dangerous to think too much about the future and not the present, she knew that. But now she wanted to consider taking Scarlet to that seer in Florence. Help from a master would go a long way.

Donya also couldn't stop herself from thinking of when she got out things she would do for Nera.

The seal's glow dimmed. Grazia prodded the ground again. "This place might be feeding off of you Donya. No signs of collapsing yet. I'm afraid we need to be leaving. I changed the seal to sever our magics from this place. We don't want any troublesome old gods trying to come for us after he finishes with you."

Donya took that as a sign both of them thought Scarlet and Nera were in real trouble. Donya too of course, but the Kraken had made her opinions on Donya's luck clear a few times.

The Kraken blinked at Grazia.

Grazia grinned in reply to her lady. When she spoke to Donya again her tone dropped to something more serious. "You need to work on untangling your power from this place. If those two will be turning you back, you need strength to help."

Donya nodded. The seal flared up.

"I hope Scarlet likes her presents," Grazia called.

And then Donya was alone.

Presents. What presents had the Kraken and that old alchemist sent to Scarlet?

⟞⟝

She wandered most of that day thinking on how to separate herself from this spell completely. She had spent much time in the water that Nera used to help build this spell, which gave her the connection and now let the spell feed on her. The dream sun moved across the sky. The Sky God arrived during the night before. Leading Donya to believe he was not a god of the sun. Good news for her.

When he appeared now he stared right through her.

"Only you," he questioned.

"Only me," Donya answered.

They stood and regarded each other. Donya knew he'd grown stronger already. But also, his eyes were changing. Mars did not have green eyes.

"What is happening to you?" Donya asked. She doubted such a simple question would cause him to lash out.

"I am unsure. I have never tried to inhabit a mortal body before. This one, it brimmed with young darkness before."

"Do you dislike the darkness?"

"No, it is a part of me."

"But this body is not balanced?" Donya remembered how Mars smelled before. Like slightly off milk boiled in an iron pot.

"Balance, yes, I enjoyed that. I will have it again." He did not change into a bird of prey this time. He simply disappeared as quickly as he'd appeared. Donya felt him leave. She felt the ripples it made in the white-blue sky. The sky of a dry desert.

It was time for her to leave this place as well.

CHAPTER 21

SCARLET

Sunday lived up to its name. It was bright out and time seemed to fly by Scarlet. Juan stood outside, he'd driven her to her last dress fitting. But he wasn't even allowed inside the shop so that he could have no chance to see the dress. Normally Scarlet wouldn't care, but she couldn't stand the thought of any more bad luck.

Her dress was perfect. Nothing popped out, the corset thing from Japan made her cleavage defy gravity and yet still seem natural. Afterward, she walked out and took Juan's hand beaming. Today Scarlet got to feel optimistic, today she wanted to feel accomplished. They walked to the beach to meet Nera and Ariel. Ariel would try and move Nera all the way from Marina to Carmel.

Juan squeezed Scarlet's hand as they walked past a silver and blue Bugatti. Only in Carmel would you see luxury cars parked on the street. Scarlet wondered if Donya would like it here, it boasted all of the fancy brands she enjoyed. She once again thought of the cheese shop that continued to be her favorite place.

Scarlet peeked over at Juan. He looked better; when he'd picked them up at the airport, he'd sported dark circles under his eyes and he appeared almost dingy. Now only a hint of the dark circles clung under his eyes. Another good night of sleep and he would be fine.

"Hey babe," Scarlet started to get his attention.

"Yes," he said, meeting her eye.

"Maybe you should take this whole week off, you have the time, I'm sure your boss would say yes."

"Only if you call in the next two days too."

Scarlet grumbled. She didn't want to do that, and he knew it. It hadn't even been a full year since she got that job and she wanted to keep it. Right now, they needed the money, and more importantly, she needed to feel normal. And having a regular job that anyone with a bachelor of science could do made her feel that way.

They made it to the beach and walked the short distance across the sand to the lapping waves. Nera left the apartment with Ariel at sun up, to teach her. Before they even left, Nera found that Ariel could sense Scarlet and Juan very well if they interacted with water. Much like her mother had back in Italy.

Scarlet kept her eyes out on the waves.

"It's so relaxing. I'm glad we made time for us today," Juan said.

"Me too. We won't have much time for the next week." Scarlet kept an eye on Juan, his jawline tensed again. Something must be bothering him. Between the wedding and everything else, it would be strange if he wasn't agitated. "It's just us here. What do you need to tell me?"

Juan's shoulders sank. "No, it isn't anything you don't already know about. I wish things could be smoother I guess."

"I'm sorry about what happened," Scarlet started.

"No, wait it isn't that," Juan interrupted. "It's my family, why can't they behave? My Tia is still inviting people even after the talk we gave her."

Scarlet giggled then threw back her head and let out a good laugh. When she stopped and wiped her eyes Nera emerged out of the surf holding Ariel. Ariel bounced happily.

"Wow, that was fast," Scarlet said.

"This one is strong and easy to teach," Nera said, patting Ariel.

Ariel popped to Juan, who still couldn't see her, but Scarlet noticed how he reflexively put his arms up when she clung to the front of his shirt.

"I think we'll walk a bit," Juan said, waving to Nera and Scarlet.

Nera dropped the Donya glamour sometime in the night. And with no disguise, her eyes were very unappealing. The whites sunk in and held a yellowish tinge and the irises faded even more, turning a boggy green. Plus, the shape seemed off. Juan avoided Nera's face now, practically staring at his shoes. Scarlet probably would have too, but the spell in the eyes always drew her gaze. The spell wriggled with darkness like a worm on a hook. "Juan and I are stopping by the venue after this, I'll stick my feet in the ocean to show you and Ariel where it is."

Nera hopped in place. "Perfect, may I obtain a dwelling there?"

"You can get a room, I think, just say you are with the wedding. We have a block, and they aren't all booked."

"Yes, what a wondrous day."

Scarlet had to agree, she was sure everything would work out now that they made it to California. "Will you two head back to the apartment after this? If you get a room, you can take your stuff there."

"No no, Ariel must learn more, she will be helping."

Scarlet waited a few breaths, but Nera didn't elaborate. "Helping what?"

"Helping to retrieve Donya."

෫෮

Scarlet wandered out to the balcony. Juan snored in their bed. They used their few hours of alone time for stress-busting intimacy, but now she thought she should let him sleep. The moon floated as a golden crescent in the dark sky. Scarlet wondered if it waxed or waned. A few clouds drifted on the horizon but right now they stayed clear of the moon. The shadows cast by the pale light cut across the landscape deep and dark. Scarlet searched the shadows, but nothing stirred. She loved California. Lots of free-floating magic but hardly any spirits.

They needed to wait three nights to try and get Donya out. She could handle Nera until then, and Ariel too. Ariel was very happy that she would get to see the wedding with Nera and hopefully Donya.

Scarlet found herself delighted that Ariel could watch. There didn't seem to be a way before. She once entertained thoughts of putting Ariel in one of her floating candle centerpieces, but Ariel had grown too big. Not to mention too wiggly. She would have never been able to just watch. Even now Scarlet wasn't sure that her bouquet wouldn't disappear mid-throw and end up in the ocean. But that was a price Scarlet would willingly pay.

A spark of movement flashed in the darkness. Scarlet focused on it. She could make out Nera's pale skin. What were they practicing now?

Nera held Scarlet's green bucket in front of her, Ariel sat inside. Ariel created bubbles of water in front of her and launched them. When she made one a miniscule white light formed in the center. Scarlet watched closely to study the spell's form. It grew denser and brighter when the ball went farther or became larger. Ariel tried over and over again. None flew farther than a few feet. As they drew near Scarlet could hear the plops of water hit the sidewalk.

Nera waved as they approached. They stood on the opposite side of the street. Nera spoke to Ariel. Ariel stopped her magic practice. Nera didn't know all about Scarlet's eyes. Nera could probably barely see Scarlet from that distance. It worried Scarlet that Nera might be telling Ariel to stop in front of her, that they might be keeping secrets.

Scarlet took a breath, reminding herself that Nera was one of the good guys—always had been. Nera lived through a hard situation, and she probably didn't want to worry Scarlet. Scarlet turned to unlock the front door for them. It was a few minutes after midnight. She stretched her hands up over her head. Maybe she could nap during lunch tomorrow.

"Look look," Ariel called as the door opened.

Scarlet held her finger up to her lips. "Inside voice." She smiled brightly at the little one so she wouldn't think she was mad. For now, no one could hear her but Scarlet and Nera, but someday that wouldn't be the case.

Ariel flapped her hands. "Sorry," she whispered. Then she wiggled her fingers and flexed her wrists and began to float.

Scarlet watched closely, trying to see the spell moving Ariel through space. Ariel wrapped her tentacles together appearing to have two legs and mimed walking. It would have looked better but her floating body drifted sideways.

Scarlet clapped her hands quietly. "Very good, what do you call that?"

Nera beamed. "Float, float."

Scarlet thought about it, pop pop and float float. Ariel's spells were easy to remember.

"What else did you learn?" Scarlet asked.

"Lots," Ariel said, flapping her hands again. "Scare ducks."

"Scare ducks?" Scarlet asked.

"She is working on a few things. A few more days and our Ariel will know nearly a dozen spells," Nera said.

Ariel popped herself into the fish tank and made bubbles that the old beta skittered away from. Ariel pulled at the fake water plants and curled up in her corner for sleep. It had been a long day for her, Scarlet never thought she could be active for this many hours.

Scarlet's mouth popped open, she shut it quickly. "Nothing dangerous."

"Not yet," Nera said.

CHAPTER 22

DONYA

Time flowed differently here in the dream. The sun paused in what might be the west. It never really set but it did move. It was not the real sun, and it did not hurt her. Donya prepared herself to sever her energy from the dream. To return to the void. If she cast herself out as far as she could, she felt almost sure this could be the hours before dawn. When it was darkest. The best time to cut ties.

It felt like severing strings, she repeated three old words to help with concentration, mostly the troll word for cut. She said it over and over again. And as it always had, the sky began to crack. Chunks of that dry white blue sky fell crashing to the ground. This was the last time Donya would be here. She knew this for certain. The darkness that waited outside of the desert dream would be all hers.

Donya moved around avoiding the brittle sky shards. But soon there were almost no places to stand on the dirt. She tried standing on one of the fallen shards of sky. It held her although she did not feel as though she stood on the ground. Instead, a strange weightlessness, like swimming in a warm salty sea surrounded her. She enjoyed the feeling while the last small piece of sky fell. When it struck the ground, the dream faded.

She emerged in the void. She could see and move, her spirit still free of the stone that trapped her body.

Once again, she was not alone.

"I have never been more popular than when I am a standing stone," Donya said.

The shrunken figure laughed and met her gaze.

"Grandmother," Donya said, shocked.

"Eii, where havve ye been? Here I come to visit my progeny all stonestuck and ye'r not bout." She took in a few sniffs through her prodigious nose and cleared her throat.

Donya still could not believe her eyes. "I became mired in a dream spell. It is a long story."

"All ye have is time now, spill it," commanded the old troll.

"That isn't all I have," Donya said with a smile and started telling her story again. She felt like she did that a lot lately.

Several times she needed to pause, as her grandmother cackled and cackled at something in the long story of how she got here. The parts that brought her grandmother the most amusement were when Donya traveled to the new world, and the part with the cow spell on Scarlet's eyes. She whistled at their confrontation with the Wolf Kings but didn't seem interested in Heldrig.

"It sounds like you may not be stonestuck long, and here I used mi best cowhi to see ya. Tossed it to the northwind I did."

"Grandmother, is this what every stonebound troll is in?" Donya asked.

"Na-ta-tall. They have the bright light of the sun, no seeing out, but still more tha this lot." She stroked her chin whiskers. "It was the human, ye can't cast a spell for shit, but you right about the shadow."

"Do you think they can do it?"

"Sounds like."

"If they free me, maybe that means others could be free."

Donya's grandmother shook her head. "Ye do that too much, pushing, changing. It can be done, but consequences come after."

Donya couldn't fault her logic. Donya messed up a lot.

"If you unbind, then ye must find that god, think of the future. Do not rush at it. Slowly slowly." Donya's grandmother held up her hands. She was a henkie, a type of river troll.

An image formed between her hands, viewed from far below. The view of a mountain from a stream. Donya could hear the flowing water, she could smell the dry grass past the water's edge and the plants that clung close trying to drink up the moisture without drowning their roots.

"Here," the old henkie said while continuing to move her hands. "He only needs ta be appeased, na bowed to."

Donya tried to memorize the lay of the mountain peak. It was not sharp. Broken down like many of the mountains near the coast in California. In the sky circling the peak glided a hawk. Troll eyes were not good but even she could see the hawk was off. It seemed far too large and its eyes glowed green blue.

"I know this one," Donya's grandmother said.

Donya nodded. Her grandmother kept to herself but somehow seemed to contain a world of knowledge and spells.

"He came far, over mountains. Ye cannot kill a god. Binding em will do. Mortals bound this one. Angry so angry."

"Angry and after me and my allies," Donya said.

"Angry and confused." Then Donya's grandmother clapped her hands. "Time for better spells."

Now Donya was the one who was confused.

⤜⤛

"This's tha last one, nine spells are all I got for ye tonight," Donya's grandmother said.

Donya couldn't believe the amount of spellwork her grandmother had tried to teach her. In Donya's youth, she would teach her one per visit. She was happy that the elder believed she really would get out and could handle a heap of ancient power. Her grandmother explained to her many of these should not be tampered with. One she taught her would work with Nera's binding. They could use it on the god. Donya had too much to lose now not to fight with everything she possessed.

"Thank you for the spell craft, Grandmother."

"Come visit me when ye can move about." The elder sniffed and turned her ear to the side. "Something is coming," Donya's grand-mother said with a gleam in her eye. She exited the void suddenly.

Donya braced for whatever else could be on its way.

Her sword shimmered into existence, floating in the darkness, covered with seeds, many different seeds. Donya exhaled slowly, then inspected each seed. She took pleasure in knowing they were meant for her. Although she worried they were meant as provisions for a long time, not to be consumed all at once. Troll metabolism was not like many others. Those seeds she did not need would simply sit inside of her. As seeds sit in soil.

She started on the smallest ones first—California poppy. They loved the light and tasted of hot sunshine. She regretted eating them somewhat as it reminded her of the sun on her face as she turned to stone. The next were acorns, their wet shells still smelled of leaf mold, like they'd been collected only moments before. She inhaled the scent of each one as she ate it.

What an ingenious way to bring her objects inside this space. The magic of the sword had not been used at all. Instead, another's magic powered the translocation. One she did not know yet, but that she recognized nonetheless. It must be the human's young ward. Ariel, Scarlet called her. What an amazing amount of power, incredibly steady for one so very young.

She was a baby Kraken. Donya got the sense that eventually, she could grow to be even stronger than her mother.

Where the hilt met the blade balanced a seed she never thought she would see or eat. A coconut. It still wore a sticker on it. Bought at the store. She unlatched her jaw and placed it in her mouth. She popped it open and juice streamed down her throat. It clung to her tongue. She picked up the rest of the seeds, none as impressive as the coconut for sheer unexpectedness but many with more power for her. She couldn't name all of them, but they intrigued her. A small black seed had been gathered in abundance. She placed these in her mouth, and she knew they came from a yellow flower that liked to bloom in the shade. Each one pulsed through her. This would do nicely. None tasted as good or satisfied as well as her mountain saxifrages, but the sheer quantity made up for that.

When she picked up the last seed, a pine nut, the sword righted itself and then snapped out of the void.

She was alone again, now armed with a new wealth of spells and power. This should have made her very happy. But with no way to use them, she only felt frustrated.

CHAPTER 23

SCARLET

Monday morning turned out misty and cool. For most it would be hard to see on the highway, Scarlet was thankful for her eyes. She could see brake lights much farther out than others. She watched for the red glow. This weather obscured all the beautiful scenery but occasionally Scarlet would catch out of the corner of her eye a dead egret. Their white feathers a sad mound on the wet pavement. It happened on days like this. They thought the slick black road to be a river. No fish swam here, just quick death by car grill could be found.

She pulled into the lot. Her body remained sore from the plane ride. Her hips still stiff. She wasn't excited for the long day in front of the microscope, but someone had to count phytoplankton and this girl was going to do it.

Nera would not let her leave the house today without the sword. It stayed useless, very fast asleep. But she took the beautiful opal sword. It sat in her trunk.

She thought about the sword and her tether to Donya. If they couldn't get her out of the stone, what would happen? How long would they keep trying? Nera and Donya were damn near immortal. It could take all of Scarlet's life to fix this. She'd almost entered the building when movement high in the mist caught her eye.

Wings flapped, a hawk, circling slowly. It was too big though. Scarlet's mind stuttered; it carried an aura. Green, like an unhealthy sky before a storm, looking at it made her eyes itch.

Scarlet used her key fob and quickly ducked inside the building. She tried again to cast out her senses. She never could sense a mystical thing to save her life. No, she would need to use her eyes. But who's eyes would be sharper, her's or a Sky God's?

Scarlet clocked in and headed down the hall to her workstation. Once she sat at her desk she could stare at the ceiling and see what she could see. She popped through the door and her black swivel chair and microscope never looked so appealing.

She took her seat and let her eyes stare. She arrived first in her section of the lab. She needed to do this quickly before everyone else showed up and distracted her from staring at the ceiling when she should be working.

Her eyes saw through the ceiling to the inside of the roof, a rat gnawed on a copper wire, but that wasn't a concern for her right now. Scarlet was pleased she grew better with her eyes, all she needed to do was practice. She didn't blink and the clouds above the building came into view. If she stared a little longer she would see through them too. From what she could see right now there no longer seemed to be a hawk circling. Maybe it hadn't seen her. Maybe she was overreacting like she had with that song that had disappeared as quickly as it came.

Her phone rang and Scarlet gasped loudly. Trina, a woman in the other lab, looked up from her scope and glared at Scarlet.

Feeling sheepish, Scarlet said, "hello," into her phone. Normally she wouldn't answer an unknown number but with so many vendors involved in the wedding, she felt she needed to this week.

"Is this Miss Scarlet Burke?" a woman's voice asked.

"Yes, it is," Scarlet answered. She waited, it'd either be a vendor or a spam call.

"My name is Olivia, I'm Guy Morgan's assistant. Or I was," Olivia said.

Scarlet held her breath. Guy was her private investigator, but he took too great an interest in the case she gave him. She should have known better than to hire a former cop. Scarlet paid the man upfront, with the option to either get a partial refund if Mars couldn't be found or sink more money in for travel and incidentals. She didn't need his services anymore. Mar's body had found them. "Oh, yes," was all she could think to say to Olivia's statement.

"I have unfortunate news. Guy was found dead."

"That's terrible." Scarlet stood and walked back the way she came as Trina had gone very still in the other lab like she listened in.

"And it appears he continued to work on that case you gave him. Perhaps the two are even linked."

"Wait, do you mean not dead, but murdered?" Scarlet asked. She stood out in the hall fixing her eyes on the linoleum floor, but her head swam, and her stomach clenched.

"Yes, I'm sorry, it is all very sudden and strange. It is just I am going through his notes, and they don't make a lot of sense. But he did find your cousin. Alive and well. But now I'm not sure that is still the case."

Scarlet realized with a murder the police would be getting involved. Perhaps even the FBI if one of Guy's old comrades felt like it, he'd worked with them a few times. From behind Scarlet, she could hear more people filtering into the lab, she chose her words carefully. "If you could send me some of the information I would appreciate it."

"Of course, I'll email you everything I have. One thing. Guy's eyes they'd been removed. It is a terrible detail I know, but I felt like I had to share it with you. Because of his notes."

"Thank you," Scarlet said, when really her mind rattled off a string of curse words. She stared at the same tile throughout the end of the phone call. Her eyes refocused and she could see the sand beneath the foundation. It reminded her of how unstable her life was right now.

Monday passed into Tuesday, and both Scarlet's work days flew by. Nera brought Ariel to meet Scarlet after work on Tuesday afternoon. Nera and Scarlet walked and walked to get away from the tourists along the beach. September had just arrived, but even with school back in session, people didn't stop visiting the beach. Nera was blind again. Her eyes finally completely disintegrated. She refused to put another pair in yet. But would not tell Scarlet why.

"Tonight will be very good, the waters are right, the moon is right," Nera said.

"I think one more night of rest would be better for the sword. Tonight is barely three nights. Donya said three nights," Scarlet argued, clutching Ariel to her chest. Ariel seemed like her usual self. Nothing different. But Scarlet could see the difference being around Nera made. Ariel looked more solid like she had been eating more, like she thrived.

"I have everything needed," Nera said, spinning around as a wave coursed up the sand. Her feet danced in the water.

"One more night is not that long, Nera. I am surprised you are in such a rush, you two have forever."

"No, no, any day could be our last," Nera said, pointing up at the sky.

Scarlet shivered, she didn't like being out in the open like this. She'd seen the one who was after Nera not far from here. She scanned the sunset orange sky. Nothing now.

"Tonight, tonight," chanted Ariel.

Scarlet had the rest of the week off work. Guests started arriving tomorrow. Her wedding was coming up. "Okay tonight, once she is back I won't have to worry about you two as much."

"Worry, you worried about us?" Nera asked, putting her hands to her cheeks.

"Of course, what if as you mentioned, he came and stole you away? I can't do anything by myself," Scarlet said. Also pointing up for emphasis. She didn't mention that Nera was a touch flighty and teaching Ariel god knew what.

"Oh yes, but you might be able to burn him to a crisp. Or smash him like father."

"Smash?" Ariel asked, bouncing against Scarlet's chest. Then she hit her tiny fist into her open hand.

"No smash." Scarlet lightly patted Ariel on the head.

"I will gather items, to make the way smoother for your beautiful sword. We need many candles. Ariel, will you help?" Nera asked, holding out her arms.

Ariel popped into them.

"Where will I meet you?" Scarlet asked.

"Stay right here, relax in the water," Nera said. Then she and Ariel popped out of existence.

Scarlet sat with a huff. She hoped they didn't take too long. All she'd eaten for lunch was a salad and dinner would be waiting for them at home, a healthy poached chicken breast for her, and delicious corndogs for Ariel.

CHAPTER 24

DONYA

With nothing to do but think, that is what Donya did. Mostly she thought about Nera. She managed to think of her so much she got annoyed with herself. But all of the thoughts were constructive. Donya decided firmly that after everything with the Sky God was sorted out she would find Nera's eyes.

She wondered if she'd become overconfident about the Sky God, but those times she'd seen him he contained no malice toward her or her allies. He wanted to use Nera. And Donya could not allow that, even if Nera went with him willingly for whatever strange reason. Nera's father used her for a lifetime, she deserved peace. And she deserved her eyes.

Donya held a few clues to the whereabouts of her eyes already. During Donya's search, she occasionally got led off in an entirely different direction. Ones she would know were wrong in her gut, but she would follow them anyway. She knew they were wrong because the earth around the area felt dry. Nera reveled in water, water made her strong and tied her to a community of other water folk. Water folk who wanted to assist her long before Donya showed up.

When she first sought Nera, right after the events in Italy, she had made her way to the Greek Isles. That jaunt almost ended her, at the time humans still lingered in her system and the sunlight in Greece fell strong, sparkling off the water at every angle. But on a rocky outcrop one night she met a siren, one that managed to help a young Nera. The siren warned Donya about Heldrig and Donya got to bite back a triumphant smile knowing he'd been killed, and she'd helped in that. But Donya did not tell the siren. She didn't want anyone to call her an oath breaker or betrayer.

That siren wouldn't be any help to her now as when she'd tried to get Nera far away from Heldrig, by purifying the blood magic he used to track his daughter, Nera was already blind.

Decades had passed since Heldrig removed Nera's eyes, and now it was more than a year since Heldrig met his end. What if Nera's eyes ceased to exist? It was possible.

She wouldn't tell Nera of her plan, if she found the eyes it would be a wonderful surprise.

Once she gotten a lead to Nera that took her to a high desert in Mongolia. No water, but that black ooze Heldrig used permeated the ground. Donya had gained strength by that trip, she took time to sniff the upwelling. Oil mixed with tar in a foul amalgamation greeted her nose.

Water and oil do not mix, if Heldrig kept the eyes he would have stashed them in oil in a dessert.

A smell rousted Donya from her thoughts and planning. The sharp tang of the ocean drifted to her, a salty savory scent with the underlying musk of life and death.

Donya stopped and luxuriated in the sensory experience.

Being trapped in this place came with rewards. It caused her to stand still long enough to rely on her allies, which she should do more often. Together they defeated Heldrig because Scarlet, Donya, the Kraken, and Grazia had worked together.

Donya could always sense Scarlet out in the world after they forged the sword. In here that shouldn't be possible but perhaps Donya never tried either. Too caught up in her initial despair and then fantasy.

This scent was around Scarlet or perhaps the sword. Donya concentrated, the two were together. She could feel it.

Donya breathed deeply. She could catch the whiff of Nera, and even the baby Kraken who already smelled too strong, maybe stronger than Nera. She kept teasing out the other smells. Another human lingered on an inland breeze. A woman who used a perfume Donya recognized but never much cared for, Chanel no 5.

Donya got a shiver up her spine. Distantly she smelled lightning. It never frightened her before. She often enjoyed it when thunder burst up on her mountain. But lighting was of the sky. And in her year in California, she'd never encountered lightning, not even in winter.

The current season was the tail end of summer in Scarlet's home. Donya wanted to be mistaken, but the terrible feeling in her gut told her she was not.

How could they get the Sky God to leave them alone? They couldn't win in an all-out fight. With her grandmother's spell maybe she could imprison him again. That would be the safest, especially if they could get him before he realized his full power. Mar's body was mortal, and he needed time to adapt to it.

Of all the gods why did it have to be a Sky God? They were the worst, always passing judgment from on high when they had never struggled down on the earth.

Donya originally hoped Scarlet would give the sword enough time to recover fully, but now she hoped they tried to get her out soon. Outside she could help.

Donya concentrated. Besides the smell she could feel tingling on her face. Donya blinked a few times. The fading light of the sun washing over Scarlet and the sword felt very much like a dozen kisses. No troll had ever experienced such a feeling. Again, Donya got to be the first.

CHAPTER 25

SCARLET

Scarlet blinked awake, her vision blurred, and for a moment she saw a grove of canary yellow leaves, and white trunks shaking in the breeze. It should have been a happy vision, but it felt oppressive. Cold water lapped at her foot, and she sat up with a start. She didn't remember falling asleep. Nera and Ariel were there. Ariel waited right by her hip playing in the sand.

"You are very quiet," Scarlet said. Her mouth felt dry and grainy.

Ariel bobbed her head and mimicked a small snore. She'd blended her color to match the moonlight-illuminated sand.

Scarlet ran her tongue around her mouth, apparently, she'd been snoring on the beach. Scarlet blurrily searched for Nera. The dark-haired beauty kneeled farther up in the sand. Nera dug an intricate shape into the soft shifting substrate. A circle on the outside but every line inside the circle lay perfectly parallel, and tiny candles flickered at set distances. The night air did not move, like all held its breath for the enchantment they would produce. Nera worked blind, feeling the sand but what she made was perfectly precise.

She stopped moving when Scarlet stood right behind her.

"Maybe you should put in new eyes? You have more, right?"

"No, dark magic made those. I don't want it to touch this spell. It must be clean."

Scarlet still didn't understand the difference between light and dark magic. It was not as simple as in the children's tales. It seemed more to do with a balance, like a universal scale weighed intent and cruelty. And it certainly didn't have to do with using light and shadow. Donya used shadow magic, but it was not dark, at least not anymore.

"How much longer till the spell is ready?" Scarlet asked.

"Three, two, one," Nera counted.

Scarlet watched her as she stood and started singing. Water surged up the beach. It moved as though it would wipe away the etching in the sand, but instead, the water gently filled it.

Ariel crawled her way to the opposite side of Nera. Scarlet could see her watching the nymph. Ariel's eyes filled with wonder and hope. Scarlet felt the tingles of jealousy in her belly. Ariel had never looked at her like that. Maybe Nera would have been a better godmother.

"The time is now, Ariel move the sand, Scarlet use fire with the sword," Nera instructed, then she spoke a different language, ugly and guttural.

Scarlet recognized it—troll. She ran back to where she'd napped. The sword lay in the sand. She picked it up, then felt a tingling all over her body. Ariel moved her. She stood to the east, while Nera and Ariel presided over the north and south. The space to the west sat empty.

The sword woke easily enough. Scarlet wasn't sure where to point the fire, into the ground or to the west. The pocket of shadow pooled on the ground when it caught Donya, so she pointed the sword down. It occurred to her that Nera must have explained to Ariel, she could have explained to her.

Plunging the sword into the ground she let fire slide over its length. It beget a beautiful red and orange flame. Ariel smiled over at her, Scarlet saw her turn the yellowish color of the moonlight. Then the magic really began.

Scarlet watched as Ariel raised the water from the circle in the ground. Now the circle became a sphere with the water swirling around inside of it. Nera raised her hands. And the water stopped, bound, it began to freeze over. But Ariel would flex her fingers and the water would unfreeze and move again. Their magics pushed and pulled. Movement and stillness battling it out in a liquid dance. Scarlet's magic seemed dull in comparison. The moon hung overhead. It was bright, growing fatter each night. When the light caught on the frozen water it sent prisms bouncing about the sand.

The tug of war in front of Scarlet went on for several minutes before anything changed. A puddling of shadow appeared at the western side of the sphere. Scarlet could see it through the swirling water. The shadow formed a column and crept into the water.

Scarlet pulled the sword up, flames continued to lick the stone blade. She held it up and the flames shot forward, a delicate tendril of fire. It was caught by the shadow. Scarlet braced her legs to keep from stumbling at the pulling and tossing of the sword.

Inside the water now danced a flame and shadow. The flame flickered and railed, turning from brighter colors to blue then back up to gold. Scarlet tried not to be too dazzled by the brightness of the flame, she kept a watchful eye out. Ariel's arms shook slightly from strain. She was just a baby, this spell might be too much for her.

Scarlet let her attention wander too much, the sword stuttered, and the flame cut off. Scarlet let out a gasp, she'd probably ruined everything. The shadow pulled forward, overwhelming the last of the flame. Ariel let her arms drop, then flopped backward on the soft sand. Nera's magic froze the sphere, winning the tug of war at last. But something manifested inside the ice sphere. The shadow. It had also won. It formed a shape.

Scarlet dropped her sword. The ice rose like a great bubble around the shape, but she could recognize it. Donya. They did it.

Nera yelled a sharp happy word and the ice bubble burst. Sending shards of shining white in all directions. Those that went up came fluttering back down. It was snowing. Snow on a beach in California, during summer. Scarlet giggled with excitement. They did it.

Nera ran inside the circle first. Scarlet wanted to give them a moment, and she needed to check on Ariel who sprawled on the sand. She scooped up the little one and cradled her.

"You did good," Scarlet said. "That was very brave and strong."

"So fun," Ariel said.

Ariel and Scarlet smiled and caught their breath together seated on the moonlit beach. It took Scarlet a moment to realize the sounds from behind her were not happy. Nera sobbed and wailed. Scarlet clutched Ariel tighter to her.

Nera's lament became a high keening rolling out over the sand and waves.

Scarlet whirled around. Donya stood there, but she was stone.

And now that Scarlet faced west, she could see darkness out in the sea. A large bubble of shadow. Similar to the one that produced Donya's stone form. The stone form that Nera clung to and cried on.

Scarlet couldn't speak, so she moved forward. The shadow formed a shape in the water. Ariel started to scream.

The sword wasn't asleep yet. Scarlet managed to raise it and a shield formed around them. It was all she could do. The shield shuddered when struck. Even with Scarlet's eyes, she couldn't see what attacked them, too much sand and water swirled around the shield.

The tempest that wailed outside faded and Scarlet could see again. Sand had piled up around the shield she'd formed; it built an octagon around them piled at least four feet high. Nera never reacted to the chaos, instead crying, draped over Donya's stone shoulders. One of Donya's arms remained raised. She stayed frozen in the awkward stance she used to struggle against the tengu. Ariel trembled up against Scarlet but was unharmed. They were all fine.

Scarlet scanned Donya's stone figure. One thing wasn't stone. Her outstretched right hand. The fingers wiggled. A thin flake came off of the wrist and more of her less stony form became exposed.

"Nera, Nera look," Scarlet managed. She thanked her lucky stars that Donya wasn't completely stone. They needed to move. Whatever resided in the water was dangerous.

Nera swiveled her head and patted at her empty eyes.

"Here, feel." Scarlet raised Nera's hand to Donya's free hand.

"It worked," Nera crooned. "Oh, it worked."

"Maybe too well," Scarlet said, cradling the trembling Ariel and pondering the dark ocean.

CHAPTER 26

DONYA

Donya might have preferred the void to this. She thawed slowly from the extremities in. Her right arm was almost free, and both her feet were out, but her knees lingered locked in stone so she couldn't move in a meaningful way. All of the fingers on her left hand had broken free, and blessedly her head.

She remained mostly helpless, except that she held the sword, and it was tired but would wake quickly if needed. Nera had dragged her to a small marina. She'd been planted under a dock. Boats bobbed above her in the sunshine.

There were upsides to being down here though. Nera kept swimming back and giving her kisses.

At this rate, she wouldn't be completely out of the stone until Friday. It took a lot of her strength to break out. She was thankful for the meal they'd sent her in the void. It allowed her to pull herself back into her body.

Another section of her left leg turned back. She could feel it when the sensation returned. When she could feel the cold of the water against her skin.

A curious otter swam up to her, twisting and turning in the dark green sea water. It appeared silver with the air trapped in its dense coat. She wiggled and flexed her free right hand. The otter paused, ran a whiskered cheek along it, and then swam off.

The small spirit that accompanied Nera came shooting up from under a boat. She slammed into Donya's hard belly and popped up with a smile.

"Win, win," she said.

Nera swam up right behind. "Oh, you beat me again, my you are fast."

Donya was struck again that Nera's voice sounded even more beautiful underwater.

"Ariel and I raced," Nera said with a smile.

"You two must go ashore, stay with Scarlet. It is not safe. You were attacked," Donya said.

"We are of the water, it is safer for us here. Up there he waits," Nera said, wriggling herself to be in the crook of Donya's still-frozen elbow.

Donya wrapped her free arm around her. Nera's hair tickled her face. "And what of Scarlet?"

"She is resting, very safe in her fiery shield," Nera cooed into Donya's ear.

Ariel giggled and made smooching sounds.

"Please do not leave again, we can discover what sings in the water when I am free," Donya pleaded.

"I cannot stand still," Nera said, stretching herself out. "I think that which is in the water is a friend, a sad friend, or even lonely."

"It didn't feel friendly." Donya remembered the first thing she felt upon getting back to her body. The anger. It had been stuck in shadow as well and used the spell meant to set Donya free to break out.

A melody began out in the deep. Here in the water, it resounded much louder. Donya instantly recognized it as Scarlet's singer. The song for the storm. This explained it. Scarlet managed to lock it away and now it escaped with Donya. It couldn't be friendly.

"It is here, Ariel come," Nera said, retching herself away from Donya and streaking off into the brighter water.

"No come back," Donya yelled.

Ariel looked at Donya then back to where Nera had disappeared, she opened her hands.

"Wait, wait little one," Donya managed.

Ariel paused.

"Remember how I feel. If anything is very bad, bring yourself and Nera back to me."

Ariel blinked her too-large eyes at her. "Sure, sure."

Then she was gone. Donya stood alone again. Perhaps she should have tried to explain to Ariel how Scarlet had trapped whatever wandered out there. But Ariel was very new. And Nera would always be hard to communicate with.

The dirge continued, Nera was right that the melody rang tinged with sadness. It went on and on, and Donya watched as the streaks of sunlight in the distance darkened, and clouds blocked out the sun.

❧❦❧

Nera and Ariel did not return by sundown. The song stopped. Donya's right side broke free of the stone much faster than the left. Perhaps the left side absorbed more sunlight. Donya managed to pull herself ashore, much to the consternation of a colony of sea lions, who barked and snorted at her.

Her right arm and leg were free. Her left arm was almost free to the elbow, and her left knee had thawed more than halfway. She dragged her left leg behind her as she trudged toward Scarlet's home. She would arrive by dawn.

As she moved through the night air she recited a few of the spells her grandmother taught her for the sword to overhear. She did not have enough energy to activate them. It was important to get them right, grandmother had explained that her constant tampering with spells caused her nothing but trouble. She didn't have the experience to go about mucking with things. Maybe in another few millennia, she could wing it.

She headed along the Highway, keeping far enough out in the muddy wetlands that no cars would see her, when she felt a pull. It wasn't Nera or Scarlet. No, this came from the earth. A place called to her. Donya stopped. It lay in the opposite direction of the way she headed.

She could not bend to place her hands in the earth. She was brittle, but the wetlands were full of soft mud and short reeds. Donya let herself fall forward into the mud. The earth got into her mouth and nose. She held her eyes closed. She used her good arm to push herself up and cough out a mouthful of mud. She was depleted but not totally out of magic. She concentrated, the earth was one of her elements. She let it whisper to her, slow and strong.

She did need to turn around. There stood a mountain. She remembered its outline. Her Grandmother had shown it to her—the mountain of the Sky God.

It was better if she went alone, he was uninterested in her. She could sneak about the mountain and know more of him. Talk to the rocks and find if he had weaknesses to exploit. Also, his perch was closer to her than Scarlet's place.

The journey still cost her several hours. She made it to a trailhead with a sign for Mount Madonna. Lush trees covered its sides, and the earth smelled sweet and clean. She reached the base as her left leg finished thawing. It would make climbing it much easier, many paths were cut into the mountain, but none seemed direct to the top. She would follow a path only to find it barely climbing and ending at a waterfall. Then she would wander up away from that path, it stayed moister here than in many other places, and the moss grew thick on the north sides of the trees. Another path would appear, wide and manicured, she would follow it for a short distance then realize it looped back on itself.

The sky to the east paled with the coming dawn. The tree cover lay thick, but she wanted to find a true cave for the day. It felt like ages since she'd rested properly on a mountain in a cave. A longing stirred in her chest. A longing for her cave on her mountain. She could not wait to take Nera to her home. If they could defeat the Sky God and the other unknown threat, the one that sang out at sea, then they could go.

Donya thought of Nera swimming off into the ocean earlier. She tried to picture her on that great northern mountain Donya called home. She could, Nera dancing in the snowflakes by the light of a crescent moon. The long days of summer in the cave curled together.

But a memory crept up of Nera, sadness painted on her face under the setting sun in Florence. Nera would not want to stay with Donya on a mountain. Her great wish was to be free. And she finally attained that. Donya thought that all her longing spawned from wanting to see Nera again to apologize to her. But every time they were together, with every kiss—Donya wanted more. Greedy, that was what Donya had become.

Donya sighed. The ache in her chest changed. Homesickness was replaced with another kind of melancholy. Her grandmother taught her nine new spells, she thought about using one now but couldn't build the strength necessary. The pebbles on the path squeaked at her for several minutes. It might take a while, but conversation would be nice. It could pull her out of the sad thoughts she currently wallowed in.

She picked up a small piece of granite. "What have you all been squalling about?"

"You, you are stone like us?" The pebble asked in a high excited voice.

"For a short time, yes." Donya touched her stomach. Once the transformation is completed it would be time for new clothes. These still smelled of cedar and bore holes from wear and battle. And turning to stone has strange effects on cotton and whatever fiber lay in this dress's weave.

"You should smell the air, do you smell that?" The pebble said.

Donya could smell dead animals. Once she began to climb the whole mountain smelled of it. "I keep smelling dead animals, but I do not see any."

"You need to look up."

Donya did as instructed. The tall night-black trees did not appear to have any corpses dangling in them. But they smelled like they did.

Donya walked on still scanning with her eyes and scenting the air. The smell became stronger at the base of one tree. She couldn't climb as she was right now. The pine stood very tall with no low-lying branches.

"Would you mind helping out?" Donya asked the pebble.

"It would be my pleasure."

Donya sniffed a few more times narrowing down the source of the noxious odor. Up above her, she could see the bottom of a bird's nest. That was where one of the strongest smells seemed to be emanating from. She aimed the pebble and with a flick of her wrist shot it up into the air.

"Weeeeee," it called as it flew. It landed with a thump.

The bird's nest and pebble came falling to earth.

Donya scooped up the pebble first. The smell of rot permeated the air now that she dislodged the nest from the tree.

"I humbly request a bath," said the pebble.

A feather and a smear of decayed flesh stuck to the pebble, Donya would have to clean the poor thing. She studied the fallen nest. A dead blue jay lay on a late batch of broken eggs. The jay's eyes were gone. A normal consequence of decay. But the missing eyes were not right. Scorch marks ringed the empty sockets. Burned feathers. The eggs had been days from hatching. Tiny dead pink birds lay in their shells. Their eyes burned away as well.

One more thing had fallen from the branch.

A human hand burned off at the wrist.

CHAPTER 27

SCARLET

"I don't ever wanna get out of bed," Scarlet mumbled into her pillow while Juan lazily rubbed circles on her back. She wiggled under the blankets, burrowing deeper, farther away from reality.

"If you want to get out of your bachelorette stuff, I'm sure your friends will understand." Juan came in closer, nuzzling the back of her neck with his nose. "And I can stay here with you and take care of your every need."

Scarlet laughed but felt tempted. They had spent a very lazy day in bed Wednesday because Scarlet stayed out so late on Tuesday night. At least that's what Scarlet said out loud. If she was being honest, she was hiding—hiding away from all of her responsibilities, paranormal magical ones, and wedding.

Her friends would understand if she told them she wasn't up to the bachelorette. This agitated Scarlet, why did her friends have to be compassionate and kind? Bertha of all people would be the only one to put up a fuss, and possibly never let Scarlet live it down.

"I'm gonna shower," Scarlet stood up, not bothering to cover herself, and walked to the bathroom. Their cat watched her and judged as she walked past. Juan watched too.

She turned on the cold water. September had begun but the late summer and early autumn days often got warmer on the coast. The shock of the cold water set her mind ticking off everything she'd ignored the past twenty-four hours.

"You know what, I'll ask one of the biologists at work next week for a GPS tag. I'll put it on Ariel. She better get back here," Scarlet yelled. Since Nera arrived Ariel had been out with her a lot, and as of Monday morning, Nera took her duffle bag to a room at the hotel where the wedding would be held. Scarlet suspected Ariel hung out there sometimes when she should be checking in.

"That's not a bad idea, I could order her an AirTag. It might even arrive tomorrow." Juan walked into the bathroom and started brushing his teeth.

"We can try that, I think those can get wet but if Ariel dives deep it will probably get squished." Scarlet lathered up with the special moisturizing wash her mother had bought her. Then she scrubbed at her face with the delicate exfoliator Elise had sent her. When she got out she owned three different bottles of moisturizer to put on, several of them gifts as well. Seeing the physical evidence of how much the wedding meant to her friends and family made her feel like she needed to join in today.

She turned up the temperature to rinse off. She would blast the cold again before she got out because that was supposed to make her hair less frizzy. She'd let her hair grow out for the wedding. It fell to her mid back now, the weight of it helped tame the frizz she was used to beating into submission with product. It wasn't princess hair, but it appeared and felt healthier than it ever had before.

She turned the temperature down and shivered. Then she heard a pop.

She turned around and Ariel sat at her feet. "You called, you called, I heard."

"I suppose I did call," Scarlet said with a smile and a shrug. "But you better go with Juan, the conditioner I use might bother you."

"Mm-hmm," Ariel nodded enthusiastically with a big smile then popped away.

Scarlet wondered about the smile, it suggested mischief.

"Oh my god, oh my god," Juan said loudly.

"What," Scarlet threw open the shower curtain.

Juan stood holding Ariel out away from his body, looking at her. His hands were under her arms. His bottom lip quivered.

"You can see her?" Scarlet asked.

Juan nodded yes and hugged Ariel to the fresh white T-shirt he wore.

Ariel beamed over at Scarlet.

Scarlet grabbed her towel off the rack quickly wrapped up and joined in the hug. "What should we do to celebrate?" Scarlet asked without loosening her grip.

"Ice cream," Ariel said in a muffled way as she was getting rather squashed.

Some things would never change. Scarlet giggled while Juan nodded, and the hug broke up.

"Let me rinse off and I'll come join you guys, don't eat it all," Scarlet said.

Juan walked off whispering to Ariel about the special ice cream he had hidden in the back of the fridge. Scarlet smiled, she noticed the sly trick yesterday while practicing with her eyes. Inside an empty bag of frozen broccoli at the back of the freezer was a full box of ice cream sandwiches.

After Scarlet finished, she quickly dressed. Then she gathered her makeup and made her way out to the living room where Ariel and Juan sat on the couch, three empty wrappers on the table in front of them.

"What happened to mine?" Scarlet asked walking to the kitchen to get a new one.

"You took too long, it was melting, Ariel had to eat it to save the table." Juan sounded like he was walking on the moon.

"What does she look like now to you?" Scarlet asked before she took the first bite of the new sandwich, already the chocolate cookie part was sticking to her fingers.

"A cute toddler, big green eyes, red hair almost the same shade as you, she might be a little pale. She is wearing a familiar dress, it's blue, very fancy. She does have six toes and one missing finger on each hand."

It took a while, but Scarlet and Juan worked out that Nera had taught Ariel how to show herself and how to make a glamour. Scarlet was happy Nera tutored Ariel in useful magic. Scarlet wondered who came up with the idea. Ariel always wanted to interact more with Juan, she might have asked Nera. The glamour was a rip-off of the little mermaid, which definitely seemed like Ariel's idea. Ariel was still working on her numbers, which could explain why her counts of fingers and toes were off by one.

Scarlet couldn't see the glamour directly, she could see the spell hanging around Ariel. And out of the corner of her eye, she could catch glimpses of the glamour. "Can you see that she is getting tired?"

Juan studied Ariel. "She is getting purple under the eyes."

"She is getting purple and blue all over to me."

"Ariel, if you are tired you need to rest. We can both rest. I will stay on the couch, and we can start a movie," Juan said to Ariel, gazing earnestly into her eyes.

Ariel nodded.

Scarlet stood in front of the full-length mirror near the window. Her foundation and eye shadow were on, now she needed to do her mascara, not easy as somehow her eyes always went out of focus when she brought the small brush up to them.

"Wow, this is even more exciting!" Juan called.

Scarlet glanced at them. Juan swung Ariel around the room again. It proceeded like a scene out of a movie. Long lost family reunited. Scarlet could see the spell for the glamour had dropped away, but Ariel continued to work to keep herself visible. That spell hung around Ariel's shoulders like a cape, and it appeared she needed to recast it regularly. Scarlet noticed a few times her lower tentacles wave and ripple then the cloak would grow longer.

"You are so cute. Look at her cheeks and her big eyes," Juan said, holding Ariel up to Scarlet.

"Yes babe, I'm glad you can finally see the real her."

Ariel giggled but it sounded nervous to Scarlet's ear. "Juan like me?"

"Like you, aww sweetie, we love you," Juan said, he patted her on the head, and she grabbed his hand and pulled him in for a hug.

Scarlet walked over and made it a group hug again. Feeling sorry that Ariel had ever doubted Juan would like the way she looked.

Scarlet left when Juan put his feet up on the coffee table and Ariel floated peacefully in the fishtank.

Once she walked out the door though she opened her phone. She'd run late.

"Hey Joy, I'm on my way. Is everyone else there?" Scarlet asked into the phone.

"No, no, take your time. Elyse and your sister can't make it tonight. I'm sure this won't even be that fun for you. I bet you come here all the time."

"Nope, I've never even been to that mission. In grade school, we did a field trip to the San Juan Batista. And umm I did make a sugar cube mission in fourth grade, but I don't remember which one. I'm excited to explore it with you," Scarlet rambled into the phone as she started her car. Her palms sweat but not from the heat of the sun that landed on her shoulders and back.

"That's good, I thought I hijacked your bachelorette. Making it a sightseeing tour instead."

"We can't drink wine the whole time," Scarlet said, trying for a laugh.

"Oh yes, we can."

The drive took twenty minutes. She met Joy outside the mission.

"I'm not kidding. Here, swig this before we go in," Joy said, handing Scarlet a can of wine cooler. The can appeared to be a fancy soda from afar, which was good, Scarlet didn't want to get in trouble for drinking in public two days before her wedding. It wasn't the best alcohol she'd ever tasted, but not the worst either. The two of them sat in companionable silence regarding the facade of the mission while they waited for more of the group. Dakota had made it down from Sacramento, but she needed to finish a business call in her car before she could join them. Scarlet glanced at her, her friend gestured with her hands. She held one of the wine coolers too. Scarlet hoped she kept the call short, not for the sake of starting the party, but so Dakota wouldn't start to slur.

"Didn't you say a few other friends might show up?" Joy asked, cracking open another can.

"Yep, but if they do it won't be till tonight. I invited them last minute because they aren't from around here but happened to be traveling in the area."

Scarlet finished her first can and Joy put the newly opened can in her hand. "I can't keep drinking. It isn't even three pm and we have to drive our cars out of here, it's a tiny parking lot."

"That is all taken care of."

"What?"

"Great timing, here it comes now."

Scarlet could see. An old-school white stretch Hummer pulled into the parking lot. It had penises drawn on the windows in fluorescent pink and purple paint. Here comes the bride was scrawled across the back window.

"This is all tradition, it must be done," Joy said, as Scarlet's other bridesmaids came piling out of the back. Bertha stumbled as she hit the pavement.

This didn't explain how they would move their cars. But Scarlet had been thinking hard for weeks now. She felt mentally exhausted and for once just wanted to let go. She tilted the wine cooler back and let it slide down her throat. Who cares about a hangover tomorrow? The important part would be the rehearsal in the evening, she could nurse a headache and sore stomach all morning.

Never before had such a rowdy group toured the mission. They didn't take any wine into the hallowed grounds, but they did traipse around the old building. They viewed the statue of the founding priest and finally wandered into the graveyard.

It was the graveyard that got Scarlet. She'd managed to cut loose. Not worrying. Not thinking about monsters and scary songs and Sky Gods. But in the graveyard, it stayed silent. Where were the singing birds? And the ground. It was too dark. Scarlet studied the streaming sunshine. The glittering magic. It did not hang around the mission. And here it would not touch the ground.

It was the graves. The shimmering Ged stayed far away from them. And it wasn't just the marked graves. Scarlet could see areas, areas that bore the same dark aspect as the graves. They made her shiver and want nothing more than to go home.

What did she read about the missions? Recently, not back in her school days. That they had been very unhappy places. Indigenous people were trapped there even by armed guards. Scarlet hated the real story and she hated that she'd built a stupid mission out of sugar cubes.

Bertha leaned over by a gravestone for a selfie. She wobbled a tad on her espadrilles. And that darkness that clung to the ground rippled and stretched to touch her.

"Time to go. Time to drink wine," Scarlet practically shrieked.

The other women seemed startled. And Lettie who'd watched Scarlet strangely the whole time narrowed her eyes.

Scarlet hadn't told anyone other than Juan about what she could see and do. He'd promised to keep it between them. But he and his sisters were close. Maybe he wouldn't have told them, but he could have let things slip—little things. Lettie was calm and observant, which would make her a good vet, she could notice what was wrong with a patient without needing to be told.

"Wine wine wine," Dakota sang and held up a fist and they all marched out of the graveyard after her.

Scarlet left the mission second to last. Lettie followed after. Scarlet could feel her soon-to-be sister-in-law's eyes on her. And she was thankful, they were eyes full of concern.

205

CHAPTER 28

DONYA

Several body parts stuck out of crevices in the cave. The hand with the mauve manicure. Most of a thigh, a scalp, but it was the purse and wallet within that illuminated the identity of the human victim. An assistant private investigator. Scarlet had mentioned hiring an investigator.

Donya remained pleased with herself that none of the human flesh sparked her appetite. Although it did not disgust her either.

Danger stalked Nera and crept around Scarlet. Donya wanted to tell Scarlet to call off the wedding. Perhaps it would be better for them all to retreat to Italy. They enjoyed a strong ally of the Kraken.

But where could one hide from the sky?

The woman the hand belonged to kept notes on a paper pad. The notes were simple. Places and names. Those places and names lead here to this mountain. She must have been very good at her job. Pity. Trolls admire proficiency, and Donya admired this woman's fashion sense, even her Chanel perfume. Perhaps not the purse though.

Earlier Donya held a conversation with a boulder at the front of the cave. It noticed the smell but did not pay attention to the killings. Animals and humans died all the time, it wasn't anything new to rocks. The rock let her know that indeed the Sky God frequented this place, but it could not say it was his main roost.

As the sun set Donya emerged from the cave mouth. It was a small opening. She needed to wiggle her way out. Soil and moss crumbled around her. It would be easier if her torso had thawed more. She still retained a large stone patch, completely inflexible, she could not bend at the waist. The cave had another opening, far larger, but it would be risky for Donya to use it. That opening lay on the cave ceiling and the walls around dripped with moisture and loose mosses. If she fell with her stone center she could crack.

The smell of dead flesh did not bother her. She snacked on a pine cone as she walked. She carried the woman's purse. Her ID declared her name to be Olivia Murata. Once Donya finished sniffing around this mountain she would find Nera, so they could search Olivia's home. And a few of the other addresses in the notes. Although one would be hard to get to. It was in Denmark. What could have been there?

Clouds once again shrouded the sky, but darkness did not fall. The clouds were still illuminated by the sun below the horizon. The light bounced around between the vapor and the atmosphere. The trees were silhouetted black but with a pink and orange background.

Flapping wings in the clouds above Donya surprised her. Another bird, it would soon be a victim to the Sky God if he returned. A new smell hit Donya's nose, it was not like death, it almost smelled like the opposite of that.

If it was not for the smell Donya would have probably exploded with the force of the impact. But she'd jumped, to find cover behind a rock. Where she stood the earth burned and smoked.

Her thick hair was still hair. It stood on end with the electrical charge. She couldn't see where the attack came from. But the smell took over the air again.

"Thank you, grandmother," she said, then chanted her troll words. The ground rose around her. It was an earth prison. She should have been using it on her enemy, but right now it protected her. The lighting hit the dome. The electricity bounced around but ultimately dissipated by the displaced earth. Small cracks opened in the dry earth, Donya walked up to one of them and punched a hole out into the twilight. "Show yourself."

The flapping hovered over her earth mound. A large bird landed. It was too beautiful. It possessed feathers of pure gold and silver. It maintained the shape of a raptor, but the splendor could only be of the godly realm. Although Donya wondered if even the gods were supposed to be this opulent and glorious. Each feather shimmered with iridescence. The great green eyes stared in at her. Donya was thankful for her poor eyesight. If she could see better, take in all the beauty and details, she didn't know what would happen. Perhaps her eyes would blaze up and burn. Like what had happened to the birds.

"You are a strong one," he said. His bird voice grated on the ears. The form shook and a man stood before her. It was still Mars' body, but different, even from the last time she had laid eyes on it. Its hair fell lustrous over broader shoulders, the skin dewy. A breeze moved the air and the god's veins glowed through his skin. They ran like veins but also like cracks in the flesh.

"That body, it is deteriorating," Donya said. She averted her gaze, her eyes felt hot and sandy.

"It cannot hold me much longer. I must attain my priestess. Bring her to me. You will be rewarded."

"Never," Donya growled.

"I am a god. You cannot deny me."

"It is not the old time, and this is not the old world. Gods are weak here. Have you not noticed? You are alone," Donya said. The wind picked up turning into a gale that lashed at her earthed dome, it would erode the dirt given enough time.

"You will bring her to me, behold, the rewards." The god's words rose over the now howling wind.

In his hand was a large glass bottle, in it sloshed a viscous liquid Donya had not seen in a while. The black ooze that Heldrig once used. It absorbed the light emanating from the god's veins. In the dark substance floated an orb.

Donya's nose remained almost overwhelmed by the hot ozone from the god's lightning strikes, but she could detect the rancid smell of the ooze, and another scent, one familiar. The orb moved in the darkness, and Donya could make out a purple iris. It was one of Nera's eyes.

"How could you have that?" Donya growled.

"I know other's wants, this is what you want."

Not for the first time Donya thought that this god's brain to be addled. She wanted Nera's eyes, yes to give them back to her because it was right, but also so that perhaps he would lose interest in her. Not think of her as his priestess anymore, as she would have nothing in common with his old priests.

"Bring her to me, all will survive if this is done."

Dagaz, a rune for a breakthrough. She etched it deep. Dragging her finger over and over it. The seeds sent to her in the void burned up fast in her stomach. She needed all of the power she could get, another minute could make all the difference. Goading him wasn't the smartest, but her instincts told her this god was beautiful and dumb. "Like I said the gods are weak here."

"There is no weakness in me." His eyes flared.

Two sinkholes opened up, one mere inches in front of the God. It was small, centered under the jar but extending under his toes. He lost his footing for a moment. A spirit of the sky would not be sure-footed on the lowly mud of the earth. He fumbled the jar. It slipped from his hand falling into the quicksand before him.

Donya smiled triumphantly. The second sinkhole was taking her into the earth. Where she would be safe, where he could not reach. The dome over her rocked with another lightning strike.

Lighting is very quick. So was this god. It took Donya completely off guard when he struck again, through a newly opened gap in her dome, at the moment her head dipped into the soil. When she gasped in pain her mouth filled with moist earth.

It was dark and cool. Donya could feel herself and the jar. Above her shrieked a great angry bird. Donya's side ached, strange that was the part of her that remained stone.

Donya held the jar. She could move quickly through the earth like this. The spell was far simpler than the one she had used in Rome. But it did not tie her to anything. She must find her bearings before she moved too far. Her side burned, occasionally taking her mind off of her direction. Pushing through the soil she felt the ocean and its rhythm to the west. Tree roots faded and the stone the mountain sat on gave way to looser earth, filled with fields and a stream. Donya thought about coming up to the air, but she decided against it. Best to make it to water where she could escape if attacked again.

The sand shifting above her felt warm when she made it close to the ocean. Heated all day by the California sun. This would be a good place to come up but perhaps a few miles farther south. The mountain sat north of where she had last been with Nera. Nera would be greatly excited to have an eye, one that was truly hers. There were many things she wanted to see and do.

Donya's side pulsed with pain.

Curiosity caused her to stop and emerge from the dark embrace of the earth. She could have gone farther but what had that god done to her?

She could smell the tang of burnt hair. She raised her hand to her head. A few spikes of her hair crumbled off black and dry as charcoal. Of all the things on her, it would be most susceptible to electricity. The rest of her was closely related to rock that should not allow the current to flow. So why did her side burn?

It remained hard to lean over. Her middle was indeed still rock. But in that rock dwelt a large crack above her left hip. She pressed at it. It did not hurt any worse to touch it. The crack went all the way to her navel. She poked a finger inside. It went in as far as her digit would go. A very deep wound.

That last bolt of lightning must have found her head in the spot with burned hair but exited to the earth through her stone stomach. A very unlucky happening. But Donya had never felt lucky.

Food, she needed food. Her limbs felt light and chalky. All that she accomplished came at a price. But it was worth it. She cradled Nera's eye. Words were meaningless. Her apology. It stayed as thin as the air that held it. This would make up for her betrayal. A gift.

She had accused the Sky God of being weak, and he was. A strike from above should have killed most spirits and creatures. This wound was serious, but unless she did something stupid not fatal.

It occurred to her that doing stupid things had become a bit of a habit of hers as of late.

CHAPTER 29

SCARLET

Scarlet was way too drunk, she stood and swayed out on a wide wooden deck that overlooked the Pacific Ocean. Draped over her shoulder hung a white sash announcing her as the bride, the letters sparkled in the moonlight. Fingering the cheap fabric and rough glitter Scarlet sipped water. She did not want to vomit tomorrow, there would be too many family members around.

Bertha's voice rang out from inside where she leaned against a stone-topped bar surrounded by old dark wood paneling that hearkened to the nineteenth century, not the cheap smoke-stained 70s.

Then two arms wrapped around Scarlet and a chin rested on her forehead.

The arms were cool and palest blue. It was a loose hug.

"You made it. I'm glad," Scarlet slurred.

"Drink all, your poor head," Nera said, pulling the glass of water back up to Scarlet's lips.

Scarlet took a large gulp. Her lips felt dry. The air off the ocean blew in cold. A clock ticked off the time in the tasting room. She turned to check the hour and caught sight of Donya standing behind Nera.

The troll had never looked so bad. Not even that first time on the plane. Even her style looked off. She wore a baggy oversized shirt with what almost seemed like biker shorts underneath, and she stood strangely, favoring her left side. Her hair was also missing from the left side of her head. Finally, a large burnt orange purse slung over the troll's shoulder completed the uncharacteristic ensemble. But at least she could move.

"You're more mobile," Scarlet said, sticking with the positive, but she couldn't contain a question about the burnt hair, "but what happened to your hair? Did the fire do that?" She thought of the spell.

"No, the Sky God," Donya said.

Scarlet nearly fell over. She glanced at Nera for help. Nera had eyes again. One was not from an animal, it sat right, like it belonged. That eye boasted a purple iris, and with Scarlet's gifted night vision, she could see the white held the blue tint that all of Nera exhibited. The other eye was a brownish color with a slit pupil, it didn't remind Scarlet of a cat, the iris was too large, it seemed more reptilian.

Scarlet touched her face under her eyes.

Nera nodded, a single blue-black tear brimming over and falling. "It is a wonderful thing."

"We should drink to that," Scarlet said then gulped the last of her water. Her head felt less fuzzy, but her face was still numb from alcohol and cold ocean air.

Nera danced into the bar, she slapped several hundred dollar bills on the bar top. "The prettiest bottles," she said, pointing up at an array of rose on a high shelf.

The young woman behind the bar took the money and shrugged her shoulders. "That will cover two bottles."

"Only two?" Nera pouted.

The barkeep opened the first bottle and poured a glass for Nera, Scarlet, and Donya. Bertha waltzed up behind them extending her glass. "Don't forget me."

Scarlet watched the shadows on Donya's face change. Something dark passed over her features. A predatory glance.

"Snacks," Scarlet said. "We need snacks too. One of the board things. The one with all the fancy nuts."

"Which charcuterie board would you like? There are two with an assortment of nuts, our Tuscan board and our Bordeaux board." When the barkeep spoke, her blond bob bounced and small hoop earrings caught the dim light.

"Tuscan," Donya said, quietly placing another couple hundred dollars in front of the bartender. "For old time's sake," she said, holding up Nera's hand for a kiss.

"Who are these friends? I don't remember meeting them before," Bertha asked sipping at the wine but eyeing the money as it was collected.

Scarlet wished she would take a step back. But at least that look that flashed across Donya's face vanished. Now her eyes were only on Nera. It was hard for anyone's eyes to not be drawn to Nera. She wore a tastefully cut silver satin gown that caught the light with emerald earrings and slingback stilettos that matched the green of the emeralds. It would come across as overdressing on anyone else. But not on Nera.

"Friends from work," Nera answered.

"You work in a laboratory?" Bertha gaped.

"Not at this one, we met at that conference in Europe I went to. Collaborated on a couple of papers. It's all very boring," Scarlet rambled. She started to sweat. It wasn't hot in the small room. "Why don't you get back to the other girls, we will bring over the board when it comes out."

Bertha shrugged. She'd almost finished her glass of fine wine. She grabbed the nearly empty bottle and poured the rest in then sauntered off.

Scarlet let out a very loud breath. She held up her glass and clinked it softly against Nera's then finally took a sip of the rose. It tasted light and fruity and of everything one could want in a mouth full of wine. Just what she needed after that encounter.

"I would not eat her," Donya said. Her mouth pulled down at the corners.

"I know," Scarlet said too fast. "Well, I think I know."

"Perhaps you should," Nera said with a coy smile. "It would make Scarlet's life easier."

"Ugh, I can't argue that," Scarlet said, the tension broke, and they all laughed. But Scarlet noticed the little wince Donya gave when she moved.

❧❧

They were all piled in the limo. Dakota and Joy slumped unconscious on the leather seats. Bertha's skin paled and shone green on her cheeks and neck and she kept putting her head down between her knees. Donya and Nera enjoyed themselves playing Never Have I Ever with Lettie. Thankfully Lettie stuck with lewd questions that kept Nera giggling. Scarlet sipped a bottle of water through a penis straw.

They pulled up to the hotel, the one the wedding would be at on Saturday. Dakota and Joy both had rooms there. Chad, Bertha's boyfriend, waited at the bar to take Bertha home. They wouldn't be staying at the venue until the wedding night. Scarlet could see him playing a card game with what looked like Deacon. Deacon was Juan's best man. And as most best men are, he'd been pretty useless.

"Here," Lettie said, unfolding a cardboard man. He was dressed in a leopard speedo. All six-pack abs and ropes of muscle. "You guys can start playing pin the junk on the hunk while we try to unload the drunks." She laughed and let a bunch of cardboard penises litter the ground. Some were small, some were large, and some sported mushroom-like shapes. One was a hotdog in a bun.

"This is amazing," Nera held one in iridescent bright red. "A mortal has been dallying with a fengor."

217

Scarlet almost spit out her water. She looked around but no one heard. Lettie worked at waking the bridesmaids from their drunken stupor and Bertha stood outside, leaning against the vehicle.

The headache Scarlet barely kept in check was starting to pound now. Tomorrow would be very bad for her. She pulled her high ponytail out and ruffled her hair, then searched her purse for the pain pills she needed.

"What is that?" Nera asked. Nera pointed with a very small male member at Scarlet's wrist.

"The scrunchie?" She asked, trying to clarify.

Nera nodded. Here new eyes wide. "I use ribbon in my hair."

Scarlet pulled the sparkly stretchy band off of her wrist and handed it to Nera. Tonight, Scarlet had straightened her hair. Considering the chaos of her apartment before she left, she felt she managed to appear casual chic. Cute charcoal pumps, loose-fitting jeans, and a charcoal blouse. Makeup and dangling earrings to finish it off with a very high pony. She might have worn a dress but feared falling and flashing her bridesmaids.

Nera held the scrunchie in front of her, stretching it back and forth. She pulled her hair back and tried to make a ponytail, but she didn't have the twisting action down.

"Let me help," Donya moved to assist—her hands quick and nimble.

When Nera's hair was up, she jumped from the open car door and began dancing around the brightly lit parking lot.

"We don't get a lot of time alone," Donya started. "I need to ask you a question."

"Go ahead," Scarlet said with a touch of apprehension because the troll's expression radiated her discomfort.

"How do you keep Juan?"

Scarlet's mind froze up, she didn't keep Juan on a leash or something. "Wait a second, are you asking me for relationship advice?"

Donya nodded.

Scarlet let out a breath. "Mostly you have to communicate and compromise. And I mean communicate a lot. About the big and small stuff. And well, you're gonna have it hard in that department." Scarlet saw Donya's discarded bag jump.

Scarlet eyed the bag, could it be a cell phone, she wondered. It did not seem like vibrating. "Donya, um, your bag?"

Donya seemed to be attempting to formulate a follow-up question, when her bag jumped again.

Then a human hand popped from the top of the bag.

"What is that?" Scarlet yelled, scrambling back. She made it out of the open hummer door without falling.

Bertha stood outside the door leaning against the shiny limo exterior, waiting for her boyfriend to come get her. The others had all managed to shamble inside. In the bright light of the parking lot Scarlet found herself squinting, she didn't know what to say.

The hand scrambled around the inside of the limo and then flopped out onto the pavement, despite Donya jumping for it. Nera also made a dive for it. It was fast, moving on its fingertips. It wasn't heading for anyone it seemed, instead, it scurried in circles and loops. Scarlet made to stomp on it, but she hesitated and lost her balance, then fell on her knees.

Bertha unfortunately raised her head at the commotion. Her eyes watched the hand move under a car. Before this, she'd been a slight shade of green and pale, but now red splotches appeared on her cheeks.

"I knew it," Bertha said quietly. "I fucking knew it. Witch. Satan worshiper!" She screamed the last few words, staggering away on wobbly legs.

Nera shimmied under vehicles in a way that no human could—trying to get the hand.

Donya made it out of the car. She took one look at Bertha and Scarlet lunged toward Bertha. Putting herself between the two. "No eating."

"It's a cult!" Bertha scream-slurred. Her hair was wild around her face. Between screaming about the cult, she also shrieked at the top of her lungs.

Lights flickered on in the hotel, but Scarlet noted the limo driver stayed firmly in his seat and looked away from the scene. Scarlet felt helpless to stop whatever happened next.

"The walnuts were enough," Donya said as she pushed past Scarlet.

Then Donya hit Bertha on the back of the head. Bertha fell to the ground like a sack of potatoes.

CHAPTER 30

DONYA

The song started shortly after Scarlet helped buckle Bertha into a car. Donya was sure the unconscious woman would be fine. Donya hit her very softly. No bone broke, no lump formed, it would most definitely bruise but under her hairline. If need be, Nera promised she could bind Bertha's memory of the hand. Water held memories very well.

Scarlet had followed them out to the dunes but turned suddenly and walked to the limo once the song began. Donya did not understand her fear. It seemed misplaced, although the old tune was odd.

"It stopped moving." Nera held up the human hand victorious in her pursuit. The hand now lay limp, it had scrambled a long way from the limo out onto the dunes.

"Did it stop right as the aria began?" Donya asked.

"It did, have you been fibbing this whole time?"

"Fibbing." Donya couldn't follow Nera's train of thought, which happened fairly often.

"About your diet?" Nera bounced her eyebrows. "It is alright, we can pick out a cruel stranger not with the wedding. Many humans deserve worse than being eaten."

Donya was still confused. Then it dawned on her, Nera thought she'd reverted to eating human flesh. Donya hadn't found a chance to talk about the dead body to Nera or Scarlet. Nera had been concerned about Donya's injuries when she found her. Donya might have given Nera her eye to actually stop the concern emanating from Nera. Nera was elated. She did not even try to purify the eye before placing it in her right eye socket, which worried Donya. That black substance, even Heldrig handled it with care when harvesting it.

"The hand came from a body on the mountain. I brought it and the purse down. For Scarlet."

"How dull," Nera said. She watched the waves. "I must go, the singer is close." She tossed the severed hand at Donya.

"And do what?" Donya caught the hand easily.

"Make it our friend. It helps us already," Nera said. She took off running for the shore.

Donya could hear the delicate stitching on her dress rip as Nera pulled at it. Donya would follow, but first, she must see Scarlet on her way and give her the body part. It had always been her intention.

She hauled herself back through the sand to the closed-up limo. The driver made to get out and open the door for her, but she waved him away. She didn't want him to see the hand. Donya crawled inside the older vehicle. Scarlet huddled inside, her eyes shimmering in the dark. She watched the ocean though, not Donya.

"Where did Nera go?"

"To find the singer," Donya answered as she grabbed the orange purse and placed the hand inside. "I leave this with you. It is connected to your human investigator. I will come back; do not try to dispose of it."

Scarlet turned toward her; she smelled the sour of fear. Donya wanted to do something to hearten her. "Would you like to take the sword? It will keep you safe."

Scarlet shook her head. "No, I want to feel normal for the next few days."

Donya understood. It was Donya who would wield the sword, Donya would keep them all safe. "I must go."

"Good luck," Scarlet said as Donya departed the vehicle.

Taking a shallow breath Donya shambled in the direction Nera had gone. Catching up would take a long while, but this was something that shouldn't be done alone.

Donya waved back at the limo, hoping Scarlet would see and head home. With Scarlet's eyes, she could certainly see Donya even out here in the dark and through the distance.

Donya waded into the black water, taking one last breath of air. She didn't need it, but it would help keep her slightly more buoyant. A smell lingered over the ocean. It smelled like old copper green with age.

Donya walked into the rolling waves. The throbbing in her left side synced almost perfectly with the breaking of each wave. Donya pushed through the pain, thankful that Scarlet procured food for her. She ate walnuts, pinenuts, and cashews. All the humans seemed more interested in the cheese set before them. Hopefully, Scarlet would not be cross with her about that small violence she perpetrated.

Donya easily followed Nera through the water, her scent tickled Donya's nose and tongue. It smelled fresher than this water. Nera belonged in a quick-moving mountain stream. But her attar was not only of fresh water, a sharp taste and smell, like a newly broken blade of grass played as an undernote.

The sound grew louder. The water was dark, and her eyes were poor. She could see nothing above her. The ocean here dropped off steeply, and she could feel upwellings of colder denser water. There were trenches out here, deep ones. She moved quickly but needed to be careful. If she fell into a deep rift, it would take time away from aiding Nera.

Nera's voice joined that of the unknown troubadour. Donya picked up the pace, taking large bounds despite the crunching coming from her side when she did.

She came upon the two at a high point on the ocean floor. Fluorescent jellyfish swarmed around them, lighting the scene. The smell of copper mingled with that of Nera's smell. Donya did not know what she expected to see, but a horse was not it. Yet that is what Donya saw swimming away from Nera. A very large horse with forelegs that ended with webbed feet instead of hooves and it possessed a whale's tail where its rear legs would have been. A hippocampus, she had seen one other before, but it was nothing like this one. A smaller beast, with shining scales, a lavish main, and it that liked lakes, not oceans. This one's mane was cropped and it wore a harness around its neck with glittering round gems in the center.

It barely seemed to notice Nera or her song.

Donya watched the horse. It pranced and swam about like it sought a person, but not Nera. Its colors in the dimness shifted between green and shimmering bronze. It reminded Donya of a place and power.

It reminded Donya of Venice.

Donya remembered Grazia and the Kraken's visit inside the dreamscape. When they came to pull their connections from the place. They told her an important message for Scarlet, that she should use her cards. But there was another piece of information that now seemed very important. That she forgot to mention as she thawed. The gift.

Donya sat on the silt of the ocean floor. The Kraken had sent a gift for Scarlet's wedding. And here it was.

∽∾

"Try calling her again," Donya said. Donya, Nera, and the hippocampus swam in the shallows now, having traveled farther south. Large rocks jutted out of the ground while waves splashed off of them and sea lions barked in the distance.

The hippocampus became interested in them once Donya removed Scarlet's hair ornament from Nera and waved it in the water. It indeed was there for Scarlet and Ariel.

"She is very young. It could take her a while, or she waits to ask Juan's permission."

"A spirit asking a human permission, pffff," Donya blew out her mouth in exasperation. Her side never stopped aching now.

The thawing continued around her midsection. She could bend better, so she pulled up her new sodden shirt and considered the wound.

The rocks behind her were visible through the crack in the stone. None of her flesh had thawed to the injury yet. She wasn't sure what would happen when it did. The crack gave off the slight smell of lye.

The hippocampus raised its head and began singing again. When it let its voice out, clouds gathered over the sky.

Mist rose and obscured the moon and stars.

"I am sure it will work, you can trust me," Nera cooed in Donya's ear.

Nera had conceived a plan, Donya wondered if she worked on it for a while or had just come up with it. Nera's mind did not flow the same way as many others, nor did her plans. It occasionally seemed as if she had planned for an event far longer than she could have even known that the situation would present itself.

"If you use the circlet, you will lose dream," Donya said, it was her only qualm with the plan. Otherwise, it fell along the lines she had been planning. It was more complicated though.

Nera wanted to borrow Scarlet's power. The circlet she wore at her temple allowed her to do it. It was a powerful tool, one gifted to Heldrig her father, but it could only be used by women. And so, he required that his daughter use it in his stead. With her binding abilities and Scarlet's shield, they could reimprison the Sky God. The sword could make a space in the void for them; it had already managed this twice.

Donya liked it, there was beauty and symmetry in the working. The Sky God grew stronger, if not sharper every time she had seen him. Yes, she only had one problem with the plan, but she had another problem. The timing.

"Scarlet is getting married in a little over twenty-four hours from now. We cannot interfere with her. Did you not see her tonight? She is under much strain."

"Says the one who is almost split in twine," Nera scolded, shaking her finger.

Donya scowled up at the big hippocampus. It was large, but clearly a new creation. Something Donya had not seen before, a life perhaps solely achievable by the Kraken collaborating with a legendary alchemist like Grazia.

"You called, you called, I heard," a high voice burst from the water.

Ariel arrived. At the sight of the hippocampus, she screamed and popped into Nera's arms.

The water horse reared in the shallow bay and splashed its tail sending water in all directions. It looked threatening but didn't all large animals?

"Calm calm both the sweet babes," Nera sang. She walked up slowly to the hippocampus, who as his head dried appeared even more coppery in the dim light bouncing from the clouds. "Your mother sent a present, it is for you and for Scarlet."

Ariel was a deep green color. She made no move to stretch out her hands or tentacles but continued to curl against Nera.

The hippocampus flared its nostrils. Which made Ariel sink deeper into Nera and change her shade trying to match the silver dress Nera wore and her palest blue skin.

"A name," Donya said.

"Brilliant, oh you are the most clever of trolls my darling, my rock," Nera said, flashing Donya a smile that could have launched a thousand ships. Without moving the cowering Ariel, she leaned closer and said, "he is very new like you, a present your mother sent here. He needs a name, give him a name."

Ariel perked up. "Scuttle." She pumped her fists. "Flotsam, Jetsum, Grimsby, Chef Louis." Ariel puffed out her cheeks.

"One name," Donya added.

"Price Eric, Flounder, um um Sebastian," Ariel called.

"Sebastian," both Donya and Nera said in unison.

"Sebastian," Ariel repeated and turned herself a bright red and made small pinching motions with her hands.

Donya didn't understand any of it. Children were quite a wonder.

CHAPTER 31

SCARLET

Scarlet tapped on the partition between her and the driver so he would take her home. She heard him start the car, yet they didn't begin to move. Donya's purse sat on the far side of the vehicle from her. The hand inside tucked in a side pocket below a compact. Concentrating with all her might she tried to visualize the shield she used naturally around the entire purse. It took a few moments, but it formed. She'd acquired increased control over her ability to manipulate her shield now. But making a sustained shield not held to her person wasn't something she normally did. Still, a small box big enough for the ugly orange purse would do. Closing the bottom of the box last she opened her eyes. Her head pounded.

The door next to Scarlet opened and one of her future sisters-in-laws climbed in—the nice one. Scarlet understood now why the limo didn't move.

"I thought you were staying here?" Scarlet mumbled. She needed time to process everything from the last ten minutes and hoped for a quiet car ride home to do it.

"Is it okay if I stay with you?" Lettie asked, opening a bottle of water from the mini fridge that hummed between the cushy seats.

It was not okay, but Scarlet could not say that out loud. "Sure, sure," she said instead.

Lettie lowered the partition to the driver and gave Scarlet's address. He began to drive almost immediately like he was ready for this job to be over.

Scarlet got two water bottles out of the minifridge, one to drink and one to press on her forehead. Her hands shook and she almost fumbled the water bottle she brought to her forehead. Lately, her emotions didn't feel logical to her, not in the normal illogical emotions way either, like how your brain will replay an embarrassment from fifth grade just before bed for no reason. It didn't even feel like overwhelm from wedding planning and stress. But she didn't know what it was. She felt stuck.

Perhaps magic could be the problem. She worked and worked at it, but it seemed to be eluding her. The few things she managed to pull off on her own were hammer moves—big, showy, destructive all around. But something that required control and precision, a scalpel move, she couldn't do on her own. She could hit hard and hit a big target, but her finer operations failed.

It hadn't even been two years since she started actively practicing though. All of her supernatural allies refined their abilities for hundreds if not thousands of years. She remembered the surprise and frustration on Donya's face when she showed up in Japan. Donya could probably be classified as a hammer too.

There they were pounding away at the world together.

Scarlet opened her eyes to take another sip of water. Lettie studied her, not unkindly.

"Do I have something on my face?" Scarlet asked.

"Did I see your friend hit my sister, while your other friend slithered around under cars chasing thing?"

Scarlet thought no one besides the driver stood close enough to see. The parking lot stayed brightly lit. There was not one puddle of shadow in that place, and even if there had been with her eyes she would have seen Lettie. Scarlet looked long at the other woman, trying to see the emotions on her face. She looked washed out, and perhaps a bit sweaty.

"I was getting Dakota into her bed and saw out the window. She's got a room facing inland," Lettie said, then looked out the dark window, giving Scarlet space to form an answer.

Scarlet didn't scan the windows on the upper floors of the hotel. God damn it. "Would you believe me if I said no? Or that one of the drinks had LSD in it?

"Definitely not, but I wouldn't press you anymore for a while." Lettie managed to sound cool, but her arms kept crossing like she was holding herself together.

"Really? Shouldn't you be freaking out? Or asking a million questions? You are such a curious person."

"I mean I freaked out at first, not as bad as Bertha. But I screamed pretty loud in Dakota's room. She didn't even wake up."

Lettie stopped to sip her water. "My mom has been taking us to Bruhas forever. And I don't know, Juan started avoiding it suddenly. He wouldn't wear any charms mom got him. Wouldn't respond to anything when she would talk about curses on the phone with all of us." She paused again, this time taking a large gulp of her water. "And I've always noticed the weird way you move and stare at nothing."

"Thanks," Scarlet said, closing her eyes again. She didn't think she moved strangely. "Listen, I will explain, but not tonight. It's a long story. And things are nerve-wracking again." Scarlet hated admitting it out loud. Donya said speaking names held power, but sometimes even ordinary words carried a sort of power. She felt like she could see long story and nerve-wracking floating around in the air of the limo, haunting her.

"So, the stuff my mom believes is real? That's exciting."

"Maybe, but every charm she has ever sent is bogus, just balls of string or ugly bracelets. Big waste of money. I haven't found anyone in California who can do anything." Scarlet felt pleased with how upbeat Lettie became. Although it probably meant she was naive.

"But there are real practitioners?"

"Yeah, but none around here. I have a list at the apartment." Scarlet opened her eyes and took a drink of water. Donya had to answer her questions. It was the payment for a freely given gift. Once Scarlet asked about other humans who could interact with the supernatural, and Donya listed all of those she knew of and even found a few more. That was an area Scarlet would love to spend more time studying, but Donya warned her even other humans could be dangerous. Scarlet did know that of course but it didn't stop her from wishing she could fly to Italy right now and go to that seer in Florence. Maybe he could tell her what she needed to do.

"I'm going to need that list," Lettie said.

Scarlet looked at her, really looked at her. She watched the way the shadow moved over her face as they passed by streetlights, excitement, curiosity, restraint, fear, and affection. Scarlet could see it all. Lettie was short with brown wavy hair and brown eyes. Her body type wasn't far off Scarlet's, a touch heavy in the bottom. When they had first met, she'd been skinny but then college happened to her—and getting older. The human metabolism was a cruel mistress.

"My brother knows right? He can be pretty dumb," Lettie asked rhetorically.

"You say that like you are sure I told him. I almost didn't, I probably wouldn't have if it wasn't for that troll, you saw hit Bertha."

"That friend of yours is a troll! Shit. Okay, how did he react?"

"Not as enthusiastically as you, but similarly. He said the same thing about your mom and the Bruhas." Scarlet took a big breath. Ever since they pulled Donya and the dreaded singer from the void Scarlet harbored a terrible gut feeling. "With what you saw tonight do you think I should call off the wedding?"

"What, no, no, oh no. I hadn't even thought about that. How bad is it?"

"Girl, there's a human hand in that purse," Scarlet said with a laugh. "And as you saw, it comes to life and moves around."

"It's in here with us? Oh, this is bad." Lettie squeaked and moved closer to Scarlet. "Why was it moving?"

"Don't worry, I think it's contained. And I don't know, but I have a terrible feeling."

"Think? Don't know." Lettie's voice rose.

"Shh," Scarlet motioned toward the partition. Also, the louder Lettie got the more her head hurt.

"Wait till you get to the house. If you are gonna know, I can't be sure, but things might be even weirder there."

"Might?"

"We'll see," Scarlet said as the limo rounded a curve. Her buzz had completely dissipated. She hadn't thought to have a human ally that wasn't magical. Juan didn't count because he emitted something weird, something she had tried to find in Grazia's old books but so far had not come across. And Lettie would be family. Scarlet relaxed into the seat. Things could get a lot easier if two people covered for her. Juan accepted the supernatural but other than his bond with Ariel he didn't seem interested in monsters and spirits. But Lettie was interested.

Now wasn't the best time, but Scarlet might not get around to it if she was left to her own devices. "Lettie let's go through the purse. Before we get to the apartment."

"What? Really?"

Lettie's voice rose, but Scarlet smiled to herself as Lettie leaned toward the purse not away. Like she'd become excited, not afraid.

"You do it, it should be safe," Scarlet said. She was also running an experiment.

Lettie grabbed for the purse, but her hand bounced off. Scarlet did make the shield very dense and strong.

"I can't touch it," Lettie said, sounding very confused.

"I know, here I'll get it out of the box."

Scarlet took off one side of the shield and pulled the purse out. She didn't dissipate the whole thing, as it would be too hard to make it again.

Lettie dumped it out on the floor among the cardboard penises, the hand landing with a soft thump. Scarlet used a cheap cocktail napkin to pick up the hand and place it gently back in the purse. She used the same napkin to pick up the compact, Tic-Tacs, snack bar, and bottle of ibuprofen. Lettie riffled through a spiral-bound pocket notebook.

"What's the story behind this?" Lettie asked with a gleam in her eye.

Scarlet rubbed at her aching head trying to think of the most important details because it was a long story, and they would be at the apartment in maybe five more minutes. She'd seen the sign for her exit flash by in the dark.

"Nera's half-brother died in a dream spell, so his soul died but his body didn't. When Donya and I kept having dreams related to the spell we realized something was wrong and I hired a private investigator to find the body of what would seem to be a coma patient. He found that the body had gotten up and left. Monday, I think, this lady called to let me know the investigator died, or more likely was murdered. Now she's probably dead too. I guess it's just a hand, she could be alive." As Scarlet spoke, she realized the other two non-magical humans who'd become involved were dead. She snatched a stack of papers away from Lettie. "I take it back, you can't see these, can't risk it."

Lettie held onto one page. "It's too late. I'm gonna go at this like a dog with a bone. You went to Japan last weekend?"

"How did you know that?"

Lettie held up her credit card history. She saw a couple of charges highlighted. Lettie's finger tapping next to the hotel Scarlet got for that one night in Fukuoka.

"Man, I hope they didn't contact Interpol," Scarlet whined as the limo came to a stop in front of her apartment.

CHAPTER 32

DONYA

Finally, the hippocampus sang a different tune, a happy one. It leapt about in the dark ocean water frolicking with Nera and Ariel. Donya couldn't currently frolic nor would she if she could, but she thoroughly enjoyed watching—and listening. With Ariel around Sebastian became compliant, allowing Donya and Nera to inspect it. Sebastian contained a lifeforce with a heartbeat and warmth above that of the ocean water. However, it's skin was metal and although one should not look a gift horse in the mouth Donya did inspect this creature's teeth and throat which also appeared metallic. Its song sounded almost like a hymn played on wind instruments.

The stones of the harness explained to Donya what Sebastian was doing. That it sang when the Sky God flew nearby. Donya was glad that Scarlet had reacted with such fear at the song. The song was harmless, but what it sought to hide her and Ariel from was not. The storm obscured the sky. The stones explained that in a handful of years, this creature would probably be able to do many more things but now it was meant mostly to entertain Ariel. The Kraken had thought the song of storms an excellent idea, that Ariel would like to ride large swells brought on by high winds and raging seas.

The stones also showed Donya where the second present was tied, behind the harness a small bottle had been strapped. The stones did not know what it was, but when Donya opened the bottle and inspected it, she found water from the Kraken's grotto with a small scent of extra magic. It was meant for Scarlet to drink.

Eventually, Donya would ask Grazia for a full story of the hippocampus' making, for the stones were set in it last and did not now. It was clearly a creation, akin to the bronze horses famously abiding in Venice. But also, one could see inspiration taken from the Trevi Fountain of Rome. He would be an excellent companion for Ariel. However, she wished either the Kraken or Grazia would have thought to warn them before sending him. Also, although he was a gift and boon, he was new like Ariel. In the end, Scarlet would have to teach them both. A very odd way for things to play out.

Although perhaps they did not think the human would have to do all the teaching of the young. Perhaps they believed Donya would stay here and help.

Now with Nera here that did not seem to be the worst idea.

Nera jumped through the air, this section of the coast remained rugged and bare of humans. The long snaking road that would allow them to visit had collapsed north of their location. If they stayed, Donya would have to engineer more collapses to give them privacy along the shoreline.

Donya knew she thought too much of the future. Making plans when she was not sure she could keep Nera. Making plans when a Sky God hunted them.

Donya felt a fool.

"Whatever do you glower for my rock?" Nera asked, dancing up to her side.

Donya was caught off guard. "You like to sneak up on others don't you?"

Nera giggled, "you got me, my you know me."

Donya could smell the other eye, the one held together by dark magic. They needed to find Nera's real eye. Donya could not lose the feeling that Nera would be set more to right with her own eyes given back to her. That Donya would have set something right in the world.

"Come let us find you food," Nera held out a hand which Donya gladly accepted.

They marched up into the forest, and Donya sensed that Ariel moved quickly North. Her energy did not flicker, Sebastian traveled with her. His energy was harder for Donya to track but now that she had smelled him and felt him up close, she could handle it for a short time.

Nera picked up a dark tightly shut pinecone and handed it to her.

"Where are Ariel and Sebastian going?" Donya asked.

Nera paused as though now she'd been surprised. "They are headed back to Scarlet. Ariel is very tired, she must sleep, and I want her away."

The trees in this area grew close together, a true forest where many of the areas they passed through were more woodland. Donya smelled acorns and headed in that direction. These still smelled green unlike those sent to her in the void, but she would check and see if a few were ready.

Nera fell silent next to her although she kept pace. Donya thought of the last thing Nera had said.

"Why do you think Scarlet does not order us away?" Nera asked.

Donya was pulled up short. She did not think Nera wondered about the human. "We can protect her where she cannot protect herself. She holds a great fear of Sebastian. We must let her know she has no need to fear him. That the Kraken sent him to aid her and Ariel."

"I will tell her. I must go to her soon. But still, she should send me away."

Donya did not understand, she made a frustrated noise letting out a low puff of air causing her side to ache.

"If I leave the Sky God would follow, he is the bigger threat."

Donya had not thought of that. Nera and her could run, at least for the next few days, to allow Scarlet her wedding. And if they were caught, then what?

"She is human, but she does not smell the type to do that," Donya finally said. She remembered the smell of humans who would push their friends down to get away from her. One thing they all carried was an anise-like smell. Sweet and cloying. She had pursued several of them over the years, passing by easier prey. And they did have a fairly wonderful flavor.

"It probably has not even occurred to her as it did not cross your mind," Nera said.

Donya noted she sounded agitated by that. She sounded agitated in general. Donya had never seen her like this. Perhaps hunger could be to blame, she had not eaten since the night before like Donya. Donya picked up her pace, Nera would probably enjoy acorns, and wonderful mushrooms grew around and under oak trees.

Nera leapt at Donya, tackling her to the ground. Donya landed on the soft pine needles rolling and allowing Nera to pin her. Donya would never struggle against Nera again. She remembered the hours she spent trying to break free from her binding, the terrible things she thought at her. Nera endured it all, all while she planned on escaping with Donya and Scarlet. Saving them from her father. Then Donya pushed Nera. Donya and Scarlet were indeed saved, but Nera was left behind.

So, Donya did not move as Nera madly ripped at her clothing. Exposing the crack in her side. Nera clawed at the earth by the crack screaming at the sky.

Donya let her wail.

"It will heal," Donya said, understanding that Nera's anger did not lie solely with her. Donya had not hidden the wound from her, but also not allowed her to inspect it.

"How long will it take?" Nera's breathing continued to be ragged, and her eyes were shut tight.

"I won't know until it thaws out of the stone. I suspect a year at least." Donya did not add it would go much quicker back on her mountain. In her home, if the winter fell hard, it would be even better, but many years had passed since her mountain experienced a hard winter filled with snow and ice that clung into the months that should be spring.

"It is because of me, I know this," Nera said, then stopped Donya from speaking with a kiss.

Donya let the kiss linger, wondering what would happen next. She could never be sure with Nera. She loved that about her.

Donya was startled to realize she loved Nera.

That explained why she hunted Nera so. Not because of the apology she owed. Or any other reason she'd entertained on the long trek.

Donya stopped moving and Nera pulled back.

"Oh," Nera said, caressing Donya's face with a smooth hand.

Donya wondered what her expression betrayed. What Nera could read in it? Donya knew she would not simply declare her love at this moment. She must do it right.

Scarlet had mentioned communication was important for a relationship. Donya would tell Nera. But Donya knew acts were important, more important than words, humans often forgot this. If communicating about large and small issues was a key to maintaining love, then it followed that accomplishing acts large and small for your love should be of equal importance. Nera found pinecones to feed Donya after all. Small things that meant so much. Donya would do those small acts, but also, she would find her eye—

and soon. It would be a great act. Then she would communicate her love to her.

Donya slowly moved her hand up Nera's thigh, Nera shivered slightly but leaned into the touch. Her silver dress was held together by a slender bow which Donya tugged on. It fell open and Donya thanked the pale sky behind Nera. It illuminated all of her perfection. To the east on the other side of the mountains, the sun rose, but it would take time to climb into the sky and bother Donya.

"Me on top or you?" Nera asked with a sigh.

"How about side by side?" Donya asked, pulling Nera into the pine needles.

"Oh yes this will be wonderful, and next time we will find the stream and be in the water."

Donya moved her hand over Nera's stomach up to her breasts. "You have a list started?"

Nera tipped her head back and arched into Donya. "Yes, and a list of bridges to go under with you."

After that they spoke no more, their mouths otherwise busy.

CHAPTER 33

SCARLET

"You two have fun at breakfast," Scarlet said, it was nearly ten am, but Juan's family insisted they show up for breakfast at the local diner.

"I have never been more disappointed to leave anywhere in my life," Lettie called as she walked out into the morning mist.

Juan followed her.

"Don't forget if your sister says anything, she saw a giant rat, lay it on thick, gaslight her if you need to," Scarlet called down the stairs while she pulled a purple robe around her. She was not going to breakfast, the thought of food was more than she could stand.

Ariel had shown up an hour earlier. All Lettie could see was the fish tank water splashing around. Ariel seemed exhausted. She told Scarlet three words before she fell asleep. "Read cards," Ariel said, paused thought then added, "Dawnya."

Scarlet knew exactly what she meant. Scarlet needed to do a tarot reading. Scarlet didn't like doing them. The cards Grazia gave her were antiquities, they should be in a museum. But they were too magically charged for Scarlet to ever donate. Scarlet neglected most of her practice; she had pulled out the antique cards once a month, but according to the *Liber Unguium* magical tools needed to be handled at least every full and new moon, every night being preferred. But what she saw rarely made sense, which discouraged her. She bought a few books for help, one book seemed to say everything was doom and gloom. Another leaned too new age. Death meant change her ass—sometimes it meant death.

The deck hadn't been complete. It still wasn't. But she did acquire more cards at antique shops and online. They were not of the same deck. But it would be unlikely she could ever find more of the Visconti-Sforza deck. Those were all in museums and rich people's private collections. But antique cards from the rider deck floated around. They were about a century old but that was good enough as far as Scarlet was concerned. And the newer cards came labeled, which helped her get through the readings.

One time she foretold the announcement of a pregnancy at work. That thus far ranked as her greatest accomplishment with the tarot. She wondered how she was supposed to be helpful with it now.

With everyone gone in what might be the only alone time she would have till Monday she needed to dig in and do it. She pulled all the blinds, not because of what she was going to do, but because the bright light bothered her hangover. Then she lit a pretty white scented candle she'd picked up at a farmers' market over the summer. It smelled of iris and clean cotton shirts and sat on her bedside table. She washed her hands three times, touching the cards was better for readings or she would have worn light gloves. The oils in her hands could really deteriorate the pigments of the five-hundred-year-old cards.

Laying out an aubergine silk scarf on her bed she shuffled the cobbled together deck. It still had a couple of holes. A five of cups, and a few of the sword cards needed to be added. The most important missing card was a page of coins. But all of the major cards were accounted for. It took her a second to start. Shuffling the deck remained a delicate affair. It would never do to bend any of the cards, so she cut the deck then cut it again and shuffled that way. Then she would fan the deck and pull cards that looked like they wanted to be pulled.

She should have decided on a spread. She grabbed one of the books and opened the section she needed. It opened to the horseshoe; she took that as a sign. Also, that spread answered a question.

What needs to be done against the Sky God? She thought at the cards as hard as she could. That part always made her feel silly.

She concentrated on her question, pulling out cards and setting them in the U shape.

She flipped over the first card, the hermit. The first card referred to the past. She wondered who the hermit referenced. Not her, maybe Donya. Or maybe the Sky God. They'd both been alone.

A knock sounded at her front door, and she heard a splash from the fish tank.

Before she got up, she flipped over the second card. The seven of wands reversed. She had no idea what that meant.

Her front door opened, it always squeaked briefly.

"What a lovely smell," came a voice from the hall.

Scarlet recognized Nera's singsong tones. Ariel had opened the door, she wondered if Donya would be with her. The sun hid behind the mist, so it was possible for the troll. Scarlet worried about Donya's appearance the night before.

"Come in here, maybe you can help," Scarlet called.

Nera walked in, her violet eye shining in the candlelight. She held Ariel who lay limply in her arms, Ariel's eyelids drooped heavily but she wore a toothy smile.

Scarlet stood up. "Maybe Ariel should go back to sleep."

Nera handed over Ariel and Scarlet walked her to the fish tank placing her in the corner away from the filter. The ancient betta swam over, and Ariel wrapped a tentacle leg around the heavily finned fish. Her eyes already firmly closed before her head even sank below the water.

Nera perched on Scarlet's bed when she entered the room. Nera sat neatly with her legs tucked under her, studying the two overturned cards.

"Is something wrong?" Scarlet asked.

Nera shook her head. "This card is not good. The present is not good. You must be a young seer."

"Let's not go making me any more weird things."

"Before you continue, I need to borrow your shield, with this," Nera said motioning to the silver circlet she wore on her brow. It did not match the light-yellow cotton sundress adorning the rest of her.

"How do you do that?" Scarlet asked. She wasn't sure she had the energy for many more spells or things. Her body was angry at her for last night, and even with her limited sense of magic, she could feel her exhaustion from freeing Donya. It felt almost like cold water sitting in her belly.

"It will be very easy. I need to bind you for but a moment. You are tired, it will be quick."

"Will it hurt?"

Nera laughed and giggled. "No, not even a little. We don't even need to get naked."

"Fine," Scarlet said and let the nymph lead her into the bathroom.

Nera put an inch of water in the bottom of the bathtub—she didn't have shoes on—and stepped in. Scarlet followed after.

"Turn your back to me and let me hold you," Nera instructed.

"I'm too heavy, you won't be able to." But Scarlet turned around and leaned back, she kept her weight mostly to herself though.

"Go limp, I am stronger than I seem, although I could not lift Donya easily."

Scarlet remembered Nera dragging the mostly stone Donya the other night. She was strong. Scarlet let herself sag and felt pleasantly surprised when Nera caught all her weight. A warm sensation took over her. A stray hair tickled her face, she wanted to swipe at it but realized she couldn't move her arm. She couldn't move anything. It made her want to shiver but she could not even do that. She began to panic when the warm feeling faded.

"All done, you are light as a feather."

Scarlet took a couple of deep breaths. Her heart drummed wildly in her chest. "We will see if Juan thinks I'm light as a feather tomorrow night when he has to carry me over the threshold."

"I love that ritual," Nera said with a wistful sigh. She stepped out of the tub and held up her hands. "Oh, this will be hard to work with. I am accustomed to dream. This is more solid, not like water at all."

Scarlet got out too and walked to the front room, the horrid hand still rested in the shield box she'd built around the orange purse. "I thought that this would disappear when you took my ability."

"Oh, I did not take, now I can use it too. This is a very fine tool. We will use it in a few hours. We will use shield, darkness, and my binding to trap the Sky God."

"In a few hours, you mean during the day?"

"Yes, with Sebastian we can shroud the sun. He sang this into being for us."

"Nera, Nera backup. Who is Sebastian? And sang, do you mean the creepy evil thing that has been haunting the shoreline."

"Oh, don't say that in front of Ariel, Sebastian is hers, and yours. The Lady sent it. He is the gift. It is a hippocampus."

Scarlet could not understand how a part of the brain was a gift. More body parts were not what she wanted to deal with. "Ugh brains," she moaned.

Nera cocked her head to the side and placed a hand on Scarlet's forehead. "Are you well? Usually I confuse those around me."

"Hippocampus, it's an area of the brain," Scarlet said, rubbing at her skull. It might have been the spot where her hippocampus was located, but she couldn't be sure.

"It is a water horse," Nera said, her brow still creased under the shining circlet.

Scarlet recalled the sight of water horses in the Trevi Fountain and other art. That kind of Hippocampus. "Okay, I think I understand, an actual aquatic horse, who is named Sebastian?"

"Yes, yes that is it. It will keep the clouds for us all day long. And tomorrow for you, sun, only after lunch and ending at sundown. Ariel was very clear in the instructions."

Scarlet doubted that Ariel could barely form a sentence.

They wandered back to the cards. Scarlet had completely overreacted to hearing that song. "I made such a mess," Scarlet murmured. "Donya never needed to come here."

"Wrong, you are clever like Donya, but you are both wrong often. It is very strange to watch."

"What do you mean?"

"Danger lurked; the god came here for us. Sebastian sang to bring the clouds and mist. The sky was covered. You should finish this," Nera said, motioning to the cards.

"Why? I'll just be wrong again." Scarlet grimaced a tad ashamed of how childish she sounded but it was almost her wedding day and everything was going wrong.

Scarlet flipped over another card that stood for hidden influences. It was the reversed four of cups. Scarlet opened the paperback book. "Fear of being alone."

"Who does it mean?" Nera asked.

"How would I know?"

"Use your eyes, they will tell you, I am sure." Nera picked up the card and held it very close to Scarlet's face.

For a second Scarlet lost focus on the card. Her vision blurred.

"Huh, my vision blurring could be more important than I thought." She snatched the card from Nera and moved it away from her face. Then closer again. When it hovered a few inches from her nose the blurring happened again. She put down that card and picked up the hermit. When the blurring happened, she did see Donya. She picked up the four of cups and again Donya flashed before her, a crack split her almost in two.

"Is Donya hurt?" Scarlet asked.

"Yes, yes, you will be a seer, very good. Flip over the rest."

Feeling buoyed by the encouragement, she flipped over the next card. It was the sun reversed. She picked it up to look closely at it. But Nera quickly snatched it out of her hands. "Hey, that is what the obstacles are."

"Obvious, is it not?"

Scarlet nodded. The sun, a Sky God, it made sense. "If I get good at this it will be even more useful than counting."

"Counting?" Nera smiled at her.

"I can count large numbers of objects if I try, it's one of the new things my eyes can do with Donya's spell."

"Yes, I could feel you have more in you but nothing I could borrow when I bound you."

Three cards remained. The next stood for the environment. It was the tower. "Oh, that's bad, right?" Scarlet picked up the book.

Nera shook her head.

The first words that Scarlet noticed on the page for the tower were exhilarating change. But no matter where she held the card, she could see nothing.

The sixth card, the one Scarlet wanted to know the most, stood for what should be done. It was the nine of wands. Scarlet flipped through the pages of her book. Strength and prudence. She held up the card. Donya came clearly into view—she no longer bore a crack and Scarlet stood with her. The sword glowed between them, the crack dark in its hilt. But the image was not like the others, it shone in a strange color like sepia but more blue. Often now Scarlet contained no name for the colors her eyes showed her.

"What did you see?"

"It's me and Donya and the sword."

Nera's mouth fell into a frown. She quickly reached down and flipped the last card. It was the hanged man reversed.

"That should be good right, he is standing up," Scarlet said, smiling a bit in relief.

"No, no, I will speak with Donya. Our plan is faulty. She keeps information from me."

Scarlet held up the last card, but her vision didn't blur. She just saw a painting of a man smiling with a rope around his foot like he'd stepped into a trap that had not yet sprung.

CHAPTER 34

DONYA

Noon passed by, and Donya found it strange to be lying outside on a flat wet rock. But Sebastian had called in a thick layer of mist. The ocean, the sand, the rocks, and the sky were all the same slate color. Donya blended right in. An ocean cave waited behind her, inviting and moist. The tide rose slowly bringing more and more water with it. She and Nera would be using the power of high tide and the shadows of the cave in a few short hours.

Grandmother warned her against augmenting spells. And this really would be the last time. How could one use simple spells against a god? After this, she would stick to the basics for a good long time. The earth prison, with Nera's binding and Scarlet's shield, could strengthen it enough to hold him inside the void. At least until they were all long dead. Then who cared what happened? He seemed a bit crazed. Perhaps more time bound would mellow him out, or the opposite. Either way, it wouldn't matter to her.

Her thawing picked up again after she ate pinecones from the shore. They digested slowly but held strength in each sharp seed and even the thick protective scales. Unfortunately, the thaw reached the first fissures of the crack in her side. The wound did indeed show her tender entrails. They swirled with color and sparkled like a geode's inner crystals. The wound would take years to fully heal. Nera wouldn't be pleased.

She wondered what delayed Nera. She said she would get a ride to Scarlet's. It shouldn't take so long.

Donya closed her eyes. Would she be able to sense if Nera needed her? If the Sky God captured her while they were separated?

When she woke it was from a kiss.

The tide rolled in, and Donya was wet with salt water, Nera stood over her smiling. Nera held the sword.

"We should not do this now," Nera nearly whispered.

Donya sat bolt upright, much to the dismay of her wound, and her still sleepy mind. "Nera, now is the only time we have. That god, he will come for you if we don't."

"And what is wrong with that?"

Donya was unsure what to say. He would burn out her eyes and use her for powerful rituals. Hasn't she been used enough? It must stop.

"You have everything, we complete the spell at high tide," Donya finally managed.

"It will fail, you and I will fail. Scarlet saw you and her," Nera said, tears pooling in her violet eye, the other remained dry.

"She is too new to magic. Come, we should prepare." Donya stood and unsheathed the sword. She walked over to the runes carved deep into the stone at the back of the cave. This spell would be altered, but she wanted to involve the elements closest to a prison. The shield and the binding. The shadow and water of the environment would fuel the spell. Give strength to her and Nera. But nothing else.

"No," Nera said and stamped her foot.

Donya let a few breaths pass by her lips as her ears absorbed Nera's protest, and her shoulders sagged. Nera was right. Compromise, Donya had never undertaken it before, but she could try now. Yet she did not want to, and she didn't know how.

"I feel strong, we should attempt something if not our plan," Donya responded.

Nera flashed her a brilliant smile. "You listened to me."

Donya felt a lightness around her chest, she placed a hand to it surprised. Scarlet's advice about communication worked. Worked better than she thought possible. And Donya did not even need to speak useful words. She supposed part of communicating was listening, not only speaking. Donya decided to delve further into listening. "Please tell me what Scarlet saw."

And so, Nera told her.

By the time Nera finished with her tale, which contained a few digressions about butterflies she saw on the way back, Donya formed a new plan. "Let us form the prison but not attempt to trap the god. It could be useful later."

"I need more time, the shield is not easy for me yet," Nera said.

More time would be just what Donya needed, as she had a new idea, riskier than the formation of the prison she had spoken of. Donya moved her rough hand through Nera's silken hair. "You practice and take your time."

Nera cocked her head at the tone of Donya's voice. But still smiled delighted that she had been heard out, and not pushed to do anything.

❧❧

Donya watched Nera practice from the cave for a few hours. The sun stayed behind the clouds, but Donya preferred to hide around the hours when the sun lingered at its highest. Also, she needed to concentrate. Working with the sword she used a locator spell, one she knew. It required hair like many locator spells. Donya snared a few strands when she touched Nera earlier.

Nera's other eye lay on an island. Donya once visited this place on her quest, a very dry island off the coast of Africa. The sun would set there soon, she needed to kill a little time. She could use the sword to move her there and be back quickly.

"I will return," Donya promised. Making a show of picking up a pinecone from the beach and eating it.

Nera hunched over a small heap of seaweed her hands spread, she flicked her gaze to Donya and her face looked frustrated. Donya was surprised Nera seemed to struggle; a shield was similar in a way to a bind. Shields kept things out while bindings often kept things in. Perhaps the opposite nature threw her off, as no shield formed around the pile of kelp.

Donya wandered up into the forest eating more pinecones although she felt quite full after all the nuts yesterday. But this movement and then building the prison would probably drain her. She wandered until she found a tree blackened by fire last year. It still held ash in a burned-out hollow cavity. She collected the ash and a sprig of pine off a sapling that grew near it then made for the brook that bubbled not far from her. It wasn't much of a water source this late in the year, but it would do.

Donya made her trench and drove the sword into the ground. It obeyed and shadow climbed up her body. Donya possessed no fear of the darkness. Even now having spent time in the void she found the cool shadow to be a comfort.

When she landed, she was not alone on the hot dry island. Perched above a puddle of black ooze huddled the Sky God. His current form an amalgam of man and bird. His legs were from a bird of prey and his wings where his arms should be, but his head and torso were that of Mars's body. He stared up at the stars, not even noticing Donya.

Donya landed awkwardly, as this was the side of a steep mountain. The black ooze worked its way from a rock and collected in a depression. One that implied construction, dug out from the side of the brown stone.

Donya moved slowly, keeping the sword at the ready, not that it could do much against the great power. The air smelled of tar and of ozone. Donya worked to catch the smell of anything else, all while knowing if the god hit her with another lightning strike she was finished. She crept closer to the puddle of sticky ooze and sniffed. Glass, under the scent of everything else, there was glass inside the darkness. Donya recalled the jar that contained Nera's other eye. Heldrig must have used a very similar jar here. Donya reached into the earth and stone underneath the ooze and pushed. It did not take much; the earth wanted the tar and ooze to run and not puddle, the makeshift dam broke, and Donya saw the jar tumble down the side of the mountain.

Unfortunately, the motion drew the eye of the god.

"You, how pleasant," the god said but did not boom.

Donya let herself slide three paces and gave a small bow. "I am honored you recall me at each of our meetings."

"I can remember you before I knew you. Much like my priestess. This time I think I would like all priestesses."

Donya nodded and took a few more steps toward the jar which had stopped rolling. "I am sorry to disturb you, I will be going."

"This is not the place I ruled. I cannot find it. But you were right, I recall what you said. There is more power here."

"I was correct about power," Donya started before she remembered what she had once told the god about being weak. She had been goading him, but the information was true. "If you found your land, would you still need a priestess?" Donya asked.

"Perhaps not, I need to know my place and name. I need that. I want a priestess."

"I understand," Donya said, not understanding all of the logic but understanding the hunger in his voice. Donya would always understand hunger. She stooped and picked up the bottle. "Good-bye, I must be on my way." Donya never turned her back on him, sensing where she needed to put each foot to not roll down the mountain. If she ran or moved too fast she knew the predator in him would notice.

He ruffled his feathers and was on her in an instant.

Donya struck out at him with the sword, but it did no damage, making a dull thudding sound when it hit his leg. He grabbed her by the shoulders and began to lift her. His talons could not sink into her stoney flesh, his grip slipped, the talons making an awful noise against her skin. Already they were too high, Donya knew if she fell the stone section of her middle could continue to crack and split her in two.

They flew over a town filled with humans and light, then over a white sand beach. Donya realized he might intend to fly her back to California, which given his speed should only take a few hours. But she didn't plan on allowing that. She hammered at his talon with the hilt of the sword, but he didn't seem to notice.

The ocean below her grew dark and deep. To use the sword to move back to California she needed ash, pine, fresh water, and land. She must escape.

Donya bit into the Sky God's foot. It took a second to realize her mistake. Her diamond teeth sunk deep into his flesh, and he screamed releasing her. But her mouth filled with his hot salty blood. It washed down her throat, burning, like the burning she suffered as the light of the sun drenched her from many directions. Would she turn to stone from the inside out?

The Atlantic Ocean closed over Donya as her eyes shut. She sank quickly and there was nothing she could do about it.

261

CHAPTER 35

SCARLET

Scarlet arrived home from the salon where she'd gotten the full beauty treatment, lash extensions, a facial, mani/pedi, and a wax. Some of those treatments were torture, but Fizzy her long-time hairstylist, kept Scarlet talking about all of the wedding drama. Fizzy would be coming to the hotel in the morning to do everyone's hair and makeup, and she literally couldn't wait to meet Bertha and see if she could get her talking about the rat. Scarlet thought when she retold the rat story, she made it quite believable.

There had been one stressful part of her visit right near the end, while Scarlet's toes were being painted the sword materialized in her right hand. Thankfully Fizzy was looking away. Her green and blue hair was a fluffy veil between her and Scarlet. Scarlet opened her hand and the shadow sword instantly dissipated.

Scarlet sipped on a smoothie as she walked into the apartment. Lettie waited for her inside with her dress. Scarlet felt like a new person, well almost, even with pain pills she still endured the slightest pinching headache. Both Ariel and Juan were out. They had a few hours until the rehearsal but still Scarlet expected them to be at the apartment.

"Juan didn't peek at the dress, did he?" Scarlet asked.

"No, I guarded it the whole time he was here."

"Where did he go anyway?"

"Ice cream run."

"Another one, did you manage to see Ariel?"

"No, but I could hear her, it was probably the weirdest experience of my life. Ugh, I think I squealed a few times, she probably hates me. I feel so uncool."

Ariel must be still too tired to use some of her spells, Scarlet thought.

Lettie slouched on the couch. Scarlet noticed a notebook out in front of her. Surely, she hadn't taken time to work on the notes from Olivia. Scarlet walked around to the kitchen. After the near half gallon of water she drank this morning and the smoothie, she was finally hungry. The apartment was small, inside the fridge sat unopened bags of baby carrots and perfect stalks of celery. She could see a few yogurts pushed to the back but didn't want to risk getting bloated tonight. A partially full container of hummus caught her eye, and she grabbed it to go with the carrots. Sunday she would go grocery shopping and buy chocolate donuts and pizza, and a cartload of other unhealthy foods.

Scarlet walked back to the front room with her haul. Lettie scribbled a quick sentence in her notebook. It was slightly larger than the pocket notebook from the orange purse. She guessed Lettie had copied everything over in her own hand, because they would destroy everything they stole from Olivia, eventually. Scarlet really hoped Donya would show up soon to do that.

She also really hoped Donya didn't plan on getting rid of the hand by eating it.

"What is it?" She asked Lettie.

"I didn't tell Juan."

Scarlet wasn't sure what she meant. "About what?"

"The hand and the murder. I found the report about Guy, Olivia had it."

"Juan knows about Guy. I told him on Monday night." Scarlet put a carrot in her mouth and watched Lettie. She could see the way the light moved over her face. Funny, Donya often bore the same play of light and shadow on her face. Scarlet recognized it as risky behavior face. "Where did Olivia have it?" Scarlet bit her lip.

"At her apartment."

"No, noooooo, why would you do that?"

"At least I didn't go into their office. I thought about it but didn't do it."

Scarlet took deep breaths. She wanted to end this conversation. Her armpits burned from sweat hitting the angry recently waxed hair follicles.

Lettie didn't meet Scarlet's eyes. "I wore a hat, and gloves, and parked outside her complex. I don't think anyone has even reported her missing yet. Her mail was piled up. I wouldn't have gone in if there was crime tape."

"Did you find anything useful?" Scarlet asked.

"Maybe, she had pictures, lots of printed pictures." Lettie got out a thick folder.

Scarlet leafed through the photos, they were all time and date stamped. The photos told a story. Either Guy or Olivia had picked up the trail Mars' body left behind. The body went to Colorado to a logging town. The logging town suffered a major bird die-off. A series of twenty pictures documented dead birds, their eyes burned from the sockets. Another series of photos were of scorched trees, the green leaves burned to ash.

Scarlet recognized the trees. She'd seen them before. Quaking Aspen, they were an interesting tree in her opinion, not really an individual. Each tree was part of a colony. She needed to read into them and do a little internet research.

"This town, it is near where the Sky God's body must have been bound," Scarlet said. If they gave the Sky God back his original body would he leave them alone? Mars' body couldn't be as good as his godly form. Donya had needed to pay her back for a freely given gift. If they gave him the body, would it work the same way? Maybe not because she did want something for it. Still, this was great information.

"What you did was dumb. Really dumb, you are one of the smartest people I know, and I can't believe you did it." Scarlet paused, watching as Lettie shrank in her seat. "Never do anything like that again, but thank you. This is a big help."

It was a big help, but Scarlet didn't know what to do with it now. Perhaps nothing this instant. On Sunday they could do more reconnaissance.

But now they needed to get the evidence out of her apartment. Scarlet desperately wished Nera or Donya owned a cell phone. If Ariel was here, she could pop over to them and bring one back.

Scarlet remembered when she called out to Ariel, that she could hear her through the water like her mother could. Scarlet got up and walked to the fish tank, her betta swimming over hoping for fish food. Scarlet stuck one finger into the water and asked, "Ariel, Ariel can you bring me Donya?"

Lettie watched her with her lips slightly parted. "What did you just do?"

"Called out to Ariel. I don't know if it will work, but maybe Donya will know what to do. And she can at least take the evidence far away when she gets here."

Scarlet picked up the photos and shuffled through them again.

"Can you magic those photos, like make them come alive and tell us a story? Oh, or summon Olivia's ghost to let us know what happened?" Lettie asked. "Also, your nails look amazing.

"Thanks, I got my nails painted to match the earrings I'm going to wear. Antique pearl clip-ons that were my great aunt's. Ugh, I wish she could have taught me more stuff. If I'd known more from a young age, I wouldn't get into all these dangerous situations. And I would be able to explain to you why I can't just get the pictures to tell us a story." Scarlet paused on that last sentence. She couldn't get the pictures to tell them a story. But maybe she could get them to tell her a story. Almost like with the cards.

"Sometimes people who are self-taught come up with novel ideas," Lettie said.

Scarlet tested that hypothesis. She held up picture after picture, bringing them close to her face and backing them off. Finally, one blurred. It almost looked like a rock but on closer inspection, it carried tool markings. It had been shaped, pointed at either side like a bird's wings, although one was freshly broken. Her vision blurred then snapped back into focus.

"Lettie, you've done it again," Scarlet said feeling relieved.

"What?"

"Helped. I don't have much, but I know this picture is important," Scarlet said and could feel the wave of disappointment radiate off of Lettie. "Listen, I'm sorry I'm not better at this stuff. I don't practice enough, I guess. But I have been studying."

A splashing sound came from the bathroom followed by a high whine. Scarlet got up to see what had happened. Nera and Ariel stood in the small space, Nera showing Ariel how to magically move the water sloshing all over the floor into the bathtub. Ariel pouted but tried.

"I swam deep in the ocean when she came," Nera explained.

"Missed tub," Ariel put in.

Scarlet picked up Ariel. "You did great Ariel. Messes are fine as long as we clean them up." She wanted to ask about Donya but didn't want to upset Ariel more. Nera might be helpful, but Donya was easier to understand. She would show Nera Lettie's findings.

When the floor was mostly dry, Scarlet rang out the bathmat, hung it over the curtain rod, and led them out to where Lettie studied the picture of the artifact.

"It's cracked," Lettie pointed at the bird.

Scarlet took the photo, and she started hoping her vision would zoom and not x-ray through the photo. It worked, but only for a moment. She could see the crack ran through scratches. The scratches could be an ancient alphabet.

"Give me a blank piece of paper," Scarlet motioned for Lettie's notebook.

She let her eyes focus and zoom. Scarlet thought that was the difference between zoom and X-ray, the level of focus in her eye.

Scarlet drew the symbols she could make out. The crack obscured one, but before she could work on it more Nera grabbed the paper and the picture from her hand.

"Do not gaze upon these, and do not remember what you have seen. If you find you think on it, tell me, I will bind the memory," Nera said with an edge in her voice.

"Wow," Lettie said.

"Oh dear, another human. I did not notice," Nera clutched the paper and photo to her chest.

"It's fine, I told her. This seems pretty serious." Scarlet wanted an explanation. "Could you tell me what that is at least?"

"No, oh no," Nera said. Ariel popped over to her shoulder and tried to get a peek at the photo. "Not even you may see." Nera clutched the photo closer to herself. "I must go."

"Wait, where is Donya?"

Nera paused on the threshold of the door. "Far far from here, perhaps she has abandoned me. Or perhaps she means to sacrifice herself." Then Nera was out the door.

Scarlet stood in the hall, thinking she'd made a giant mess of things.

CHAPTER 36
DONYA

Donya did not fight the smoldering blood in her throat. Instead, she opened her mouth and let the cool ocean water run in. It did not quench the flames, but it gave her room to recover herself. And in those moments, she realized the gift the god unwittingly gave her, blood was one of the ingredients needed for the ninth spell her grandmother had taught her in the void. Blood and sand. Donya let herself sink and when she hit the ocean floor she ran her fingers through the substrate and was rewarded with the grit of silt and sand.

Quickly she worked the circle for the spell into the sand around her, moving her body as little as possible so as to not disturb her pattern. She had never done a spell under the sea, but there was no reason it would not work. When she finished sculpting the circle she gathered a handful of sand and gagged into it. Bringing up material from her stomach was not pleasant, and the clenching involved pulled at her wound, but Donya pushed through the discomfort.

She never let go of the jar holding Nera's other eye.

The ocean was not pitch black here; her short fall through the water left her still in the shallows where light could reach, and the moon rose above her. A great squid glided by giving off a purple glow. The god's blood shimmered too brightly with the sand. Donya waited, when the circle activated the runes inside it shifted of their own accord melting away until the ocean floor appeared unmarked. Then Donya lay in that spot and the memories came. Not all of them thankfully, but a large amount, Donya retained the will in the spell to pick and choose which recollections she wanted. Although a handful of memories were very clear and almost insistent. She chose several of mountains and stars, the steady nature let her know this was from the time when the god stayed bound. Then she chose several of Nera in a forest, she stood tall, her hair longer than she wore it now, these would be borrowed memories from the body the god now inhabited. Nera did not smile in those memories, but she worked spells with great skill. The body's recollections remained as strong as the gods own, Donya could understand why he went to California and stalked Scarlet first as those were some of Mar's last thoughts. In comparison to the body's the god's memories were unorganized, she found several recent ones, where he used the birds around him to help him move in Mars' body. And his attempt to make a found human woman a trial priestess, she did not survive, but he had been gentle with her. Even the birds, he never tried to kill them. And in these memories, she saw his power over their bodies. Something he did not understand was that he could control those whose eyes he burned out. Finally, Donya took in one memory that seemed to be the oldest, it brimmed with other gods, and they spoke a language Donya could understand a few words of. It came from the old world, far to the east of her mountain.

The constellations from the tree though, it hurt Donya's head, but she understood the god was bound in the new world. Yet his original home was in the old. Neither spot lay on the coast. His betrayal, he'd mentioned other gods, they must have transported him across a great distance.

In the memories of the trees, there were several terribly frustrating sensations; the god could sense his body out in the world. Yet could not escape to find it. And by the time he did, his sense of that body was gone. Over and over, he thought the tree that held him died but the talisman connected to the roots, and the roots would put up more trees.

No wonder he seemed broken. Donya had thought in the void she would eventually lose her mind.

Donya lay in the cool sand, here on the ocean floor it was very still, and she felt the last part of her stone stomach come loose and move again as her flesh should. She thought of the few healing spells she knew. Now that she'd become entirely free of the stone bind, she could cast one. But the one strong enough to help with the crack in her side was the second spell her grandmother taught her in the void. And it took three nights to complete. Three nights soaking in a slow-moving stream chanting. And she didn't have three nights to spare.

She must return to California. With any luck, that confused god would travel elsewhere, or maybe get distracted. But Donya felt it in her troll bones that she never enjoyed that type of luck.

∾◌∾

Scarlet and Juan were startled when Donya landed by the stove in the kitchen. Scarlet gave out a small yell and lost control of her shield. But she recovered quickly. Donya noticed Juan wore black slacks and a crisp white button-down. "The wedding is tomorrow, correct?" Donya asked.

"Yeah, we are leaving for the rehearsal in a few minutes," Scarlet said, as she closed the blinds to their balcony. The large sliding glass door faced west, and the sun streamed through the glass but did not hit Donya where she stood.

"Please inspect the sword, what do you see?" Donya took a few steps to Scarlet and handed over the sword. Scarlet and Juan's apartment was not that much larger than her cave, but the ceiling stood higher.

Scarlet considered the sword; to Donya it shimmered more than usual, but it did that after completing a spell. It was made of opal and caught the light from every angle. It produced its own luminescence occasionally, Donya had noticed it did this after a spell casting finished, like it was pleased.

"It's glowing a bit, hard to see I guess. It's more red than purple and yellow."

Donya thought about the other times she'd used this spell to move herself. The sword liked to take one to the heart of a place. Where the warmth came from, and the life.

"Thank you," Donya said to Scarlet then walked over to the fishtank, surprised to see Ariel resting inside. "Why are you not with Nera or Sebastian?"

Ariel peeked over at Scarlet.

Scarlet's attire consisted of a dress, pretty navy with pink flowers, she picked up the orange purse. "Nera told me that Sebastian doesn't understand restraint yet. Ugh, two baby monsters. If they stay together, they play all day and night, running amok. Here, do something about this purse before the police come and search my apartment."

Donya could smell the stink of the dead flesh coming from the purse, but she could not touch the purse.

"I'll take the shield off of it when we leave, otherwise it gets very smelly. Take these too. Lettie went to a lotta trouble to get them. Nera already left with one. When the sun sets you better go find her."

Juan walked to the front door. He fidgeted with a set of metal keys.

Donya opened the folder to groupings and stacks of photographs.

"I think that is from the area the god was bound in. He was stuck to an aspen tree. Those are clonal, the oldest colony is supposed to be eighty thousand years old," Scarlet said, fixing a pearl earring on her ear.

"I appreciate all you have done. Go, do not be late. May I wait here for darkness?"

"Of course, that is what I implied when I said go find Nera when the sun sets." Scarlet threw up her hands but gave a wave as she walked out the door.

Ariel watched from the water.

"Humans are very strange young one."

Donya slumped down onto the couch holding the jar still, catching glimpses of the purple iris in the tar. It was easier for the sword to bring her back to Scarlet, and she currently required that ease. Her throat still ached, and her side throbbed. She didn't think she could do much right now. Rest, she needed rest. Donya closed her eyes for a moment.

Water flicked across Donya's face.

"Newa," Ariel said from a brightly lit fish tank.

Donya let her senses move out into the sandy ground far below the upstairs apartment. The first thing she noticed was that the sun had set. The second thing was that she could not sense Nera's whereabouts. It felt like the old emptiness when she reached for Nera. The emptiness that meant Nera hid herself. Donya opened her eyes with a panic thrumming through her veins.

"Ariel, can you take me to Nera?" Donya used the words of a question, but her tone came out as a demand.

Ariel shook her head. "No find." And her tentacles turned black at the bottom where they were normally purple.

Donya stood and stomped to the door. She could smell the dead flesh of the orange purse, but she could also smell Nera. Her scent wafted fresh and heavy in the room. Nera may know how to hide magical traces; she could not be sensed easily, but Donya could sniff her out with the trail this fresh.

Donya picked up the purse and the folder of photographs. She did not believe she would need these things, but it was better to be safe than sorry.

She flung open the door and descended the stairs two at a time. A popping noise sounded behind her, and wet tentacles wrapped around her shoulder and over her upper arm. Apparently, Donya wouldn't have to find Nera alone.

CHAPTER 37

SCARLET

Scarlet fell asleep on the car ride to the rehearsal dinner. It felt strange, almost like the pull of a spell, but it could have been extreme exhaustion.

The rehearsal went off without a hitch. Her wedding party was medium-sized, but overall, the wedding stayed small, and Juan wanted a short ceremony, which Scarlet and the officiant were more than happy to oblige. The venue was an older hotel, but the staff kept it well maintained. It sported a fresh coat of dark blue paint and the chairs they set out for the guests were a bright white.

The dinner was held at the attached restaurant. Scarlet kept her right hand under the table while they ate appetizers and listened to speeches, as the sword kept materializing in random short bursts. But if it showed up at the wrong time it could be a disaster. Scarlet harbored the feeling that there had already been a disaster. Where did Nera go with that photograph? What word could have been so dangerous that Nera did not want her to know it?

If they could just keep a lid on this situation for one more day, then the wedding would be over and maybe Scarlet could devote more mental energy to the whole Sky God situation. They needed to stand together. In legends that was how mortals tended to fare best against a god.

Scarlet hadn't realized she stared at the wall while Deacon gave a weird long speech about how much Juan meant to him. Her vision shifted and she could see Donya sitting in a car outside. A very flashy, very fast-looking, cherry red car. Why would Donya need a car? Scarlet hadn't even realized she could drive. And what bounded next to her? Ariel. Ariel sat in the passenger seat, more accurately the passenger dashboard, her tiny tentacles suction cupping her to the windshield and dash.

Deacon finished the speech and Scarlet took a sip of champagne. The food already sat out; it was a simple buffet. Thankfully Deacon's speech should be the final one.

Scarlet leaned over to Juan. "Hey, I gotta go outside."

He nodded and gave her right hand a squeeze.

Scarlet drew a few smiles as she passed her parents, but they were more focused on the buffet line than her. Juan pointedly looked away. She needed to ask him how worried he was about the wedding being ruined when they got home tonight. He had been the one excited for their day. Juan helped with so many of the plans, problem solving if necessary and putting personal touches here and there. If he'd seem-ed even a little less excited, she realized she would have called off the wedding long ago, right when the trouble started, but she wanted to make Juan happy.

The sky was a dark gray, covered over with clouds. Far off in the distance, she could hear Ariel's water horse singing its still slightly creepy song.

It took Scarlet a moment to recognize what kind of car Donya drove. A trident decorated the front of the car, a Maserati. Even standing still the play of the light across the paint made it seem as if it would dart away at any second. The driver side door handle crooked strangely out away from the smooth surface. Stolen. It was a very fast, very expensive and very stolen car.

Scarlet didn't mention it, the troll looked melty. Her hair lay limp and still singed. Donya rolled down the window but said nothing.

"How bad is it?" Scarlet finally asked.

Donya didn't respond, she rolled up her shirt. Scarlet could see the wound in her side. The troll's inside glittered pink, purple, and blue. They didn't seem wet, but they did not seem totally solid either. Scarlet never wanted to have to touch that wound. A slight chartreuse miasma wafted from it, but although Scarlet could see the fumes, she could not smell them. Scarlet managed not to gag at the sight.

"And Nera?" Scarlet asked.

"He has her. But you knew that would happen didn't you," Donya said.

Scarlet was taken aback by how angry the troll sounded. Even Ariel stopped her bouncing to eye Donya.

"I don't know anything Donya. Sorry."

"Get in," Donya growled.

Scarlet glanced at the restaurant. It wasn't like she needed to do anything right then other than eat. But if she got this over with now, and they went and got Nera out from the Sky God's nose, then she could have her wedding tomorrow and not have to worry. "Ugh fine, let me go tell Juan."

Scarlet stomped back to the restaurant. A fresh salad on a plate sat in front of her empty chair. Juan's chair sat empty as well. Grabbing her champagne, she chugged it. Lettie and Elyse were in conversation, neither met her eyes as she scanned the room. Where was Juan?

All the parents were talking to uncles and other relatives in town for the event, Scarlet didn't want to interrupt and possibly get sucked into a long conversation. She smiled when she realized she could make Lettie give excuses for her. Elyse was one of her oldest friends and would smooth things out with the elders if feathers got ruffled by her leaving.

"Hey something came up last minute I gotta go. Can you two cover for me?" Scarlet asked.

Lettie nodded enthusiastically. "Should we say there is a rip in your dress? Or maybe the veil, that seems important but less drastic."

"The veil is lace right, easy enough to pretend a quick mend is almost seamless. I'll pour more wine in everyone's cups too and they probably won't even question it," Elyse offered.

Scarlet recalled her and Elyse's high school shenanigans and felt choked up for a moment.

"Thank you," Scarlet said as she walked away, still looking for her soon-to-be husband.

She visually searched one more time for Juan. The longer it took to find Juan the more second thoughts popped into Scarlet's mind. Could they do this on Sunday?

No, it wouldn't be right to leave Nera with her captor that long. Even if Scarlet was pretty sure Nera could take care of herself far better than Donya believed. Scarlet held the lingering thought that Nera must have gone to the Sky God. Probably with that picture and paper that Scarlet gave her.

Out through the backdoor Juan talked to Deacon. Scarlet breathed a sigh of relief but didn't know why they hung around out back, then she saw Deacon pass Juan the pen. She could smell the slight scent of vanilla in the air. Of course, Deacon owned a vape pen.

On the street an old silver van came squealing into the parking lot. Scarlet stopped short as the van screeched to a halt by Juan. Several guys jumped out of the back—they all wore ski masks. And then they put a pillowcase over Juan's head.

"God damn it!" Scarlet managed to yell.

Deacon laughed wildly. "I told you we would get him."

Scarlet took her shoe off and flung it at the best man. The black pump went sailing off to the right not coming anywhere close to Deacon. But something else did hit him.

"Donya no," Scarlet managed to yell as the troll held Deacon up by the collar.

None of the other men noticed. They'd taken it upon themselves to hoist Juan up into the back of the van instead of letting him sit like an adult.

Thankfully Donya paused. But Scarlet was pretty sure Deacon had been seconds away from being eaten. Donya's mouth stayed open.

Scarlet ran up as fast as she could with only one shoe on and her bad foot exposed to asphalt. Deacon didn't scream. He looked stunned and really really high. His eyes were very red.

"Put him down. This is a tradition. They are not actually kidnapping Juan," Scarlet explained.

Donya released Deacon slowly. Then turned and walked to her expensive car without a word.

"Don't keep him out too late you hear!" Scarlet yelled. She considered how close that came. Donya must be at her limit. It was impressive that she hadn't devoured Juan's best man.

Scarlet thought that if she'd been in the same situation, with Juan gone and an easy way to restore herself dangling right in front of her—Scarlet would have taken it.

Scarlet retrieved her pump and then slid into the car. Donya's breathing rasped beside her.

They needed to do something about Donya's condition. Well, she needed to do something about it. The vision, the one of her, Donya, and the sword. The only thing that made sense to her with that in mind was transference. But how would she do it?

"Donya, do you know any transference spells?"

Donya did not answer at first. Scarlet waited, watching the night speed by, the dash sparkled resplendent with small gauges. The speedometer pushed far to the right. The car stayed quiet as it ran almost purring. It didn't feel that fast, but Scarlet guessed they traveled at over a hundred. They would be to their destination in no time.

"I do know one, but I have no power to do it," Donya finally said.

"That's fine, teach it to me."

Donya's narrow eyes did not leave the road. Scarlet began to feel stupid. She began to mentally prepare her explanation, that the sword would help her along, transference came naturally to them now because of the sword. It took her a moment to clear her throat and open her mouth. "Donya—"

"Repeat after me," Donya whispered, cutting Scarlet off.

CHAPTER 38

DONYA

They pulled over before they got to Mount Madonna. Teaching Scarlet trollish words went slowly. Thankfully Scarlet was quick to perfectly draw the runes in the sand of the beach.

Ariel watched with curiosity. The young spirit absorbed information like a sponge. She practiced the troll words of the spell too but could not yet make the many THR sounds common to the language. P's gave her a hard time, there were not many in troll, but this spell contained one and it must be recited exactly.

Scarlet held the sword. She began the spell "Throth trelbble nen. Perot, thren thorin."

Her pronunciation was perfect. But she needed to repeat it nine times and then draw the runes.

On the ninth time, Donya let out her breath. Scarlet drew the runes and fire poured from the sword. It spun around and around like a small funnel cloud and came toward Donya.

It did not burn but felt warm. It was a surprise when the pain in her side doubled and then tripled. Donya opened her mouth and screamed. Her eyes closed in agony. She fell into the sand and writhed around.

What had she done wrong?

Moments spent in true pain go on forever.

Donya got time to think of her grandmother and her warnings of tampering with spells. But Donya did not tamper with this spell, she'd used it many times in the few hundred years since her grandmother taught it to her. Although she had not used it in this way.

She had never transferred a part of herself before. And this wound was indeed a part of her.

She managed to control her body, opening her eyes. Scarlet clutched the sword. A crack formed and grew in its hilt.

Donya could not manage to bend and see her side. But she let her hand feel along the length of her torso. The injury felt smaller. There were no longer any side fissures. She brought in a breath through her gritted teeth.

The pain gave one more throb. One more deep stab and faded.

Donya lay in the sand. She let her eyes close again. She needed a moment.

It felt like a second had passed when a bag landed on her chest.

"I'm trying to be more prepared," Scarlet said.

Donya lifted a plastic Ziplock bag filled with roasted nuts—almonds, pecans, walnuts, and peanuts.

Donya unhinged her jaw and dumped the bag in. Her mouth once sandy felt instant relief. She sat up as she chewed, grinding the nuts into dust. The peanuts were oily and lubricated the mixture, the oil felt like a salve to her raw throat. Donya sensed a power in these seeds, one crisp and clear.

"Wow," Ariel said. Her wide eyes round with reverence.

"You really could have swallowed Deacon whole," Scarlet said, her skin gone a bit pale in the moonlight.

"Did you cast a spell upon my food?" Donya asked Scarlet, her throat no longer hurting.

"Not really, I pushed Ged into them, only a few. I haven't had much time lately, but I finally started carrying them in my purse, oh and I've been meaning to give you this."

Donya nodded as she stood and made her way back to the car, every advantage was needed. Scarlet dropped Hisa into her hand. Donya placed the stone in the car and made her apologies as they wound their way up the mountain roads.

Donya wanted a plan, but her mind drew a blank. In the end, the only thing that soothed her was knowing that the Sky God needed Nera. That he would not kill her as he had the human woman, because she was strong. He needed Nera. But for what Donya did not know. She even had the memory of a tengu seeking the Sky God out, it knew he wanted Nera, gave him information freely, but there was never any why. Could it be that even the Sky God did not know?

Donya began to think of every strength they possessed, every ally they could call on. The Kraken and Grazia, though they were far away, both enjoyed more strength and skill than her or Scarlet.

Ariel's strength grew every day, but she must be protected, the Kraken would not spare Donya if she involved her offspring and the worst were to happen. The reason Ariel stayed in the car was that she could not be sent away.

The water horse was a powerful creature summoned into being as a plaything and protector. He would be of great use if Donya could get the Sky God near the ocean. Before any of them knew of the threat it sang to block out the sky to safeguard Ariel and Scarlet.

And if Nera could help, she had her binding and the shielding borrowed from Scarlet. Donya hoped she'd mastered the use of that shield, that even now she kept herself safe from the full force of the Sky God with it.

Donya didn't want to think about what it would be like if Nera couldn't help. It hurt her worse than the pain of the fissure in her side ever had. Even when Scarlet transferred it.

The sword slept. She couldn't rely on it. What Scarlet managed did heal her but took their greatest weapon out of use. Was Donya worth that? She didn't know.

Then there was Scarlet. She knew of her powers now, but it seemed she always held back. Nera mentioned Scarlet was reluctant to use the cards Grazia left her. She'd stifled mastering her abilities. Tonight, Donya thought a few of those abilities would be a liability, her eyes could be easily damaged by the Sky God with their sensitivity. But that shield of hers. Donya would need her to use it. Use it like she had around that orange purse, in new interesting ways.

The paved road ended. The car rattled over the dirt and gravel on what was really a large path. She'd hit several potholes. The shining car now wheezed as she did when she took it. The man in a suit holding the keys never even knew what hit him. Yet he'd been lucky, for she did not consume him and his expensive woolen clothing.

Donya stopped the car under a great redwood tree. It was time. Nera would not be abandoned again by her, not now and not ever.

Donya hesitated, she didn't open the door. "I don't have a plan."

Scarlet rubbed her face with her hands.

"It will be a difficult night," Donya said.

"Duh, we are going up against a Sky God," Scarlet snapped.

"No, difficult because you need to wear this," Donya said as she prepared a strip of shadow in her hands. It would blindfold Scarlet. She could risk herself, but she could not risk the human.

"Wear it where?"

"Over your eyes," Donya said, leaning forward and tying it around Scarlet's head. "You cannot risk even a glimpse of that god as he is now. I'm surprised with your eyes you were not blinded like the other humans."

"It did hurt to look at him, but I always put a shield between us," She said, touching the blindfold.

"Can you see?" Donya asked. No one could see through this pitch-blackness she'd created.

"Yes," Scarlet said with a shrug.

"What!"

Ariel giggled loudly as she climbed on Scarlet's shoulder and played at putting the tail of the shadow over her eyes.

Scarlet waited for Ariel's giggles to subside. "I told you I can see through things. I can see through this, but everything is much darker. I can't see through it if I blink though. It's only when I stare."

"Don't stare, you need protection."

"Eeek-a-boo" Ariel said merrily.

"You have a job too. You are to leave, go back to Sebastian, and wait," Donya said as sternly as she could.

Ariel bit her lip and shook her head.

"You can do it, Ariel, we will come to you," Scarlet's voice came out higher than usual and soothing.

"No."

Donya let out a breath through her nose, hopefully the Kraken would not be cross if they tried their best. "Then stay with Scarlet, move her and her shields. You must do this if you will not do as told." Yet if the worst happened, the Kraken would kill Donya slowly if the Sky God did not do it first. And she would deserve it.

"He's coming," Scarlet said.

"I told you not to stare," Donya said. Scarlet's blindfolded eyes were more powerful than her own senses. She couldn't feel the god yet. But he didn't need to know that.

They got out of the car, Scarlet raised a shield around them.

The night air sparkled with gold. Donya feared the lightning strike she expected but it did not come. Instead, the iridescent and incandescent great bird landed before them.

"You are late," he said as he transformed back into a man.

CHAPTER 39

SCARLET

The blindfold Donya crafted for her was not perfect, but Scarlet felt grateful for its presence. She blinked regularly to keep from seeing through it, but in those moments when her eyes wanted to see, when they started to activate, if she kept them open and fixed, or closed and fixed—they burned. She didn't even peek at the Sky God from the corner of her eye, instead tracking the luminous haze emanating from his body. And she could feel his warmth through the shield. It continued to be pleasant right now, but she felt he could change that. Go from a pleasant spring day to the burning heat of a desert in summer.

"Give her back," Donya roared to Scarlet's left.

Scarlet could feel it when Donya rolled through her shield. She wasn't giving the Sky God any time. Scarlet heard the gentle strange rasp of shadow moving.

She wished she could see right now.

No sound came from the god, Scarlet let her eyes see through the darkness, to the spot where she thought Donya was.

She could see Donya, nothing hurt, the Sky God stood enveloped by shadow, but he did not seem to fight it.

"Donya," Scarlet yelled. "Donya, maybe he will give her back. He isn't moving."

"Give her to me this instant."

Scarlet blinked her eyes obscuring her x-ray vision as Donya stopped her attack.

They both waited for the answer. Scarlet feared she was wrong. She raised a hand pushing and shaping a shield out in front of where Donya had been. It wasn't all-inclusive like hers. Only a wall, built to slow a frontal attack.

"I cannot give her, you must win her," he said.

He sounded different to Scarlet, his voice boomed in her bones. He was stronger, sharper, more of what he should have been. This would not be good for them.

Ariel moved up onto Scarlet's head, her tentacles wrapping into Scarlet's hair. Scarlet felt a gentle tug to the right.

Scarlet let her eyes refocus through the shadow, she kept them on the ground near Donya. Donya trudged up the mountain, her eyes to the sky.

Gods were not known to be fair, they didn't seem to care to pay their debts like spirits did. This game didn't seem right. Although in all her reading gods did like games. There was probably a trick involved. She hoped it wasn't a riddle. Scarlet hated riddles.

Donya stopped in a clearing filled with brush, grasses, and low shrubs. Scarlet could feel heat on the left side of her body. The Sky God must hover in that direction. She hated being cut off from the full potential of her eyesight. When Donya had cast that spell on her to give her night vision she gave Scarlet a gift, one greater than she knew. Scarlet hadn't shunned her new abilities like she once did her shield and fire natures. But she failed to practice enough with them. If she had maybe this whole situation could have been avoided. Donya said one day the spell she cast on Scarlet's eyes would fade, but until that time Scarlet realized she needed to master everything her eyes could do for her.

"Count every blade of grass in this clearing," the Sky God boomed. "You have an hour."

Scarlet could hear the hint of mirth in his voice. A troll would never be able to do this. He wandered in their dream, he probably knew about their bond, and magic types, as many could discern such things. But Scarlet's eyes and what Donya did to them. He could only know that if Nera told him. And Nera didn't explain well even when she wanted to.

Scarlet felt the warmth fade upwards.

"Can I take the blindfold off now?" Scarlet asked.

"Yes," Donya said.

Scarlet pulled the blindfold off and blinked. Her dark vision made the clearing as vivid and sharp as if seen under the noon sun. She hadn't tried counting anything this big. But she let her eyes do the work of counting samples in the lab pretty regularly. She simply needed to un-focus her eyes over the area.

Donya whispered to the stone from Japan, Scarlet couldn't make out the words. But her body partially obscured the grasses under her.

"Hey Donya, could you move outside the clearing?" Scarlet asked.

Donya didn't look up at her, clearly engrossed in her conversation, but she walked away. Scarlet scrambled up a stony outcropping for a fuller view. She stretched her arms, she did love to catalog a sample. Then she unfocused her eyes and started counting.

It took under ten minutes.

"Grass is 866,272, and if he's counting the other grass-like plants, it's up to 1,002,089. A few California asters are growing here and in that boggy section there are irises. I hope he meant the green plants because there's a lot of dry dead plants this time of year."

Donya turned her head slowly squinting up at Scarlet.

"You're right, I'll double-check," Scarlet said then started counting again. It was easiest for her to break the meadow up into subsamples—scanning areas, she didn't need to count each individual blade. Just relax and let the number come to her. She was the reason her project stayed caught up on zooplankton samples and made headway on a backlog of phytoplankton samples. And now other projects asked her to count mysids and larval fish.

Scarlet slowed her counting, as she always did to QC, another ten minutes passed.

"Yep, I stick by my numbers."

"The rocks are all very impressed, they are cheering for you," Donya said.

Ariel clapped her hands on top of Scarlet's head.

"Put your mask back on. I will signal the Sky God, the faster we get this over with the better."

Scarlet couldn't agree more. The long nights wore on her. And the adrenaline rush of earlier faded away leaving her legs shaky underneath the folds of her dress.

Scarlet managed to tie the slippery shadow on even with one of Ariel's tentacles in the way. Shadow magic always felt wet to her, she whipped her hands on her jeans. Ariel went back to gripping her head. Everything remained dark and shadowed for a few moments. Scarlet focused her eyes on the ground waiting to be able to see. When her eyes adjusted, she could see Donya watching the sky, waiting.

In the moments she wasn't active she could take time to worry, to doubt. "Ariel, how are your eyes feeling?" Scarlet asked in a whisper.

"Dry. I'll wet," Ariel said back loudly in Scarlet's ear.

Then water splashed on Scarlet's head. It was a warm night, so it felt good, but Scarlet still gasped and blinked.

The heat from the Sky God landing took Scarlet by surprise and she blinked again into the darkness.

"You wanted blades of grass, specifically?" Donya asked.

Scarlet couldn't be sure but perhaps the Sky God nodded. It killed her not to see. Fear was a normal part of these dealings, but the blindness made her feel more vulnerable than ever before.

"Eight hundred sixty-six thousand two hundred seventy-two," Donya said.

"What's happening?" Scarlet asked Ariel not being able to stand it.

"Magic numbers," Ariel answered.

Scarlet had no idea what that meant. Ariel still possessed very limited language, that was probably the best explanation she could come up with.

"You are correct, follow me."

"We played your game, let Nera go," Donya demanded.

"Two more tasks and then she will leave, free of me forever."

Scarlet kept her eyes on the ground, they walked back down the mountain without more conversation. Scarlet recognized the path to the car. Donya stopped at it, and they got in. Ariel leapt from Scarlet's head to the dash. Scarlet reached up to take off the shadow.

"Don't," Donya commanded.

Scarlet let her hand drop. She took a moment to breathe and steady herself. This happened before. Starting strong then fading. If anything went wrong, she might fall apart. It had been a year and a half since the last time she shut down in the middle of a dire situation, right after their encounter with the Wolf Kings in Rome. The time since then had been filled with studying and trying her best to accept herself and her situation. She felt proud of herself for how she handled their predicament in Japan after Donya turned to stone.

Through the shadow the night flew past, dim, but not as dim as her vision once was. The trees obscured the sky, but every once in a while, she caught a glimpse of what looked like a bright rainbow.

They came to the coastal highway and once again raced along the ocean. The red car rattled loud and rough. Scarlet glimpsed the clock, almost midnight; she would be getting her hair and makeup done in twelve hours. A shiver ran up her spine, she would be getting her hair done, if they managed to survive and remain unharmed. If her eyes got burned out, the wedding would be off, and she would never see Juan's smile again.

Scarlet pushed the dark thoughts out of her mind. If they stuck together, they would win.

CHAPTER 40

DONYA

Donya leaned over running her hands through the cool grains of sand again. Scarlet stood before her staring out at the great dark Pacific Ocean. She would see Ariel before anyone else, even before the Sky God. Scarlet's eyes were more powerful than his. Donya remained unsure of this before.

The second task was to bring water from the deepest part of the ocean. It needed to arrive before dawn. Impossible for Donya now with her broken sword, except Ariel could move herself instantly large distances through the ocean. She'd told them in her childish way she'd gone to Alaska with Nera on Monday. Scarlet had pointed the little Kraken in the direction of the Mariana Trench and off she went.

The Hippocampus swam back and forth through the bay, singing a strange song. Scarlet kept her arms crossed over her. All of her muscles tensed up. At first, the Sky God circled them, but now he seemed to have flown off to the mountain.

They were being lured into a trap. Trolls loved to set traps. Donya once considered herself an expert in them. But she'd been outmaneuvered too many times now. One of those times was by Nera. But that trap never meant to harm her. Whose trap did she stand in now? Donya thought it to be the Sky God's. But he didn't know all of their strengths and weaknesses. No, this trap felt intimate.

Last time Nera set a trap for her she managed to escape it, her rage fueling just enough strength to push Nera away right before they were all transported to another realm. Donya wondered what she would do to mess it up this time. If she indeed read the signs correctly.

"There she is!" Scarlet called excitedly.

Donya noted the position of the moon. Not even two hours had lapsed. They still retained much of the night, which they needed. Krakens usually hunted in one place, but this young one was a terrifying beast. Scarlet explained earlier that the Mariana Trench rested in the Pacific but across it. And from Donya's travels, she'd seen how large the Pacific was. The largest ocean on the planet.

Donya approached Scarlet. "How far out?"

"It's hard for me to tell distance, Sebastian is on its way to her, and she is popping towards it now. I'm sure she's exhausted."

"You are worn as well."

Scarlet broke her stare to eye Donya. "Pot calling the kettle black."

Donya did not understand the riddle. She waited silent for a moment. She answered Scarlet's questions, as payment for a freely given gift. But she found herself relying on the human as much as the human relied on her. "I have a question?"

"Go on, we have a few minutes till they both arrive," Scarlet said. She squinted back at the mountain. She brought her hand up to shield her eyes.

Donya turned, very distantly a speck of light moved too quickly. Damn. "Do you think we are in a trap right now?"

"Probably right, gods were known for tricks. We need to be ready for it to spring."

"No not his trap. Nera set up a ruse like this before. Where she used Heldrig, making him think he controlled the situation, but she set it up for us three to go to the Kraken. I ruined it. These last challenges have been too easy. Is it her again?"

"Shit, shit yes. She knows about my eyes, and she knows more about Ariel than even I do at this point. What do you think she will have set up for the third challenge?"

"I don't know but I bet it will be for me."

"Take this. It's asleep but maybe if you desperately need it the sword will wake up." Scarlet held out their broken sword.

Donya shook her head. "Keep it, should I fail, you can use it to reinforce your shield. If the Sky God comes for revenge."

"Gods do love their revenge."

Donya remembered his words in the dreamscape. He wanted his life back, but he needed revenge on those who trapped him.

Donya could see their forms from the memories she'd acquired. Like him, they retained animal features.

Sebastian surfed a wave up onto the beach beating its powerful tail and pawing. Ariel rode on its back, holding tight to the short-clipped mane, the hippocampus held still so Scarlet could reach up and collect Ariel. She needed to hop slightly. Donya realized how big Sebastian stood. If it could stand on land Donya would barely come up to its belly and Scarlet wouldn't quite reach its shoulder.

Scarlet cradled Ariel in her arms and took the clay bottle from her. Scarlet cooed and whispered quiet encouragement. "You should go to sleep now. Tomorrow is a big day. I'm sure we won't need you for anything else tonight."

Ariel shook her head.

"I could put you back on Sebastian's back, he knows where the wedding is, he'll take you."

Ariel shook her head again. Then she grabbed the scrap of shadow that Scarlet held over her shoulder and used her suction cups to climb up Scarlet's blouse.

Donya turned to the night sky. The Sky God circled overhead, preparing to dive to earth.

Scarlet tied the knot on the shadow. It remained slightly loose, Donya wanted to let her know but then the booming of the Sky God came from behind her.

"Again, you surprise me," he said.

Donya turned, he glowed, golden and every other color. His form continued to change. He stood with an easy grace, golden skin, and green eyes. Only the frame of the body hinted at its once less-than-godly existence. Still not that much taller than Scarlet.

"It is done, give us the final task."

"Short on time, are we?" The god smiled.

"Always," Donya said. She would complete this challenge. Whatever it was that Nera had set up for her. This god may be strong, but Nera was intelligent and sly. Donya hoped it would be easy and tailored to her skill set.

"Beat me to the top of the mountain, Troll, and you can have the nymph back." The Sky God took a moment to transform. His feathers sent rainbows dancing across the night water.

Donya couldn't win. Trolls were not fast.

"Sebastian grab him!" Scarlet yelled. She threw herself to the ground and covered Ariel with her upper body.

The night air rolled with heat, and Donya swore that god tried to cook them. But she understood what Scarlet instantly gleaned. He had not said unaided.

Donya sent herself into a tumble. Trolls could roll quite well. She plowed through the sand. Over the sound of the ocean waves a struggle could be heard, wings beating against water and the screams of an angry bird rang in the warm air.

Faster, she must move faster.

Ariel couldn't help Donya in her exhausted state. Damn, she could have won instantly with a few pops to the top of the mountain.

What if this wasn't a trap by Nera? What if the Sky God played them? She could have become overconfident. A misplaced hunch now could lose Nera's freedom and who knows what else. The Sky God hadn't noticed Scarlet much before, but he would now.

Water sprayed in every direction as she plunged through the marsh. She leapt out of the roll and ran, her legs heavy and sticking in the mud. She needed to make sure he didn't follow yet, indeed behind her a glow hung like an angry sunrise on the beach. Perfect. She dragged to a stop, carved her rune, and spoke her words. The earth began to open to let her in, but she did not wait, diving into the mud and grit.

The spell allowed her to move through the earth, she clawed and pulled faster and faster.

She needn't follow the lines of the road, making a straight path for herself up the mountain.

Pulling close to the surface she felt heat baking the ground. He flew free and above her. No no. It couldn't end like this.

Donya pulled herself out. Her eyes landed on the Sky God immediately. He worked hard too.

Sebastian had damaged the god. She would have never thought to go for a wing. Clever horse. The Sky God flapped but one wing lacked a section of feathers.

That gave her an idea.

She grabbed the nearest boulder. "I need your help, this might hurt," she warned.

She hurled the boulder with all her strength. It went high, but thankfully she got the arch right. The Sky God ignorantly believed no attacks would come at all let alone from above. The boulder hit him square in the good wing.

He crashed into the trees. The same strategy would probably not work again. She dove back into the soil and moved her arms, swimming through the substrate. Boulders that might not have once awoken moved now clearing a path for her, afraid of being used as ammunition.

Donya kept her senses wide open, she could feel the spot on the ground where the Sky God lay. It was a hot angry patch of land. In the back of her mind, she could feel Scarlet coming up the mountain along the road. She must have gotten in the car. Donya wished she would have stayed by the ocean, but also felt glad for the assistance.

The Sky God could lash out at any moment. Would Scarlet's shield hold up long against a god? Donya didn't think so.

Nera, if she got to Nera they could all go free. She'd climbed over halfway up the mountain. Tree roots helped to push her along. Perhaps they held a grudge at the death of all their birds. Trees were vindictive. She was happy for all the help she could get.

Then like a drink of water in the desert, Donya sensed Nera ahead.

The spot where the Sky God lay went cold. Damn, he persisted, up again.

Donya knew she couldn't make it. It was impossible to win, she'd been in the god's talons when he flew, one beat of his wings could propel him faster than she could ever hope to move. What a trap, what a trick. He would mock her when she emerged then burn her and Nera to cinders. Donya smothered a sob. And what would happen to Scarlet and Ariel? She wanted to scream, turn around and scream at them to flee. But she could not stop her forward motion toward Nera.

One minute her hand pulled her through the earth, the next, she held the sword. She could not believe Scarlet managed to awaken it with all the damage to its hilt. What was the human doing? Donya ground her teeth and pulled faster, bolstered by the sword in her hand.

She was almost there. The direct path up under the dirt had been fast. Now she could feel the stones that almost touched the sky. It was a slight movement to change the angle of her climb. She would breach the surface in a moment.

The surface of the earth crumbled away from her. The air bit cold and the sky blazed gold. Nera sat in front of her, but Donya's eyes were dazzled by the light. Had she lost?

CHAPTER 41

SCARLET

They gave it everything they had. Even the car. Scarlet drove it hard up a narrow gravel path surely meant for off-road vehicles. The car billowed steam from under the hood when she left it, but she was the one struggling. Putting up one shield in mid-air after another. The Sky God knocked against them, and they would break apart, but this slowed him.

The sword woke up for her. And even though it was the farthest she'd ever sent a shield using the sword helped it work. But she needed to do it over and over again. Aiming ahead of the flying god. Her eyes burned under the shadow. But she needed to keep the god at the bottom of her vision, or she couldn't aim properly. He looked like the most beautiful bird she'd ever seen. Her eyes picked up colors she held no name for from his feathers.

The moment Donya popped out of the earth and made her way to Nera Scarlet let go.

306

She fell back on her butt panting and cursing.

Ariel clung to her still, eyes wide in a pale moon-white face.

"I think we won," Scarlet said.

But she needed to get closer to find out. She stood slowly and limped forward. It was easy to pick out a path even in the dark for her. A game trail ran narrow but smooth. If she couldn't see in the dark, she wouldn't have ever been brave enough to take it. The night waited eerily quiet, not even a cricket chirped.

Scarlet was not close, but the Sky God's voice carried through the air. She kept her eyes off of him peering through the trees at Donya and Nera.

"It was a good game, I am done with you leave now," he boomed.

"You bastard, you did not give her back as she was before," Donya said.

"She will heal, unlike a mortal priestess," he said.

"Come my rock, we should be off the mountain," Nera said standing.

It took Scarlet a moment to see what angered Donya. Nera's body appeared unharmed. Her one real eye was still there, although the other socket lay empty. She had not been burned. Her remaining eye did appear green. That verdant green that the Sky God seeped from his body and glowed in his eyes.

"Don't forget your promise," the god said.

"No one will know your true name from my lips," Nera said, her back to him.

Scarlet found she couldn't move forward any longer. It was strange. Her feet refused to take another step, but not from exhaustion. No, they were stuck. She looked up.

The god stood before her in his more human form, their eyes locked.

The world turned a blinding white and for a moment she smelled burning hair. "I don't like losing, but I will be gratuitous, for you helped bring me to myself." Scarlet heard over the pain searing her eyes.

She could move again suddenly and fell to her knees.

Rough hands undid the shadow from behind her head. "Scarlet you must open your eyes," Donya said.

Scarlet blinked and her eyes felt cold, not hot. The pain receded but still her eyes throbbed like she'd been out in the sun at the beach all day.

"Your eyes appear uninjured," Donya said. "What can you see?"

Scarlet blinked and blinked, the fuzzy world came into view. The night still too bright and filled with color. Like a daytime scene.

"I can see the same as I have since Rome," Scarlet said, studying Nera's face. Her eye was indeed a vivid green all of it from the iris to the pupil. "What about you Nera?"

"I can see nothing, but this is not unusual for me."

"He did that because of your last-minute interference. I would have lost without your help," Donya said.

"Did what? I can see fine," Scarlet said.

"Follow me," Donya said.

They ambled and shuffled back to the car. Scarlet felt shocked that the ordeal seemed over. She felt like laughing and crying all at the same time. Her wedding, she would make it, Scarlet had stopped believing they would get away in time. And they were all alive if not well.

Donya ripped the side mirror off the passenger door. It cleaved from the door with a shrill snap. She handed the mirror to Scarlet.

Scarlet's eyes were different. Colors remained strange in the dark for her. But her irises appeared to be green and gold now. And her eyelashes were gone.

Scarlet let out a hysterical giggle. "I paid good money for those eyelashes."

"I will bring your face back to normal in the morning, I cannot now," Nera said, sounding very tired.

It wasn't a far ride from the mountain to Scarlet's apartment, but Scarlet fell asleep. She woke up groggy still holding the side mirror in her hand. The sword rested at her feet. The crack appeared as severe as it first had, but the sword shone faintly, the colors flashing off the facets flickered in purples and violet.

"Do you two want to come in?" Scarlet asked as she opened her door. Donya shook her head, but Scarlet could see once again the troll wore a strange look on her face. "What?"

Donya would not meet her eyes. "Can you see the spell on this for me?" Donya produced a jar from inside the glove compartment, it was cracked, and a dark sticky ooze clung inside but did not drip.

Scarlet took a sharp inhale but reached for the jar.

"No, do not touch it," Nera said smiling. "Thank you, I should not doubt you ever again," Nera patted Donya's arm as she took the jar and poured out the contents inside the center console.

Scarlet attempted to see the spell Donya requested. A sliding slug-like thing undulated through the ooze, it moved around an eyeball not on or in it. It was a dark manifestation, Scarlet could almost see the contempt it emanated. Scarlet could also see Nera's other eye. It was clearly Nera's with the brilliant violet coloring. Scarlet waited for it to roll away from the spell and then smashed down hard with her fiery shield on the slug.

"Um, it moved like a slug, but it's gone now."

"Father and his curses," Nera said, picking up the eye. She splashed it with water and popped it in her empty socket. She blinked twice and the only abnormality around that eye was the tiny white scars on her upper and lower eyelid. "Much better." Nera smiled.

Scarlet leaned back in and picked up Ariel who slept in the back seat. Her tentacles curled around Scarlet's arm, but her eyes didn't flicker.

"Good night," Scarlet said.

Nera turned, still smiling. "I will come by after dawn."

"Great, see you in a few hours then," Scarlet responded.

She heard the car pull out of the parking lot before she even opened the door. Scarlet's phone said it was just past four am.

The apartment sat quiet. Too quiet. Juan wasn't snoring.

"Babe," Scarlet called softly. She didn't want to wake the neighbors. Placing Ariel in the fish tank she turned to the bedroom.

It was empty.

Scarlet whipped out her phone and dialed Juan. It rang two times.

"Haha, you can't have him back, we are at the strip club."

Scarlet took a deep breath. "Deacon, I swear I will let my friend kill you if you don't have him back within an hour." They couldn't be at a strip club. There were none around and the closest one would have been closed at two anyway. She thought.

"Okay, okay, we'll call a cab. This is his last night as a free man you could have let him have the whole night."

"No." Scarlet hung up the phone. She wanted to be angrier, but she felt numb. And cold. She smelled like the ocean. Maybe a hot bath would bring her back to normal.

She sat on the couch, the blue-white light from the fish tank the only light in the room. She watched the patterns on the walls the bubbles made and thought about getting up.

❧❧

Scarlet enjoyed the most pleasant dream. A mountain of pasta sat heaped in front of her. The aroma of good cheese wafted around in the air. The pasta had that buttery yellow color of handmade noodles in Italy. Scarlet brought a fork full to her mouth when she felt a tapping on her nose.

It was a gentle tapping.

Scarlet opened her eyes.

Ariel perched in her lap. Her hand outstretched, patting Scarlet's nose and cheeks. Nera stood next to her. Nera looked refreshed, she still had one green eye and one purple.

Sunlight streamed through the window and Scarlet could see the lingering trappings of a spell in the air.

Juan poked his head out from the kitchen. "We would have let you sleep longer, but your hair and makeup starts in an hour," he said, sounding too chipper.

"What did you guys do?" Scarlet asked, her eyes lingering on Nera.

"Eyelashes!" Ariel squealed, popping over to the kitchen table where a corndog waited.

"Water can heal, and conceal," Nera said. "Ariel almost mastered the spell with only witnessing." Nera held up a small bottle. "Drink this, it is from the Kraken."

Scarlet took the bottle but didn't open it.

Nera wandered away from Scarlet to sit at the table with Ariel.

Scarlet continued to blink when Juan placed a steaming mug of hot chocolate in her unoccupied hand. "I put a shot of espresso in it." He stopped and studied her closely. "Oh, good job Ariel, they look almost like the ones she had put on."

"What?" Scarlet shot up and walked quickly to the bathroom. Her hot chocolate sloshed but did not spill.

She checked her face in the mirror. Her irises still appeared green and gold, but she could see a spell over them. And her eyelashes were grown back, there was no spell, they were real, but the wrong color. Her real eyelashes grew in light brown, and she'd gotten the same color for the extensions, but these lashes seemed almost black.

She couldn't handle this right now. Tears started to flow.

Juan walked up behind her. "It's okay. It has been a rough week. Tell me what you want me to do. Call off the wedding? We can still do that."

"Shh, no I just need a shower then I'll be fine. My eyes look brown to you?" Scarlet sniveled. She didn't want to hurt Ariel's feelings. And honestly, the lashes were beautiful in that overdramatic sort of way. Also, as Scarlet observed her face more closely she thought her skin seemed extremely smooth, even a few of her darker freckles were faded. She wondered if that happened because of the heat treatment from the god last night or Nera's spells in her sleep this morning. Either way, she did appreciate it. "Find my mascara will you." Maybe Fizzy wouldn't notice the different hue of her lashes with a coating of brown over them.

"Yep, your eyes are brown, maybe extra sparkly, but otherwise normal."

She looked at Juan over her shoulder. He suffered dark circles under his eyes but was otherwise untouched. Scarlet took a big sip of her warm drink. The water in the bottle she held sloshed slowly, it reminded her of the magical water in the Kraken's grotto. She opened the bottle and drank deeply. Instantly she felt better, her head clear and her body no longer stiff from sleeping on the couch. She held up the bottle, it had a spell in the water, a happy springy little spell with a gold sheen.

"Did you go to a strip club last night?" Scarlet didn't know why she asked, but that was where her mind went.

"No, but the guys did get a stripper for Deacon's hotel room. It wasn't my thing. I think Deacon paid extra for alone time after I left."

Scarlet felt a smile tugging at her lips. Juan always knew how to make her smile.

"You do look beautiful, and not even tired anymore," Juan said.

Scarlet glanced in the mirror again. She did. Nera or the water must have done something to her face, she ran her fingers over her cheekbone, and it felt as smooth as it did before she hit puberty and pimples attacked.

Juan squeezed Scarlet's hand as he leaned down to start searching the bathroom drawers for her mascara. Scarlet pulled off her salty dress. Juan eyed her, bouncing his eyebrows. "You know it's good luck to have sex before the wedding."

"No, it's not, you're not even supposed to see me," Scarlet said, throwing her bra on his head. He needed a sip of the Kraken's water, he was obviously delirious from exhaustion.

"Worth a shot," Juan said with a laugh, placing her mascara on the sink.

CHAPTER 42

DONYA

Nera rested on the white hotel bed, occasionally her eyes would flutter. Tonight, Donya would feast on nuts then they would find a stream and she would work her grandmother's healing spell on both of them. Only the pale shears were pulled over the window, so the ocean waves could be seen outside. They rolled and glittered in the early afternoon sunlight. The wedding would be starting at three. Donya could sense Scarlet above her in a room to the right.

Donya had brought Hisa in from the now-ruined car; she requested to be tossed on the beach after she witnessed the wedding. Hisa was not upset about being moved from her homeland, on the contrary, she seemed excited to see the sunset from the beach instead of it rising.

Through everything, the wedding gift she bought for Scarlet remained in her luggage. The packaging no longer appeared pristine, but the silk of the kimono was unspoiled, Donya checked slowly and methodically.

Nera used this room for almost a week. Her clothes lay strewn about the floor and bed. Donya needed to get ready herself. Perhaps one of Nera's shirts could be worn like a dress on her. She began picking up clothing. Most of it was very colorful, pastel peaches, pinks, and violets. Donya hung up the dresses in the small closet. Then she pulled the kimono out of the bag she had bought at the last minute. She wondered if she should wear it tonight, perhaps not the full ensemble, just the kimono with one of Nera's thick belts. And Nera could wear the golden cord.

Nera opened her mismatched eyes and watched Donya move. "You do love clothing, why is that?" She asked.

Donya turned; Nera hadn't moved. She lay on her side under the duvet. Donya came closer to the bed; so she could watch the play of emotions on Nera's face as they spoke.

"I am like the Kraken. I like beautiful things." She let her hand reach out. Nera wore the silver circlet still; she never removed it lately.

"What about when I am old, will you still love me then, when I am saggy?"

Donya tried to imagine Nera saggy, but she could not. "No troll has ever left their mate, even when changed to stone the other will stay. We do not move on."

"Good," Nera said then popped up. She skipped around the room picking up shoes, then tossing them aside.

"Tell me what you want to wear, and I will bring it to you," Donya offered. Nera had fully extended herself. Going to the god, giving him back his name, then using the name and her binding magic to tightly knit the god to his new body.

"I am not blind or bedbound."

Donya held no response.

"I'll write it for you," Nera said.

Donya turned to find Nera nude except for black kitten heel pumps. Donya felt her face warm and her mouth water. It was strange how close the physical feelings of desire emulated the feelings of hunger. After the celebration, she would take her time with Nera in this very room.

Nera didn't dress but instead braided her hair around the crown of her head twisting the end under the back of the circlet. Donya found her mind going blank. She let out a low growl.

Nera giggled. "You are not paying attention to what I say."

Donya snapped out of it but couldn't form a word, she grunted.

"I'll write his name, the Sky God. I said I would never say it, but I can write it. It will be important."

"We are not through with him?"

"Yes, but he is ambitious. I bound his broken parts. Yet his true body still exists, he will want it."

"What you did was no easy feat," Donya said. "He is a fast god. I wonder how long it will take for him to find his body."

Nera wiggled into a black lace dress with tulle around the fringe. Donya recognized the lace. It was Prada. Her favorite.

"He will need air from the highest mountain, water from the deepest sea, the hottest fire, and the oldest rock, then a finding spell that can search all of the realms," Nera said, applying a lotion that smelled of bergamot to her hands.

"We gave him the water, Nera did you design the game or him?" Donya needed to know.

"Most of the gods that betrayed him are long dead. He will reunite with his body and find the living gods he wants dead but after this perhaps he will not be satisfied. Men are hard to satisfy."

"Nera," Donya said, bringing the cord from her kimono to her and looping it around her neck. It made a beautiful ornament.

"I helped him decide." She smiled at Donya.

Donya got the feeling the task meant for her was supposed to be hard, and she felt glad of it, now Nera would know the lengths she would go to for her. Donya, thinking of the god, gingerly picked up her cracked sword. She would wear it along her spine today and tonight so it could be a part of the festivities. She worried over how she would fix the crack but decided to save that worry for a later time. "Where were his lands?"

"A desert. He despaired at how the humans live there now and the god they worship. Will we go to your mountain after the wedding?"

Donya was pulled up short. "My mountain?"

"Yes, I headed in that direction, the long way."

Donya concentrated on her outfit, putting on the kimono and belting it but she didn't like the ensemble. Instead, she pulled out the purple sash meant for under the obi and tied it around the middle with a water knot at the side. Her black leather boots completed it although they barely showed under the kimono. One nice thing about real leather boots was they cleaned up easily. Donya had knocked all the dirt and mud off of these earlier and now she scrubbed at them with a towel. Not good for the towel but the boots became soft and almost new. She focused on this while she tried to process the news.

"But I was not at my mountain, I searched for you," Donya finally said.

"Foolish troll. I told you I wanted to travel. I got that out of the way. And ran from the feeling of being chased."

Donya felt cold. She chased away her happiness.

Nera put a hand on her shoulder. "Chased by that god, not you."

The feelings of desire and embarrassment are also closely related. Donya felt her cheeks grow warm again. She chose to change the subject. They could discuss their plans later. "I must go to the upper lobby now if I want to leave this room before sunset. The walkways are only partially shaded."

Nera giggled at her gruff answer.

⊷⊶

Donya was drained but Nera seemed to come more alive as more guests arrived. Ariel as well. Donya watched them and their antics with Hisa by her side on the railing. Ariel had herded dolphins and whales into the bay. The ceremony would be outside on a deck and the sunlight covered it bright and warm as Sebastian sang an old weather charm for calm seas and sky. Nera kept strolling to the shore working a quiet casting on the bubbling foam.

The dolphins and whales spouted their breath into the sunlight and the gathering guests enjoyed quite the entertaining spectacle while they waited for the ceremony to begin. Donya could see Juan waiting at the altar now. There wouldn't be that much more time. She wished Nera would make her way back to the hotel. Or she might miss it.

A single cello began the wedding march and Donya felt Nera drape her arms around her. She wore dark sunglasses to hide her mismatched eyes. She did not want to cast a small spell on them, as it would slow the healing of the green-tinted eye.

"Here she comes," Nera said.

Donya tried to see with her dim vision, but Scarlet stood in the sunlight in a bright white dress. Donya could not hold her eyes on it for all the glare. Then she couldn't see because a slippery sea monster roosted on her head.

"Now little one," Nera said.

Donya could smell the magic and the salt in the air. The sun still shone but a slight haze rose. In that haze, a rainbow sparkled. Scarlet continued to walk the aisle.

"Like movie," Ariel said as Donya lifted her off of her head.

Scarlet was escorted by a human with a white beard.

"Not Triton," Ariel said, pointing at the man.

Nera shook her head. "There's no sea king here. You will be the queen someday."

Donya felt lost but she watched intently. The humans said their vows in front of a holy person who sang a warbling hymn for them.

"The best part is coming," Nera whispered as Scarlet and Juan sealed their vows with words.

"And now you may kiss the bride," called the holy one.

Donya always did like an action to seal a vow. She clapped her hands the same as the humans in the seats below, just as the bay exploded with leaping dolphins, breaching whales, and jumping fish.

CHAPTER 43

SCARLET

"You may now kiss the bride."

Scarlet leaned forward with tears in her eyes and a smile on her face. Juan kissed her and she could hear others clapping. For the briefest moment, she felt a tingling and knew magic lighted on their lips. The vow of marriage was real. She could feel the bond form. Not unlike when she had forged the sword with Donya.

When she pulled away Juan met her eyes, and they turned to the audience with big smiles.

But their guests did not notice them, instead marveling at the bay, where pilot whales beached, seagulls dove, pelicans flew past in their great V formations, and dolphins rode the waves. The sea seethed and roiled with activity. And the rainbow she saw as her wedding march started presided over it all.

Ariel did love that wedding scene at the end of *The Little Mermaid.*

Scarlet laughed as Juan led her closer to the railing. He accepted her for all her weirdness. And right now, he looked really happy. And she was too.

The next few minutes were a blur of congratulations and kind wishes while both sides of the immediate family filed down to the beach for a round of photography. The dolphins continued to jump and the whales to spout. Scarlet overheard one of her coworker guests mention a bait ball. Their logic made perfect sense, although the number of marine mammals was still too high for that.

The waves grew large and made a beautiful backdrop for the photos. Ariel made Scarlet smile and laugh by jumping around in the waves and riding a dolphin. The photographer eagerly snapped up the stupendous shots. Scarlet wondered if the camera would pick up anything on the dolphin's back but doubted it. They cut the photo-shoot short, opting to head back out at golden hour before the cake was cut.

Juan and Scarlet still missed cocktail hour but managed to get into the ballroom on time. Speeches went a bit long-winded but stayed well-intended, their neighbor Trun's speech even came across as funny. Exhaustion never took its toll, instead Scarlet felt alert and lively. Juan seemed to feel the same as her. At a bathroom break, Scarlet leaned over to the running water in the sink and said a quiet thank you to the Kraken. Her potion kept them both out of the fog of fatigue, allowing them to be present and happy at their wedding.

Once the sun set Scarlet fully expected to see Donya. Nera sat quietly at a table with Ariel on her lap. Ariel stayed corporal and maintained her human glamour with a cute pink dress and pigtails in her hair.

They cut the cake, and it was time for the garter toss when Scarlet finally saw Donya loitering against a wall. She looked haggard still. Not as bad as when she was injured but worn out. Scarlet's distraction with Donya made her surprised to see Juan dancing his way toward her. She'd begged him to take dance lessons with her, but he'd refused this one thing, saying he would be too embarrassed. She wondered if the potion did more than give them energy. As Juan's dance right now was what she would have thought he found humiliating. He mixed disco moves, cowboy with rope, and what she thought might be the robot. Then he did a little run and slid up to her on his knees, disappearing under the fluff of her dress to pull off her garter. She felt him nip her upper thigh and laughed.

His friends and groomsmen all jumped up and down and cheered loudly. She saw one of the kids in the crowd hide his face in his hands. Poor Vivian, his mother, would have to answer some questions from him later. And Scarlet's young niece yelled loudly, "what is he even doing?" Scarlet's sister would have explaining to do as well.

Nera's mouth gaped open in surprise, a delicate hand coming up to her lip, which Scarlet found strange, the nymph was not bashful.

Then Scarlet heard whispering from under her skirt.

"This is a kind of game. You gotta go back, it's funny, don't worry."

"No biting, rules," Ariel was loud and insistent. "Flower time, no biting."

No biting was one of the very first things Scarlet ever taught Ariel. Scarlet thanked her lucky stars they were in the middle of the dance floor away from everyone. She leaned down to her lap.

"Don't take too long, the crowd will get suspicious." She knew the flower time Ariel wanted. The bouquet toss, which was also in her favorite movie.

Juan crawled backward with the garter in his teeth. Scarlet fluffed her dress back out hoping that no one spotted Ariel.

Ariel sat on Scarlet's foot. But popped off in time to see Juan throw the band of lace and elastic to the waiting men behind him.

He used the elastic and stretched it as far as it would go. It flung high and wide, landing square on Donya's chest. At which Scarlet broke into laughter so hard she almost cried. Donya held up the garter confused, but Nera came dancing up and kissed her.

At the bouquet toss a slight scuffle occurred, Nera took Ariel into the waiting ladies to let her have a chance. Of course, Ariel maneuvered the bouquet to her, but Bertha snatched it out of her hands. Scarlet whirled around just in time to see. Thankfully Ariel kept hold of a large white rose from the center, which seemed to make her happy. A quick scan of the crowd let Scarlet see that Donya witnessed the incident and wasn't happy. Scarlet felt pretty sure Donya wouldn't eat the bridesmaid.

Scarlet made it back to the sweetheart table where a piece of cake waited for her and Juan. They'd bought a big cake for their fairly small wedding. It was the only way she could get two flavors, which the bakery managed to botch. Her mother pointed this out. Black forest cake composed all three layers, the white berry cake forgotten by the bakers.

A few other minor mishaps occurred throughout the night, but Scarlet didn't care. She remembered how upset she'd felt about the potential rain, and when the venue booked their backup event space.

None of that mattered anymore. They all survived another crazy event. And she felt happy with her wedding. Life was pretty good. In the last few days she'd even begun to rely on her supernatural gifts. It had been one thing to learn to live with them, but now she knew she wanted and needed them.

Juan stood trapped by his aunties, all wanting photos with him on their phones. She needed to get up and save him, but for a moment she enjoyed relaxing, taking it all in and thinking of how far they had come. Her innate abilities had kept her safe her whole life, and now she appreciated them. She had the tools to learn about what she could do. No one could have it all, there wasn't enough time. But with everything she'd already acquired she had choices. She could choose what she wanted in her life. Trolls, nymphs, career, baby monsters, and Juan.

CHAPTER 44

DONYA

Donya should have eaten the nuts. All of them on those tiny trays. Donya couldn't seem to calm herself. It wasn't just the violence done to the Kraken child. That woman, her dress did not match the other dresses. Donya noticed it from the shade of the balcony during the photos on the beach. The green was wrong. And her hair lay unbound, unlike the rest of the maids who followed Scarlet.

Donya's stomach gave an audible growl.

The woman she had hit in the head. She smelled like Juan. Spice but with a different scent mixed in, coconut perhaps, and on top of it all perfume. The perfume's top notes blended well with her human scent, also being tropical in nature. But one of the minor notes clashed.

Donya tracked her around the room. She hung near the photographer with her date. Getting in many of the photos. This was not her celebration. But she seemed to be making it her own.

This simply would not do.

Donya moved up on the dance floor behind the woman. Weaving between humans.

Suddenly something filled her mouth. Donya stopped moving. The music pounded in her head. Her mouth brimmed with sweet and salty and deliciousness.

"Candied pecans on strawberry slices my rock," Nera said into her ear, biting her.

Donya waited for Nera to remove her fingertips from her mouth before she chewed.

She ground the tree nuts into a fine paste, delighted that the strawberry seeds gave a fine grain texture and sweetness. But it was Nera's fingers on her tongue that tasted the best. Donya let thoughts of eating any more humans slip from her mind.

"You didn't break your pretty teeth on my ear, did you?" Donya asked.

"I am stronger than you think," Nera said, swinging around in front of her and beginning to dance.

Donya thought Nera was strong indeed. She must let her know that. And she must let her know of her true feelings. But now, she needed to let Nera choose what came next. Nera had been trapped for so long. Donya would not trap her again, no she'd decided Nera would make the decisions.

"Nera, do you want to go to our mountain, or do you want to continue to travel?"

Nera stopped moving. She stood motionless in the crowd. The children who danced nearby blew bubbles from small wands and they floated around Nera. Donya could not take her eyes off of her.

"Our mountain," Nera whispered.

Donya almost didn't hear her. But the warmth that spread through her as her slow mind caught up with her ears was undeniable. Her chalky limbs wrapped around Nera, and they stood still. Donya felt a bubble burst on her fingers and opened her eyes.

Ariel danced around too, at one with the human children. Blowing bubbles and jiggling. Donya looked around, Scarlet danced with Juan. Her arms raised above her head. Everyone was happy, everyone was safe.

"Let's go home." Donya tugged on Nera's arm.

They walked past the pile of gifts, Donya's sat on top. She hoped Scarlet would like it. They would meet again soon enough.

∾

Donya pried at the cave mouth. It took two and a half nights of travel to arrive on their mountain. The equinox was weeks off, but it felt like deep autumn this far north. The nights turned cold. Nera skipped up the side of the mountain in front of her. When Nera came close Donya could see the small bumps rising on her arms. She was cold.

Donya bore a heavy backpack. In it were things she thought Nera would need to be comfortable through the winter: a down-filled comforter, a thick foam camping mattress, and several woolen blankets. Donya could not be sure her nymph would be happy so bundled up, but she wanted to stop worrying about it.

Nera skipped right past the opening to her cave. It was hard to see with the rock Donya used as a door pulled over it. The rock was an old friend, it kept out intruders and ravens. Ravens notoriously stole away pretty stones and shiny objects. Donya rolled the stone back.

Her cave brimmed with interesting rocks and curios. They sparkled in the moonlight as her eyes adjusted. She felt Nera stop behind her. Donya had not fully recovered from their latest adventure. Her limbs felt like sandstone despite the many seeds she'd been eating. But being home gave her new strength. And starting tomorrow night she and Nera would work on healing their wounds.

"Fond greetings," Nera said to all the rocks in the cave.

Nera couldn't hear their responses, but Donya could. Many were quite enchanted by her. Several of the oldest rocks uttered crude words. Donya hastily picked them up and gave them a roll down the mountain. She would let them cool off for a few nights.

Donya took out the sword and laid it at the back of the cave, it continued to sleep. She would let it rest through the fall and winter. It would rise with the spring and then she would travel to Italy to see what could be done to repair it.

"And who is this?" Nera picked up the little bone.

"That is a good friend. She helped me in Rome, to find you."

Nera brought the bone up close to her face, inspecting it in the low moonlight of the cave. "I thought she felt familiar, what does she have to say?"

"Nothing I am afraid, she sleeps still, I overtaxed her."

"You are very taxing and taxed." Nera grabbed at the large pack.

Donya hefted off her burden and gave more greetings. Her eyes flickering back to the sword, another thing she had overtaxed.

Many of her rocks wanted to know how long Nera would be staying. Donya hoped forever. But for now, Donya was quite happy to answer all of Nera's questions and introduce her to their mountain.

EPILOGUE

Hanauma Bay was the perfect temperature as far as Scarlet was concerned. Swimming in it felt like swimming in a dream, a nice dream, not one brought on by blood magic. Fish darted around the coral in a rainbow of colors ranging in size from tiny to very large. A sea turtle even gilded between Juan and her. It quickly disappeared back out into the vast blue.

They snorkeled close to the surface, bobbing around in the water, enjoying the sunshine and relaxation. Neither had ever been to Hawaii before. They saved it for their honeymoon. Scarlet was glad they did. Even though the islands overflowed with spirits. None she recognized or even had read about in one of Grazia's old leather-bound books. But they seemed friendly enough. There were these ones that looked like golden spheres, they bounded and sang constantly. Even when Scarlet put up her shield they continued with their bouncing and singing, not particularly interested in her or Juan.

With so many spirits on the land, Scarlet expected a few in the ocean, but the only ones she saw while they snorkeled were Ariel and Sebastian.

Ariel came to check on them almost every day. And eat donuts. Scarlet suspected she'd traveled here a few times before to get to the large fresh donuts sold around the island. Ariel loved to explore warmer water. Occasionally Scarlet doubted her placement of Ariel, but a local beach was the best place for her to keep an eye on the growing kraken.

Scarlet and Juan headed back up to shore. Her shield could keep out the supernatural, but it didn't have any SPF and with red hair, she needed a lot of sunscreen applications. Juan took off his mask and snorkel and waded in the turquoise waters ahead of her. Scarlet was also feeling a bit hungry, lunchtime she guessed. She wasn't surprised when a little head bobbed up next to Juan flushed apricot and pink from exertion. Ariel glanced back at Scarlet as she started to climb up Juan's back, she held a corndog in one hand, it sagged to one side becoming soggy.

❧❧

It was early for the first snow, but it started to fall before the sun hid behind another mountain on what had been a gray day. Donya watched out the cave mouth for Nera who'd walked down the mountain and several miles east into a human village. Donya could hear her coming before she saw her. Nera sang at the top of her lungs in trollish, which Donya taught her on the lengthening nights. The song hung in the air even as the snow hushed all other sounds.

Nera wore a white snowsuit, the hood rimmed with synthetic fur that Donya did not like the smell of, but Nera raved about. Her black hair flew loose and framed her face against the white world of snow. They were both fully healed after spending many nights in the river, yet this was Nera's first outing without Donya. Only a few hours passed by but to Donya it felt like weeks.

Donya held a present for Nera, she'd worked on the carvings while Nera slept, and in the last hour, Donya wove the leather cord into a patterned knot that would be strong but supple. The present was a large piece of lapis. Donya shaped and polished it into a crescent. It was big, almost as large as Donya's hand, but it would lay beautifully on Nera's decolletage. The leather was a light natural tan, and it would not freeze in the months to come like a metal chain would.

She had laid no enchantment on the piece of jewelry. Although it would take many wards easily. If Nera wished they would work on a casting together, right now it could be a gift both beautiful and full of potential.

Nera's eyes alighted on the gift the moment she walked in. "For me?"

Donya nodded, pleased at the happy expression on Nera's face. The way when she smiled for Donya her eyes turned up at the corners, it was a difference Donya noticed in the time they spent alone on the mountain.

Still Donya's mouth felt dry, the gift was an object to help show her affection. Affection she wanted to speak of to Nera.

Nera kneeled, unzipping her thick coat. Underneath she wore a white turtleneck. Donya placed the stone on her chest and then began to tie the leather in the back. It remained loose enough to slip over Nera's head but to get the placement exactly right she couldn't do these last knots until now.

"Why did you give this to me?" Nera asked, fingering the stone.

Donya could hear the stone purring in response to the warmth and gentle touch. "It reminds me of you and as a token."

Nera moved a hand up to Donya's fingers. "Token?"

"A token similar to the ring, the human ring," Donya babbled. She was not finding the words she required. "A token to show my devotion." Donya took a deep breath. "And love."

Donya wasn't prepared for how quickly Nera spun around and enveloped her in a hug. She still surprised Donya every day.

THE END

Acknowledgments

For my second book I thought it wouldn't need as much help to get it off the ground. I was wrong. Just as much help and work was completely necessary and I want to thank everyone who assisted though the long process.

A big thank you to Erin for tons of editing. Special thanks to Analynn, Jen, Dan, and Michelle from my writing group for all the wonderful feedback. My deepest gratitude to Ivan for sitting patiently as I read the final draft to him. I'm pretty sure he didn't enjoy it as much as *Traveling Monsters*, but that's okay. Thank you, Leo, for taking naps even though he is growing out of them, Mama needed the editing time.

Infinite thanks also to Sarah and Tara for reading through it for me. Also, thanks to all my friends I griped, grumbled and/or whined to.

Thank you to Dave for the wonderful exterior design of this book.

Thank you to my niece, Panda, who has not read my books but thinks it's cool I write. Sometimes all you need is a cheerleader.

And thank you to all my friends who help me promote my books by posting on their feeds. I am no good at social media (really social anything.) The assistance is needed and appreciated. I am sure there are those I forgot. Le me know and I will make a proper apology.

FINALLY, THANK YOU
TO ALL THE MONSTERS
BABY, TRAVELING, AND OTHERWISE.